DATING CAN
BE DEADLY

Amanda Flower

DATING CAN BE DEADLY

AN AMISH MATCHMAKER MYSTERY

Kensington Publishing Corp.
www.kensingtonbooks.com

KENSINGTON BOOKS are published by

Kensington Publishing Corp.
119 West 40th Street
New York, NY 10018

All Kensington titles, imprints, and distributed lines are available at special quantity discounts for bulk purchases for sales promotion, premiums, fund-raising, educational, or institutional use.

Special book excerpts or customized printings can also be created to fit specific needs. For details, write or phone the office of the Kensington Sales Manager: Attn.: Sales Department. Kensington Publishing Corp., 119 West 40th Street, New York, NY 10018. Phone: 1-800-221-2647.

The K and Teapot logo is a trademark of Kensington Publishing Corp.

First Printing: November 2023
ISBN: 978-1-4967-3748-9

ISBN: 978-1-4967-3749-6 (ebook)

10 9 8 7 6 5 4 3 2 1

Printed in the United States of America

For Betty Seymour

Acknowledgments

A very special thank-you to all my Dear Readers, who love going back to Harvest novel after novel. *Dating Can Be Deadly* is the fifteenth book set in this world, including the Amish Matchmaker Mysteries and the Amish Candy Shop Mysteries. It's always been my dream to have a long-running series where the characters become friends to my readers and me. Thank you for reading. You made that dream come true. I'm looking forward to taking you back to Harvest again and again.

Thanks always to my amazing agent Nicole Resciniti, who convinced me to write the first Harvest novel at the beginning, and to the amazing team at Kensington, including my editor Alicia Condon and publicist Larissa Ackerman. I work with the very best.

Thank you to Kimra Bell for reading and commenting on the manuscript.

Love and thanks to my husband, David Seymour, for his unfailing support and steadfast love. I know how blessed I am to have you in my life.

Finally, I thank Gott, as Millie Fisher would call Him, for allowing my dreams to come true.

A person may hoard up money, he may bury his talents, but you cannot hoard up love.

—Amish Proverb

Chapter One

"Do you see him?" Lois asked, standing on her tiptoes as she tried to look over the line of people paying for their tickets to enter the Holmes County Fair. "He said he would meet me at the ticket window."

"How would I know if I've seen him if I've never met him?" I asked, holding my quilting basket tightly to my middle, so that it wouldn't get jostled in the crowd. "And neither have you."

"I've seen his picture on the app," Lois said. "He's very handsome. I hope that wasn't just good lighting and filters. I used a filter once and erased my nose, and then I didn't know how to get it back. I had to take a whole new picture."

I stared at her. Honestly, I had no idea what Lois was speaking about half the time. She spoke in *Englisch* riddles to me.

"I want you to be careful. You told me that people can be misleading on this dating app. They post a picture of themselves when they were much younger or use someone else's picture altogether, and if you can erase your nose, who knows what others are capable of," I said.

"The nose thing wasn't on purpose."

"It never is," I said and fanned myself in the heat. It was still morning, but morning in the August, the dog days of summer as they say, and even in my short-sleeve cotton dress, I was toasty.

Lois touched her hair. The purple-red spikey tufts on the top of her head didn't move. She told me once she had to use three different styling products to get her hair to stand upright like that. I didn't know how she did it. I had never used a styling product on my hair. I knew what it would look like every day. I would twist my long white hair into a bun at the nape of my neck and finish the look with a white Amish prayer cap held in place with hairpins. My clothing choices were just as simple. I wore a plain, solid-colored dress—usually navy blue—and sturdy, black walking shoes. Knowing what I was going to wear everyday did take a lot of the guesswork out of my life.

Lois Henry was my dearest friend in the world, but she was as far from Amish as a person could be. She had that hair—the red/purplish spike kind—she loved bright clothes with multiple patterns, and she never met a piece of costume jewelry or container of eye shadow that she didn't like. The massive patchwork purse over her arm held everything in the world, or so it seemed. Lois's purse was the stuff of legend; she could pull just about anything out of it at any time, including a brick. Surprisingly, that brick had come in handy on more than one occasion, so who was I to judge?

She always wore makeup and did her hair, but today, she had gone all out. Her hair was like concrete—not even the thick August humidity was going to take it down—and she wore a purple leopard-print jumpsuit and bright green sneakers.

There was quite the range of fashion at the fair, from plain Amish to *Englisch* teenagers in shorts so short that the inside of their pockets hung below the hems. But even in that crowd, Lois stood out.

"Virgil would never lie about his pictures on the app. He's an upstanding man. Why do you think I'm meeting him here? I don't have time to waste on deadbeats. I'm sixty-eight years old. Chances are he'll be my next husband. Possibly even my last. That's debatable though."

She wasn't making a joke there. Lois had been married four times already, so it was entirely possible she had multiple husbands in her future.

"Whoa," I said the same way I told my horse, Bessie, to slow down when she was pulling my buggy. "Whoa. Why are you talking about marriage at all? You haven't even met him yet."

"Millie, when you know, you know."

I folded my arms. "When you know you know? Could this be how you ended up being married four times already?"

"Listen," Lois said. "I'm not one of those 'slow burn' people like you are."

"What are you talking about?" I asked.

"Uriah Schrock? Need I *really* say more? The two of you have been dancing around each other ever since he returned to Harvest months ago. I don't have time for that. If I want to be able to walk down the wedding aisle under my own steam and without the aid of a walker, I need to lock Virgil down."

I rubbed a spot between my eyebrows because I felt a headache forming there. I loved Lois dearly, and I didn't want her to end up in another bad marriage. She'd had three. Her only good marriage was to her second husband, who left her widowed until she married again.

Lois sucked in a breath. "Oh, I see him. He's as handsome as his picture. I don't think he used a filter at all."

I stood on my toes trying to see. "Where? Where?"

"Millie, stop that; you'll make a scene," Lois hissed.

"*I'll* make a scene?" I asked, but I stopped trying to look over the crowd.

Lois put a hand to her heart, and the late morning light sparkled in the bright gemstones of her many rings. "He's standing by the ticket booth waiting for me just like he said he would. Isn't that the most romantic thing?" She turned to me. "How do I look?"

"Colorful," I said.

"Perfect. Now, you have to leave."

"Leave?" I asked.

"You need to get to the quilt barn to hang your quilt anyhow. You don't even have to buy a ticket. You get to go in as one of the presenters through the other entrance."

"I know I can, but I want to be with you when you meet Virgil."

"You can't be. I don't want it to look like I need my friend to check him out," Lois argued.

I believed I *did* need to check him out for Lois's sake. She wasn't as discerning as I thought she should be when it came to men.

"Shoo. Shoo." She waved me away.

"You're shooing me away?" I asked.

"Yes, I don't want Virgil to think I brought a friend because I didn't trust that he is who he says he is."

"You might trust him, but I don't. I want to see him and make sure he's deserving of you." I adjusted the heavy quilting basket on my arm. My wrist was beginning to ache from holding it for so long. The quilt itself had to weigh thirty pounds. It was for a king-sized bed.

"Please, Millie." She looked over her shoulder. "Let me meet him alone first. I'll come to the quilt barn where you'll be, and we can bump into each other all natural-like."

I frowned. "Fine, but I don't like having to wait. Don't take too long making your way to the quilt barn. I need to see him."

And approve of him, I mentally added.

"I won't. Go!" She peered over the heads of the people in line again.

Shaking my head, I stepped out of the ticket line and walked a little ways down the chain-link fence that surrounded the fairgrounds until I reached the vendor and presenter entrance. There was a small security shed by this entrance, and a large jovial *Englisch* man in overalls and a bucket hat smiled at me as I approached.

"Good morning, Millie. It's going to be a hot one today."

I glanced up at the glaring orange August sun overhead. It was slightly shrouded in a haze of humidity. Sal Dungle, the fairground's security guard, was right. It was indeed going to be a hot one.

"Are you sure you're going to be able to stand it in the quilt barn with no AC?"

"Sal, you know I don't have air conditioning at home—I will do just fine," I said.

"If you ask me, all those non-Amish ladies are going to melt right into the concrete slab. They aren't built for these conditions." Sal grinned. "That might be good for you though, right? You can't win the quilting competition if you aren't present for the judging. One of you Amish ladies will be a shoo-in because you won't faint from the heat."

"Let's hope everyone is present for the judging, so the best quilt wins. I also think judging is based on the quilting, not whether you can stand the heat."

He chuckled. "That's tough enough from what I hear." He then waved in a young girl carrying a chicken. She walked upright as if she was quite pleased with the hen she would be presenting to the judges.

"What do you mean?" I asked.

"The head judge is Tara Barron." He whispered the name.

I searched my memory, trying to recall the name Tara Barron, but no one came to mind.

Based on her name alone, I assumed she was an *Englischer*. Her name didn't sound Amish in the least.

"I'm sure I will be able to handle her, and if I have any trouble at all, I know Lois will be ready to jump to my rescue." The basket was growing very heavy on my arm at this point, and I knew it was time to move along. If I didn't set the basket down soon, I would have a permanent bruise.

Sal laughed. "I sure wouldn't mess with Lois." He waved me through the gate.

The fairgrounds were filled with the heady scent of manure, hay, and fried food. It took me back to my childhood when my family would come to the fair together. It was one of my favorite memories. That was one of the few times when we truly interacted with the *Englisch* community. When I was young, the *Englisch* and Amish communities were much more divided. Now, the lines blurred. Of course, even as a child, I saw Lois every day because she was my next-door neighbor and came to our house all the time to escape her difficult home life. However in those cases, she was entering my turf, not the other way around. Going to the fair had felt like being allowed into the *Englisch* side of the county with its rides, games, and bright colors.

To my left, I saw a line of games. There was everything from a basketball hoop to a ring toss to a water pistol shooting competition. As I walked down the line of booths, which were doing a good business by the looks of it, the operators shouted in their loud voices for me to come give their games a try. At the end of the game line was a trailer that had been transformed. One end was like a normal trailer, but the rest of the sides and the roof of the trailer were made of chain-link fencing, making a cage of sorts. AXE THROWING FOR STRESS RELIEF was emblazoned on the side.

A young *Englisch* man stood in the trailer holding a hatchet over his head. He took one step forward and let the hatchet go. The blade dug into the wooden target. "Great job!" the game operator said, and the young man inside jumped up and down with excitement.

Two young people stood by the cage. "Virgil is going to be so mad when he learns you misplaced one of the axes," said one, a young man who didn't look a day over sixteen.

My ears perked up at the name Virgil. Was it the same man that Lois was meeting at the fair? It had to be. How many Virgils could there be at the fair on opening day?

The woman he spoke to was just as young. "I didn't misplace it!" she snapped. "It was right here."

He rolled his eyes. "It didn't grow legs and walk off."

"Well, then that means someone took it," she snapped.

"That's not better than its being lost," he hissed back. "In fact, it's a whole lot worse."

I shook my head. I remembered when the fair's most dangerous game was darts. The axe-throwing seemed a bit extreme. It was a little worrisome to me that the axe-throwing workers weren't keeping track of their equipment. And how responsible was Virgil to hire these young people who had lost track of one of the axes?

Ahead of me was the horse barn and horse show paddock. I turned right there and passed the line of food stands. My stomach growled. I promised myself that I would get a corn dog just as soon as I could break away from the quilt barn. I wondered if there were any blueberry desserts at the fair. I loved blueberries.

The quilt barn was actually the barn where all the craft judging would be held, including flower arranging, needlework, photography, and other artwork. However, the quilt competition was the premier event. It even rivaled the cattle judging that would happen three barns away. At least it rivaled it in prestige for the winner. Not nearly as many spectators came out for the craft judging as they did for the animals.

The building itself was a white pole barn on a concrete floor. The barn was made of metal, so it felt as if I was walking into a hotbox just as Sal had warned me. All the windows and doors were wide-open, and three huge industrial fans circulated the humid air. I was glad I'd left my large black bonnet at home. It was far too hot for a day like this.

Presenters were all over the barn displaying their work. Quilters hung their prize-worthy quilts on giant mobile walls that could display every inch of the quilt to the public and the judges.

"Millie!" Raellen Raber waved at me from the other end of the large barn.

I waved back. Raellen was a member of Double Stitch, the quilting circle in my Amish district in the small village of Harvest. The group had five members, but Raellen, Iris Young, and I were the only ones who were entering the fair's quilting competition this year. The bishop's wife, Ruth Yoder, had also wanted to enter a quilt, but she'd missed the deadline to submit a photograph of her piece to be considered. Knowing Ruth as well as I did, I guessed that she would be at the fair sometime today to complain about that very fact.

I made my way toward Raellen but paused when an *Englisch* woman stepped into my path. "Observers aren't supposed to be in the quilt barn yet, just presenters." She had short, bobbed blond hair and wore jeans and a checked shirt. She held a list in her hand. There was a large purple ribbon on her chest that said JUDGE.

"I'm a presenter. My friend over there"—I pointed at Raellen—"is going to help me hang up my quilt." I showed her my basket. "She's a presenter too."

The woman pressed her mouth into a thin line. "What's your name?"

"Millie Fisher."

She consulted the list. "Your name is on here," she said somewhat reluctantly.

"I'm glad to hear it. May I ask your name?" I nodded at the ribbon. "Judge?"

"Tara Barron. I'm the head judge for the quilting competition and the president of the fair board. I do not abide any foolishness in my barn or anywhere else on the fairgrounds for that matter."

Ah, so I had now met the judge Sal had warned me about. As for the foolishness comment, I looked down at my Amish garb. I was a sixty-something Amish widow. What foolishness could I get into? I wanted to ask her that. Then I thought of all the tight spots Lois and I had found ourselves in over the years and kept my mouth shut.

Tara looked over my shoulder at someone else coming into the barn. Her face paled slightly, but when I turned to see who she was staring at, I couldn't tell. There had been numerous people behind me hurrying here and there to get ready for the various arts and crafts events.

"Miss Barron, are you all right?" I asked.

My words snapped her out of her stupor, and she scowled. "Good luck in the competition."

She stalked away.

I didn't for a second believe she meant that.

Chapter Two

"I see you met Tara," Raellen said in Pennsylvania Dutch when I joined her on the other side of the pole barn.

It wasn't lost on me that she spoke in our language so the *Englischers* in the barn would not know what she was saying.

I replied in kind. "She seems to be a tad on edge."

"Well, imagine if your quilt shop just burned down and you had to judge a bunch of quilts right after. You'd be on edge too," Raellen said.

I blinked. "She had a quilt shop that burned down? Where? I thought I knew all the quilt shops in Holmes County."

"It was a brand-new one in Millersburg called the Thread Spool. From what I heard, it'd only been open a month before it went up in flames. I went there once with Leah to see what fabric she had, and it was a nice selection. She also had some gorgeous quilts there. Some patterns I had never seen before. If I'd had more time to shop, I would have asked about them, but Leah had to leave because she was watching her grandchildren after school. It's a real shame about the shop. I was planning to go back."

Leah Bontrager was another member of our quilting circle. She was close to my age and the most practical member of the group. "If the two of you knew about the shop, I'm surprised that you didn't tell the rest of us."

"We didn't want to bring it up at the meeting because the quilt shop is run by an *Englischer*, and you know how Ruth feels about that."

I nodded with understanding. I knew very well how Ruth felt about what she considered Amish businesses being run by non-Amish people. Ruth was the self-appointed leader of Double Stitch. She believed she should have the title because she was the bishop's wife.

"But I'm surprised you hadn't heard of the fire." Raellen lowered her voice just a bit, but not enough that a passerby couldn't overhear. "It happened maybe two or three days ago. There were worries it would jump to other buildings downtown. Can you imagine if the county courthouse went up in flames?" Her eyes glowed as if she could see the inferno. "They say it was arson, and the fire marshal suspects Tara and her ex-husband."

"Her ex-husband?"

She nodded and took a step closer to me as if she was ready to tell me the whole story about Tara Barron and her ill-fated quilt shop. I wasn't surprised. Raellen was a sweet woman with a big heart, but she also was a terrible gossip. It didn't matter if you were Amish or *Englisch,* she wanted to know your business and you could be sure that she would talk about it. At times this tendency of hers to gossip helped Lois and me when we were in the middle of one of our investigations, but as Raellen's friend and neighbor, I found it an unwelcome habit.

Just the same, I was aware I wasn't telling her to stop. I had an odd interest in crime, and hearing about a fire that might have been arson piqued my curiosity. However, there was one very important detail I had to know before she went on. "Was anyone hurt in the fire?"

She shook her head. "*Nee,* praise Gott for that. It happened in the middle of the night. Maybe one or two in the morning to be more specific. There was no one there. This is both a *gut* and bad thing. Had someone been there, they would have called for help before the building was too far gone to save it, but at the same time, no lives were at risk."

I nodded. "Why would the police suspect Tara, and why is her ex-husband involved?"

"The insurance money, of course. You know all the *Englischers* insure everything. They don't have a community to lean on like we do." She shook her head. "It must be very difficult to be *Englisch.*"

I glanced around the quilt barn for Tara, but I could no longer see her. Raellen was right. It did seem that the *Englisch* insured everything from their cars to their businesses to their homes and even themselves. That was not the Amish way. Instead, we relied on the community when tragedy struck. If a building were to burn down, everyone in the district would pitch in to rebuild the lost structure. The *Englisch* had to depend on strangers and insurance companies to do that. It indeed sounded difficult to be *Englisch*.

Raellen gestured to the quilts around us. "I certainly wouldn't want to be around all these beautiful quilts when I had lost so much. Wouldn't it just be a constant reminder of the tragedy?" She patted her prayer cap on the top of her head as if to reassure herself that it was still there. "Then again, if she was the one to burn the place down, maybe it doesn't matter to her."

"Raellen," I said. "Watch your words. People could be listening."

"I'm not speaking *Englisch*."

"I know that, but there are plenty of Amish in this room who could overhear you, and you know how news travels in the community."

She cocked her head. "Apparently, it doesn't travel fast enough since you hadn't heard about the fire."

"I'm sure I would have if I hadn't been working at my niece's greenhouse the last few days helping her plant inventory for the end of the season. This is the first time I've even seen Lois this week; there has been so much work to do."

Raellen seemed to consider my explanation. "I'm surprised Lois didn't go find you and tell you. She must have known. I'm sure it was all the chatter at the Sunbeam Café."

The Sunbeam Café was where Lois worked when her granddaughter, Darcy Woodin, the café owner, needed a little extra help. Most of the gossip in Ohio's Amish Country ended up being exchanged there at some point. However, I think I knew why Lois hadn't mentioned it. She was far too preoccupied with her upcoming date with Virgil who didn't use filters, whatever those were. The last few days she had talked about what she planned to wear and planned to say when she met him, and little else. Under those circumstances, I could understand how the fire had slipped her mind.

When Lois fell for a man, she fell hard and with abandon. I didn't say this to Raellen of course. The only time a person told Raellen anything was when they *wanted* the news to spread. She had the loosest lips in the district. Not that she gossiped out of malice, but no matter her intentions, I had learned to mind my words around her.

I knew Raellen would love to add a little kernel of information about Lois to her gossip stockpile, but she wasn't going to get it from me.

"Uh-oh," Raellen said.

"What is it?"

Raellen grimaced.

I turned around to see what she was looking at and spotted Tara with her hands on her hips facing off with none other than Ruth Yoder. I felt sure this encounter was reason for Raellen's *uh-oh*.

"Does Ruth have a quilt entered in the competition?" I asked. "I thought she missed the deadline."

"It looks to me like she has a quilt under her arm."

I sighed. Leave it to Ruth to think she could waltz into the quilt barn the day of the fair and enter her quilt. The quilts had been selected for the show well over a month ago. Ruth had been working on her piece at the time but hadn't finished it yet. She'd blamed me for that. Well, Lois and me, actually. Because any time I was in trouble with Ruth, Lois was in some way involved.

"It looks like the conversation is getting heated," Raellen said just above a whisper.

She was right. Tara was shaking her finger at Ruth as if she was scolding a disappointing child. I could have told her right then and there that this wasn't going to end well for her. However, I also believe that people need to learn how to interact with each other on their own. Apparently Raellen Raber wasn't of the same mind.

"Are you going to do something about it?" Raellen asked.

I turned back to her. "Do something? Whatever the two of them are arguing about has nothing to do with me."

Raellen bit her lip. "That's true, but people—mostly *Englischers*—are starting to stare. It could appear as a black mark on the community, a prominent Amish wife like Ruth making such a fuss."

I sighed, knowing that she was right. I could have told her to go over herself and de-escalate the situation if she was so worried about it, but I knew that would never work. Ruth would scowl at Raellen for half a second, and the younger Amish woman would run away in tears.

Ruth couldn't bring me to tears. I had known her for far too long and we had too much history. I still remembered the time she was scolded for making mud pies on her front lawn.

I straightened my shoulders and walked over. I

knew Ruth wouldn't appreciate whatever I decided to say to help the situation, so I might as well as get on with it.

The two women were glaring at each other when I walked over. "Can I be of assistance?"

Tara's head snapped in my direction. "Who are you?" Then she glared at Ruth. "Is this one of your members who you've convinced to cause more trouble for me?"

Before Ruth could answer—because heaven knew what she might have said—I spoke.

"I'm Millie Fisher. We just met a few moments ago. I have a quilt in the competition."

Tara's lip curled. "Yes, you were the one who was late."

"What is it that you want, Millie? You're interrupting a very important conversation," Ruth said.

When she used that tone, most people would run away and let Ruth fight her own battles. But as Lois had often said, neither one of us had ever been *most people*.

"I just want to offer some help," I said in a low voice. "The two of you are you making a scene."

"We wouldn't be if she would listen to me and leave the quilt barn," Tara snapped.

"I don't see why my quilt can't be entered. The quilt barn doesn't open for twenty minutes. There is plenty of time to hang it. I even see a bare space right over there." She pointed to the wall where my quilt was to be hung.

Tara glared at her. "Entries were due one month ago."

"My quilt wasn't done then," Ruth said. "I had to finish it before I could enter it."

"Then, you cannot participate," Tara said coldly. "You can save your quilt and show it next year."

Ruth glared at her. "Do you really think I'm going to hold on to the quilt that long? I have to sell it to help my family."

"That is your choice. Now, I have to ask you to leave."

Ruth's face turned red. She wasn't used to someone kicking her out of any place within Holmes County. "What right do you have to judge the quilts here?"

"I'm a quilter myself and a quilt shop owner."

Ruth's lip curled as if she smelled something rotten. "Shouldn't you say *former* quilt shop owner since you burned yours to the ground?"

I arched my brow. I might not have been aware of Tara's shop, but it seemed Ruth knew all about it.

"How dare you!" Tara pulled her hand back, and for a moment, I thought she might slap Ruth across the face.

I stepped between the two women. "Ladies, please."

"Millie Fisher, what are you doing?" Ruth asked.

"I'm stopping you from making this worse," I said in our language.

"What are you saying?" Tara asked. "Speak English!"

I eyed her. "I was asking her to stop."

Ruth sent me a formidable glare, but it had no effect on me. She realized it and scowled at Tara instead. She probably thought she'd have a higher chance of intimidation there.

"You wouldn't have had your quilting business if

it weren't for the Amish in the area. We're the ones who bring in the tourists."

Tara had opened her mouth as if she was going to say something, when Lois floated into the barn. "Millie! Yoo-hoo!"

Ruth aimed her scowl in Lois's direction. Lois didn't even react. Ruth had been scowling at her since we were all children.

"Who are you?" Tara wanted to know. "Only exhibitors are allowed in the barn until we open. How many times do I have to say this? Why can't anyone follow instructions?"

Lois pulled up short and looked at all the serious faces around the pole barn. "According to the sign the quilt barn is open."

Tara looked at the watch on her wrist and then turned to Ruth. "Do you see how much time you've wasted? The barn is open, and we aren't even ready!" She turned to the ladies who were making the final touches to their quilts and displays. "The fair is open. Finish up."

At first everyone froze, and then all at once, they jumped into action. Women dashed about making sure their quits hung straight and didn't have a single wrinkle.

"I want both of you out of my barn right now." Tara pointed at Ruth and Lois. "The fair may be open, but the quilt barn doesn't open until I say it does. We need ten more minutes. You can come back inside when the general public is allowed in and not a moment before."

The two women looked at each other as if they could not believe they'd been clumped together for anything.

"I just came in to see how Millie was getting on," Lois said and folded her arms.

"I'm fine, Lois. Raellen will help me hang up my quilt." I glanced at the large schoolroom clock that hung above the pole barn's entrance. "And I'd better get to it."

Lois nodded. "Did you see that axe-throwing game? I'm definitely doing that!"

I placed a hand on my cheek at the very thought of Lois throwing an axe at anything.

"You both have to leave so we can make final preparations," Tara said.

Ruth lifted her chin and looked around the room. "You'll be sorry you didn't allow my quilt in this competition. In fact, I don't see anything that measures up to it. It's not even worth my time to display here." With that, she stomped out of the barn.

As we watched her go, Lois shook her head. "She's going to be talking about this for the rest of our lives."

Lois could not have been more right.

Chapter Three

At Tara's request, Lois stepped out of the barn for a few minutes. Raellen helped me hang my quilt, and the fair was underway. I told Lois that I would meet her outside the quilt barn just as soon as my quilt was displayed. I felt lucky I had a quilt to enter in this year's competition. In years past, I just hadn't found the time, or didn't have a quilt I thought was ready for such a prestigious event. Quilting in Holmes County was a serious endeavor, and to enter my quilt in the fair, I needed a quilt of the highest caliber. At last year's fair, I'd promised myself that I would enter, and I'd spent the fall and winter working on my quilt in between making other quilts that would keep a roof over my head, and helping out my niece, Edith Hochstetler, at her greenhouse.

I was very pleased with my final result. It was a blue, yellow, and green wedding-ring quilt. Every piece was cut with care and every stitch perfectly in place. It was the prettiest quilt I had ever made, and I knew just what to do with it after the fair. I planned to tuck it away until the wedding of candy shop owner Bailey King and Sheriff Aiden Brody. It would be their wedding gift.

If I chose to sell it, I would make a wonderful profit for the craftsmanship and flawless stitches, but a quilt that I'd spent this much time and love on needed a better end. I would be delighted if Bailey and Sheriff Brody would accept it.

I smiled to myself as I thought of giving it to them. When I stepped out of the pole barn, I blinked at the bright sunshine, and I could feel the small bits of my hair that escaped my bun and prayer cap begin to curl. The humidity was high. There was no air conditioning on the fairgrounds. The Ferris wheel conductor was already wiping sweat from his brow. I was grateful that I always carried a handkerchief in the pocket of my dress because I knew I would soon be doing the same.

I looked around the grounds. When I had entered the quilt barn, the fair had been quiet, the rides and games just being tested before the arrival of the public. Now, the rides spun, and the games beeped and buzzed as both *Englisch* and Amish attendees enjoyed the festivities. On a Tuesday morning, most of the fair patrons were mothers with young children, retirees, and teenagers.

I had asked Lois to meet me right outside the quilt barn but wasn't surprised to find her gone. It had taken Raellen and me longer than anticipated to display my quilt, and Lois wasn't one to sit and wait around for another person, even if the other person was me.

In actuality, the fairgrounds weren't very big, so I assumed that if I looked hard enough, I would find her.

I walked down the row of food vendors. Even though it wasn't lunchtime yet, there were already long lines of people waiting to get snacks and pastries of every type. In one of the booths, an Amish girl sold fry pies. Next to her booth, an *Englischer* sold fried treats, from Oreos to Twinkies. My mouth watered. I did allow myself to indulge in one fried Twinkie each year. I made a mental note to get one before the fair ended.

My friend Lois could have a very loud voice when she was excited, and she sounded excited as she exclaimed, "Bull's-eye! I'm a natural!"

I walked in the direction of the axe-throwing cage. Sure enough, I spotted Lois inside. She held the hatchet back over her head, took one step forward with her right foot, and threw the axe with all her might.

The axe bounced off the wood and clattered to the floor of the cage. Lois jumped back as if afraid it would cut off her foot.

"Drat! Let me try that again," she said.

"One more time," a handsome man said.

Lois picked up the axe, returned to the starting line, and threw. This time the axe's blade sank into the bull's-eye. Lois threw up her arms in victory. The handsome man who appeared to be in his late fifties held out a hand for her. He was tall and built like a retired football player with broad shoulders and a slight belly that hung over his silver belt buckle. He smiled at Lois adoringly.

"Thank you, Virgil, for letting me try that." She accepted his hand. "It was such a thrill. I really got the hang of it, and now I am wondering if I should put a setup like this in my backyard for practice."

That sounded like a terrible idea to me.

"You did amazingly well. But you don't need to put up your own target. You are welcome to come to my throwing range whenever you want. It's on me. Also remind me never to say anything that might cause you to throw something at me." He held an enormous purple elephant out to her. "Because I am sure it will hit its mark. If you keep this up, you will be better at this sport than I am, and I have been throwing for decades."

"Oh, how did you get into it?"

"It was something my father and I did when I was growing up."

"What a wonderful bonding experience." Lois accepted the elephant and smiled up at him. "I will remind you, but I can't imagine you ever saying anything to hurt another person."

I blinked. Could this younger man be her date? It seemed I had been right that he was the same Virgil the two young people had been talking about when I'd first arrived at the fair.

"Millie!" Lois cried when she spotted me. "Why are you just standing there? Come over and say hello."

I walked over to them.

She beamed at me. "This is Virgil."

He smiled at her with genuine warmth, and I felt my guard lessen just a bit.

"Virgil Rinaldi. It's so nice to meet you," he

greeted me. "Lois has been telling me about your many adventures. She said you are known as 'Amish Marple.' "

I gave Lois a look. She had given me that nickname—or codename I believed she would call it—because of the many criminal cases we had poked our noses into over the last few years, but I didn't want her to be sharing that with someone she'd just met.

"It's nice to meet you, Virgil." I smiled at him. He did seem like a very nice man, if a bit young. But I had seen matches with age gaps work before. In fact, as the matchmaker in my district, I had been responsible for one or two of them.

An old Amish proverb came to me: *Instead of complaining that the rosebush is full of thorns, be glad that the thornbush has roses.* It was a *gut* reminder to me. Was I looking for something to be wrong with Virgil? I was being protective of my friend's heart. I didn't want her to make another mistake. I also needed to remind myself Lois had to make her own decisions and mistakes.

I pointed at the trailer with the axe-throwing cage. "This is yours."

He nodded. "It's my pride and joy. I just opened the business six months ago, and we have already become a popular spot. We do especially well with bachelor and bachelorette parties. I guess folks want to get their aggression out before they walk down the aisle." He chuckled at his own joke.

My opinion of him went down just a little at that.

"You go to events like this in the trailer?" I asked.

He shook his head. "Not usually. Our main location is an old warehouse in Walnut Creek. The fair is my first outing. It was a nightmare to convince the folks here that the game was safe. I had to complete so much paperwork and prove my staff knew what we were doing. It was infuriating, but now that we are here, I'm happy with all the publicity this is giving my business. All the headaches were worth it in the end."

I glanced at Lois. "Did you know about his business before today?"

"No, we never talked about it online, but now I see why he wanted me to meet him for the first time at the fair." She looked up at Virgil. "The setup is quite impressive, and he is a great teacher. I might hit the bull's-eye every time now."

"I'm sure you will," Virgil said.

I felt my matchmaking instinct itching at the back of my mind. It seemed to me that Virgil and Lois liked each other very much, but there was just something off. I didn't feel they were the right fit, and it was something other than the age difference. Knowing this put me in a bad position because I wanted to be honest with my friend, but at the same time, I didn't want to upset her by saying that Virgil wasn't the right match for her. Hopefully, it wouldn't come to that, and she would see that Virgil wasn't right for her on her own.

"I was just telling Virgil all about the kerfuffle in the quilt barn with Ruth." She smiled at Virgil. "You have to know there is always a kerfuffle when Ruth is around. I'm surprised she didn't throw her quilt at Tara and make a run for it."

"Ruth would never put her quilt at risk like that."

Virgil smiled. "Who knew that quilting was such a dramatic art?"

"You have no idea," Lois said. "I'm not a quilter myself, but having Millie as my best friend, I have seen quite a lot. My hobbies are more along the lines of refinishing furniture."

Virgil's eyes sparkled. "Really? I love antiques. Do you go antiquing?"

"Do I ever!" Lois cried.

Maybe the two of them had more in common than I'd first thought.

"Lois has been looking forward to meeting you," I said. "I'll admit I was a little skeptical when she told me she met you on the Internet, but you will have to forgive me as I have never used a computer myself."

"There's nothing to forgive. I had been on that dating app for years and never found anyone. To be honest, I was about to delete it from my phone when Lois popped up. She caught my eye right away." He sounded sincere, and I felt more at ease.

"I have never met anyone quite like Lois," he added. "She intrigued me from the start."

That was a fair statement.

Lois changed the subject. "It wasn't until I left the pole barn that I realized the judge was the woman whose quilt shop burned down."

"You knew about that?" I asked.

She nodded.

"Why didn't you tell me?" I asked. "I would have expected you'd call me about something like that the moment you heard."

"I only heard about it last night, and you've been so busy at the greenhouse helping Edith. I planned to tell you on the drive here, but it slipped my mind. I was so nervous about meeting Virgil." She smiled at him.

Virgil laughed. "And I was equally nervous about meeting you. It's nice to hear we were in the same spot."

"My guess is Tara was in a foul mood about the fire," Lois said. "Or it could have been Ruth giving her a hard time." She tucked her elephant under her arm and reached into her giant purse. She pulled out her phone.

She struggled to tap the screen and Virgil gallantly took the elephant from her, holding it as confidently as a grown man could carry a purple elephant a third his size.

"Here's the article about it from the paper." She went on to read, " 'The Thread Spool, a quilt shop in Millersburg owned by Tara Barron, caught fire very early Sunday morning between the hours of one and two.

" 'Fire and rescue were able to control the blaze before it could jump to other buildings or the historic courthouse in the middle of town. They declared the building a complete loss, and it will have to be torn down. The fire marshal claims there are signs of arson at the site. The owners could not be reached for comment. The investigation is ongoing.' "

I shivered when I thought about all the quilts and fabric that must have been in the shop. As a quilter myself, quilting shops had a special place in my heart.

"Was anyone hurt?" Virgil asked.

"No," Lois said. "Thank the Lord for that."

"Well, that is something to be grateful for," I said. It seemed Lois and I were tied far too often to violent deaths in the county. I was relieved that this time no one had died.

Virgil shook his head. "Tara gave me a terrible time when I was applying to have this booth at the fair. She was the one who wanted me to jump through all those hoops. Even so, I'm sorry to hear about her business. As a small-business owner myself, I know how heartbreaking such a loss would be." Virgil cleared his throat. "I'm parched. I see they have lemonade over there. Can I interest you in some?"

"We'd love some lemonade," Lois said for both of us. "There is just something so refreshing about lemonade at the fair. It tastes different too."

"That's what I have always thought," Virgil said.

Lois beamed at him, and then he left to fetch the lemonades. I wasn't going to argue with him about getting me one. It was a hot day and ice-cold lemonade was just what we needed.

When Virgil disappeared into the crowd, Lois grabbed my hand. "What do you think?"

Thwacking sounds came from behind me. The axe had hit its target once again. "Can we move away from the axe-throwing booth? It's making me a bit uncomfortable." The memory of the conversation about the missing axe came to mind.

"Oh, Millie, you should be in there throwing an axe. It's so empowering."

"Being empowered is not a virtue held in high regard by the Amish."

Lois shook her head as if that was a sad state of affairs. "Now tell me what you think about Virgil. He's wonderful, isn't he?"

I hesitated for a few short seconds before I gave my answer. "He seems very kind and friendly."

"Oh, he is! He's the nicest man I know. I've never met anyone so polite."

I smiled. "How old is he?"

"He just turned fifty-nine. He looks young for his age, just like me. It's another thing we have in common. Good genes."

I cocked my head. "How old does he think you are?"

Lois shifted back and forth on her feet. "I told him I was in my sixties."

"Where in your sixties?"

She squinted at me. "Why does it matter, Millie? I'm fit as a fiddle. Age is just a number."

"That may be true, but you don't want to start any relationship on false pretenses. That is not the way to build a strong foundation."

"So what do you want? For me to shout out that I'm sixty-eight years old? He would run away from me, and I would never be able to catch him. Did you see his legs? He's an athlete. I always wanted to date a jock. I was too much of a nerd to get that type of attention when I was in high school. I'm just having a little fun, Millie. It's nothing serious."

I frowned, not believing that was true, especially because she'd said the opposite earlier. It was always something serious when it came to Lois and men. She had a habit of making rash decisions like getting married to a man she hardly knew. That's what happened with her last marriage, which had only lasted a few days before she'd pushed him into a hotel pool and asked for a divorce.

"Don't worry, Millie. I have a new attitude when it comes to dating. I'm going to take things slow. I won't do anything rash."

I hoped for both our sakes that was true.

Chapter Four

Spirits were high as the fair got underway. Not wanting to be a third wheel with Lois and her young man, I decided to go find my niece Edith and my great-nephew, Micah Hochstetler, to see how my goats were faring.

Most of the animals were in a huge pole barn that was twice the size of the quilt barn. There were cows, chickens, rabbits, sheep, and even llamas. However, not a single goat was inside the barn.

The goats were cast out in a tent in the middle of the green all by themselves. I thought their isolation was telling. Goats were known for being rambunctious. I knew this from firsthand experience of course.

"He is so cute!" an *Englisch* teenager in shorts and tank top cried as she peered into one of the goat pens that held a young pygmy goat. The little goat was no bigger than an adult squirrel. I guessed that he was only a few months old. That was very early to have the little creature out among other animals, and there was no sign of his mother. Poor thing must have been fed with a bottle."

"He's a doll," the teenager gushed. "I wish I could take him home."

"He's for sale," said the young Amish boy who was standing in the pen with the little goat. "I'll give you a *gut* price." His face was full of hope that the *Englisch* teen might buy his goat.

The teenager backed away. "No, thank you." She hurried away as if she couldn't escape the goat tent fast enough. I had a feeling she wouldn't be back.

The Amish boy's face fell. He couldn't be more than ten and had dark brown hair he wore a bit longer than most Amish boys and wide-set brown eyes. He sat on an overturned five-gallon bucket in the pen and appeared to be completely defeated after the girl hurried away.

It wasn't unusual for a child presenter to offer to sell one of the animals that he planned to show at the fair. At the end of the fair, most of the animals shown over the week would be sold. Many of the presenters were taking offers on their livestock, but I had never seen a child so desperate to sell his goat before. From where I stood, it looked to me as if it almost broke him when she said no.

I walked up to the little goat's pen. "He is a very handsome goat. I have two of my own," I said in our language. "Mine are Boer goats, and they should be somewhere in this tent. My nephew is showing them. They are Phillip and Peter. What is your little goat's name?"

The boy scratched his goat between the ears. "Scooter. He's a pygmy, and a young one at that. If you have goats already, maybe you would like to buy him. I will give you a *gut* price. He would make a very *gut* friend for the goats you already have. He comes from *gut* stock. My mother bred him herself, and she's known for her goats statewide. People come from all over for her goats."

I smiled. "I'm sure that he would, but to be honest the two goats I have are more than I can handle on a day to day basis."

His face fell all over again.

"You can't keep him? Maybe he can be a stud for your future goats."

"I can't." He looked away. "I'm not allowed."

"I'm sure you will find the right home for him."

"I have to," he whispered. "I can't keep him. I need to find him a home or . . ." He trailed off.

"Or what?" I asked.

He looked as if he might cry.

"*Aenti* Millie, we're over here!" Micah waved from the far end of the tent. Phillip and Peter, my two Boer goats, jumped up and down. The three of them looked like a pack of kangaroos that I had seen when Lois took me to the Columbus Zoo earlier in the summer.

I glanced back at the boy, but he must have slipped out of the pen when I was distracted by Micah and my goats. I wished I had asked him his name. Perhaps Micah would know him. They were about the same age. Only the young pygmy goat remained. The little goat was all black with a grizzled chin. He stared up at me with bright yellow eyes. My heart constricted, and I knew it was time to retreat before I tucked the baby goat in my apron pocket and took him with me.

Three grinning faces greeted me at the far end of the tent. Two were goats. Phillip and Peter pressed their bodies against the walls of the pen, trying to reach me. Through the mesh, I scratched them both between the ears.

"*Aenti*, I'm so glad you're here." Micah smiled up at me. He wore a freshly pressed short-sleeve work shirt, black trousers, and his hair was combed. He was taking this competition very seriously.

"Micah, you look very nice."

"*Danki*, the first round of judging is at eleven, and I want to be ready. Phillip and Peter are going to snag the blue ribbon. I just know it."

The two goats set their front hooves on the fencing that made up their pen and grinned at me. They seemed just as confident of their chances of winning as Micah.

"*Danki* again for letting me enter them in the showing," Micah said.

"You're welcome, but I don't think you were going to take *nee* as an answer. You can be very determined when you want something. You might have gotten that from me." I winked at him.

He laughed. "That is what my *maam* says."

"Your *maam* knows me well." I smiled. "I just met a boy when I came into the tent. I wonder if you know who he is."

"Is he showing a goat?" Micah asked.

"A pygmy," I said. "The black one with a little silver around his mouth. The goat is very tiny."

"Oh! That's Scooter. You must mean Zach

Troyer. He goes to my school sometimes. This is the most I have ever seen him here at the fair."

"He goes to your school sometimes?"

Micah nodded. "He doesn't come that much. I think he missed the whole last month of school before summer started."

I glanced behind me, looking for Zach, but he was still missing. "He looks like he could use a friend. Stop over and chat with him when you have a spare moment. It is very important that we reach out to those who are lonely. I believe Zach is that."

Micah shrugged. "Sure!"

My youngest great-nephew was undaunted by the task. He was outgoing and unafraid to talk to anyone, which was so different from his mother and two siblings. They were all much more reserved. At times, I thought Micah was more like Lois than anyone in my family.

"Well, I am happy to see you and the goats getting on so well," I said.

"We are!" Micah said. "Will you come to the final judging? Today is just the preliminary round. Everyone gets through to the final though. This one is practice to get used to the ring. The big one is in a couple of days."

"I would not miss it," I said.

He grinned. "*Maam* and my brother and sister will be there for the final judging too. *Maam* found someone to watch the greenhouse for a few hours so she could be here."

"That is very *gut* news." I did my best to hide my surprise. It wasn't often that my niece Edith would be willing to leave her greenhouse in the summertime. May through September was her busiest time.

Phillip cried to remind us that he was there and therefore should be the center of attention. Peter didn't like to be outdone by his brother goat, so he ran at me and jumped over the side of pen. Phillip stared at him for a second before he did the same.

"Not again!" Micah cried.

"Again? They have done this before?" Even as I asked, I wasn't that surprised. I had thought it was just a matter of time before the goats got into trouble.

"What's going on here?" asked a large Amish man whose stomach hung well over his belt. He wore an Amish beard and felt hat. The gray work shirt under his suspenders was dark with sweat stains. Reading glasses hung from a chain around his neck. I put his age somewhere between fifty and sixty.

Micah stepped in front of the goats. "I was just putting them back. They won't do it again."

"How can you say that? This is the third time these goats have escaped from their pen. One more time, and I'm kicking all three of you out of this tent."

"It won't happen again," I said. "We will find a way to make sure the pen is secure. I'm Micah's *aenti.*"

"I will not abide of foolishness in my goat tent. It's bad enough I have to be here at all. Worse if I have to deal with disobedient animals."

"Your goat tent?" I asked. And what did he mean when he said *It's bad enough I have to be here?* If he was a volunteer of some sort, wasn't he here by choice?

He turned his attention to me. "I'm in charge of all the animal pens to make sure that they are safe and secure. We can't have animals running around the fair. So, *ya*, this is my goat tent."

As he said that, I realized there might be a problem. Phillip and Peter were professional escape artists. Keeping them in the pen for the entire week was going to be tricky.

"We won't let it happen again," I said, knowing full well I wasn't sure that was true.

"*Gut*. You should have them better trained so that they will not want to leave their pen. That is what a proper goat owner does." He scowled at Micah.

"Oh, this isn't Micah's fault," I said, coming to my great-nephew's defense. "They are my goats, and I can assure you they don't listen to me either."

His narrowed eyes looked in my direction. "So it is your fault that they misbehave. I should have suspected as much from a Harvest Amish."

I wrinkled my brow. "Harvest Amish?"

"You're all from Harvest, aren't you? You think that your district is better than the rest of us. I have heard the bishop's wife speak of such things." He glowered at me.

"I'm from Harvest, but that is not true. We don't think we are better than anyone." In this case, I was speaking for myself, not for Ruth Yoder. Ruth *did* believe that our district was better than the rest, but I didn't need to share that with this man.

He grunted as if he didn't believe me. I can't say

I blamed him, at least as far as Ruth was concerned.

"What was your name?" I asked.

"Hezekiah Troyer."

I raised my brow. "I know that Troyer is quite a common name, but are you related to Zach Troyer? I just met him, and he has the most adorable baby goat in his pen."

It was difficult to believe that it was possible, but Hezekiah's expression grew even darker. "He's my grandson. His mother left him behind when she ran away from the community. Now, he is my burden."

"A child is not a burden," I said.

"How would you know?" he snapped. "You have never been a mother."

I gaped at his rudeness, and I was shocked that he knew of my childless state. I was a widow, and unfortunately my husband and I had never been blessed with children. Before, he had claimed not to know who I was, but if he knew something so personal about me, that must not be the case.

I felt Micah's small hand grab mine and squeeze it tight. I might not have had children myself, but that made me no less a mother to Edith, whom I'd half raised after the death of her own mother. I was a grandmother to her children. And the nurturing *aenti* to dozens more. All of this was on the tip of my tongue to say, but I held back. It was not the Amish way to have a public argument. Besides, what this man thought about my district or me was of very little importance. In fact, it was of no importance at all.

"Keep those goats in the pen," Hezekiah said. "You hear me?"

With that, he stomped away.

Micah still held my hand. "I'll be extra nice to Zach, Aenti. If that man is his *grossdaadi*, he needs all the friends he can get."

So very true.

Chapter Five

At the end of the first day of the fair, I was exhausted and had a stomachache. Micah had convinced me that sharing a fried Twinkie was the best way to kick off the fair. He was wrong. A fried Twinkie was never a *gut* idea.

Neither was the Italian sausage sandwich nor cotton candy that I ate later in the day. Usually, I ate very healthy except for my unmitigated obsession with the blueberry pie Darcy made every day at the Sunbeam Café. I had no self-control when it came to blueberry anything, especially her pie. However, it seemed that as soon as I walked into the fair, anything I knew about healthy eating went out the fair gates because I ate my way through the grounds and loved every second of it.

Until I started to feel queasy.

Lois was to drive me home, and we'd planned to meet at the fair gate at four. The quilt judging wouldn't happen until the next day, so there was no real reason for me to stay much longer. It was best to go home, have a cup of ginger tea, and regroup, so I would be at my very best for the judging tomorrow.

As usual I beat Lois to the gate. Lois wasn't typically late, but I was typically early. It made for a lot of waiting around on my part.

"Millie," Sal said to me from his security post at the gate. "What are you doing over there standing in the sun?" He got up from his chair. "Here, have my seat in the shade."

"You don't have to give me your chair."

"Of course, I do, and it's good for me to stand up every so often. I don't want my bones to go stiff. I've been watching the gate for the last hour. Overall, it's been a quiet day, but the first day of the fair usually is. Of course, that will change on Friday."

"What's Friday?"

"There's a monster truck rally in the evening. It's the biggest event in the arena. It can be a rowdy crowd. Friday and Saturday are always the biggest nights at the fair. I've been told I'll have extra help on those days. I'm going to need it."

"Extra security help?" I asked.

He nodded. "That's right. Until Friday, I'm the only guard here during the day, and I'm on duty until midnight. Two other guards come on at that time and work midnight until eight in the morning. Eight is when I'm back on the job."

"That doesn't give you much time to go home and rest."

"I'm sleeping in a trailer behind the stables," he

explained. "I don't mind. It beats driving all the way home that late at night. I really have everything I need here."

"I'm very glad that you've had a peaceful day then, so you can prepare for the night. It seems to me that you have your work cut out for you with shifts that long."

He grinned. "Not totally peaceful. Early this morning I was with your nephew Micah chasing your goats back into their pen."

I groaned. "Those goats. They are trouble, but I can't imagine my life without them."

"Thankfully, Micah was able to get them back into the pen, but I do worry about what I would do if they break out again. I'm not in the best shape for chasing goats." He patted his round belly.

"I'm so very sorry that they are giving you any kind of trouble." I reached into my apron pocket and pulled out the stub of a pencil and little pad of paper I carried in there. I flipped to a fresh page and scribbled down my phone number. It felt odd to have a phone dedicated to myself after all these years. It was a new development in my life.

Bishop Yoder had given permission to have the phone line and telephone installed after several unfortunate incidents had occurred when I was at the farm alone. If I'd had a phone, I could have called for help and things might have gone much differently.

"Here," I said. "If the goats give you any trouble at all, you call me."

He wiped a blue bandana across his damp brow and over his bald head before accepting the piece of paper. "Thank you, Millie. I hope I won't have to use it, but it does make me feel better about things. It will be nice to have one less thing to worry about. It seems there is so much on my plate at the moment."

"If I may ask, why didn't the fair organizers hire more security? You'd think they'd want to give you some extra help."

He pulled at his collar, and for a moment, I thought he wasn't going to answer. In the end he said, "The fair isn't as popular as it used to be. Not like fifty years ago, before streaming, video games, and cell phones. There's been less attendance the last several years, so the fair board has really tightened up the budget." He cleared his throat. "At least that's what I was told when I asked for extra help. I was relieved they relented somewhat, and I will at least have help all day Friday and Saturday. But that was all they would give me. The sheriff's department has agreed to send a deputy to the grounds to patrol every few hours, so I'm hoping between those two things, everything will go off without a hitch."

I patted his arm. "I'm sure it will."

"What will?" Lois asked as she walked up to join us.

"Sal was just telling me about his busy week."

"Ahh," Lois answered.

I peeked behind her. "Where's Virgil?"

She blushed like a schoolgirl. "He left already. He had to go back to his main building and check on things there. I just think it's adorable he takes his business so seriously."

I suspected if Virgil had said he had to go to the

supermarket, Lois would have thought that was adorable too. Instead of making that comment, I said, "I'm glad you are happy, Lois."

"Are you ready to go home?" Lois asked.

"More than ready," I said. "I ate way too much. I need a mug of tea and to put my feet up."

"No blueberry pie?" Lois asked with a twinkle in her eye.

"*Nee*," I groaned and placed a hand on my middle. "I can't even eat that."

Her eyes went wide. "Then you must have really overdone it. I can't remember a single time you've turned down blueberry pie."

"Thanks for talking to me, Millie," Sal said as Lois and I made our way to the gate.

I waved. "Don't forget to call me if those goats give any bit of trouble."

"I will." And he kept that promise.

Chapter Six

Lois dropped me off at home a little after five that afternoon. She kindly offered to take me to her granddaughter's café for a light meal so I wouldn't have to cook for myself, but I wasn't up to eating anything more and was happy to be home. My stomach was so sore; I worried I might have gotten a bout of food poisoning from one of the many fried concoctions I had eaten. You would think at my age, I would know better, but it seemed even I could be tempted by onion rings under the right circumstances.

Before going into the house, I went into the barn to check on Bessie, my horse. She was in her stall snoozing and seemed to relish the quiet that reigned, with the goats at the fair. She opened her eyes as I drew closer, and I gave her two sugar cubes I kept locked in an airtight tin on a shelf by the door.

She took the sugar cubes in her teeth and leaned

over the stall as if looking for something or someone. When she didn't see the goats, she blew a puff
of hot air from her lips. It seemed the novelty of the
goats being away had worn off.

"I miss them too, girl." I scooped feed into her
trough. "They will be home at the end of the week.
I promise. We just need to make the best of it until
then. Let's use this time to get as much rest as we
can, because when they come back, they will be
full of energy."

She gave another puff of air, and I took that to
mean she wanted a third sugar cube, which I gave
to her.

With Bessie settled, I closed the barn door behind me. It was August, and the sun was still high
in the sky. There was much I could have done with
the remaining hours of light. There was never a
shortage of tasks on a farm. Anyone who lived on
one and said they were bored I found suspect.

I took pride in keeping my farm tidy and the
gardens well under control, so my list of chores
was always endless. However, after such a long and
tiring day at the fair, I opted to postpone those
tasks for another day.

I sat down with my mug of ginger tea and my cat
Peaches on my lap and told myself shutting my
eyes for a few minutes wasn't shirking my duties.

When the ringing telephone woke me up, I
found myself in the dark. The sound was startling,
and also a little disorienting. How long had I slept?

Thankfully, I had not spilled the tea although by
the tilt of my hand I had come very close. Peaches
was no longer on my lap. Instead, he sat on the

open windowsill and stared out into the night. The phone was just on the other side of the wall.

I pulled my small pocket watch out; it was after eleven. How could I have slept so long? However, my sore stomach felt much better. It seemed the tea and nap had been just what I'd needed to set me to rights again.

I guessed I had napped for a solid five hours. It was embarrassing to think I had slept so much of the day away. If Ruth Yoder knew, I was certain she would have some choice words about my lack of accomplishment that afternoon.

The phone rang again, and I was just as startled by it as the first time. I rarely received calls, and never in the middle of the night. There were only a handful of people who had my new number. Lois, Bishop Yoder, Edith, and Uriah were the ones I remembered giving my phone number in case of emergency.

Why would any of those people be calling me in the middle of the night? Of the lot, Lois was the most likely to be making the call. I hoped she was all right, and since I would worry about her if I didn't pick up, I got out of my rocker to answer.

I set my cup on the little table, grabbed a shawl from the back of my chair, and headed to the front door. Peaches ran ahead of me. I knew he hoped to slip out into the night as it would be the best time for him to catch a mouse to later leave on my doorstep like a trophy.

Peaches dashed out around my feet as I stepped onto the small porch. With a battery-operated lantern to light my way, I edged around the house.

The phone kept ringing over and over again. It was an eerie sound in the night. I still wasn't used to hearing it so near my home.

Usually Amish don't have phones unless they're necessary for work, but Lois was insistent that I get one after a number of frightening incidents occurred while I was home alone. She said that I needed to call the police and her if I ever was in any kind of trouble.

Lois would have been happier if I had gotten a cell phone, so that she could reach me any time. However, that was far too much of a stretch for Bishop Yoder and quite honestly for me. I didn't need the cell phone for work like some of the men in my district did. Lois said crime solving was now our job but since our work was unofficial, I didn't believe it counted.

I was feeling more vulnerable at night without the goats here to raise an alarm if strangers appeared. I picked up the phone. "Hello?"

"Hello, Millie? This is Sal from the fair."

"Oh, hello, Sal, is everything all right?"

"Your goats are out, and I have spent the last hour chasing them around the fair. They're quick. I just can't get my hands on either one of them. I didn't want to call you so late at night, but they are outsmarting me left and right. Now, I have lost track of them completely." He swallowed hard. "I should have called you as soon as they escaped the pen, but I just thought I would be able to catch them."

"You're not the first one to think that, Sal. Please don't blame yourself. The goats are likely seeing their stay at the fair as a new adventure and are itching to explore." I should have known something like this would happen. Letting Micah enter the goats in the fair had been a bad idea from the start. We were going to have to think of a better way to keep them in their pen. I was certain Hezekiah Troyer would not put up with their naughty behavior for long. "I'll be there as soon as I can."

"Thank you, Millie." I might have been mistaken, but when he ended the call, he sounded close to tears. It seemed the exhaustion was catching up with Sal.

I dialed the only telephone number I knew by heart. It would take me far too long to drive to the fairground by buggy. The fairgrounds were at least twenty miles from my little farm. I needed to find a quicker way and knew of only one *Englischer* who would be willing to drive me there in the middle of the night.

"Hello?" Lois answered the phone right away. "Millie, is everything all right?" Her voice was anxious. She knew that I would only call her at this time of night if something bad had happened or the goats were up to mischief. It was always one or the other. Sometimes both.

"I'm fine. It seems that Phillip and Peter have escaped their pen at the fair. Sal can't catch them."

"Oh my!" she exclaimed. "Those goats are so much trouble."

I wasn't going to argue that point because it was true. "I hope I didn't wake you," I said.

"Oh, I'm not even in my pajamas yet. I have so

much energy after my amazing date that I'm up sanding a chair. You should see this new power sander I got. She's a beaut!"

I shook my head. Lois was obsessed with furniture. Her collecting had gotten so bad that a person could barely walk through her rented house near the square. I had to admit she made long forgotten pieces beautiful. However, after refinishing the furniture, she did nothing with it. She had refurbished so many pieces, she could host her own booth at the local flea market. I knew that she was proud of each piece of furniture she brought back to life, and I couldn't fault her for that. She did beautiful work, but she needed to share that beautiful work with someone else. Or at least that was my thought. I hadn't broached the subject with Lois yet. It was a touchy subject.

"I will be there as soon as I can. Let me just close up my paints, and then I'll be on my way."

Before I could say anything more, she ended the call.

I went back into the house and warmed some milk, which I then poured into Peaches's bowl, before I called the cat back into the house. With the promise of warm milk, he came running. The cat purred before lapping it up.

By the time I freshened up and put on my walking shoes, Lois was in my driveway beeping her car horn. I said goodbye to Peaches, who was lying on his back in the middle of the living room rug in a milk coma. He would be out until morning.

I locked the door to my little house as I left. Another new habit I had acquired since Lois and I had become "crime fighters." Those were her words not mine.

Inside Lois's car, I said, "You got here much sooner than I expected."

"I might have pressed a little harder on the gas than I normally would, but what choice did I have? The goats are in danger. We must ride to the rescue!"

"I think it would be more accurate to say the fair is in much more danger than the goats," I said. "I shiver to think what they may have knocked over, destroyed, or eaten in the amount of time they have been loose."

"You're right. I bet the popcorn trailer is completely flipped over."

I grimaced. "I hope you're wrong."

Then again, the goats really loved popcorn.

"I hope we can catch them," I said worriedly. "Those two boys are so much trouble, but I would hate for anything to happen to them. I am quite fond of them. Also, Micah would never forgive himself if they got hurt because he entered them into the fair."

Lois turned her car around in my yard and drove down the driveway. "I'm fond of them too because of the way they take care of you. They are very protective, and that is what you need."

I didn't disagree with her in the least. The last several years, Lois and I had gotten into our share of trouble around the village and made some dangerous enemies. On more than one occasion, the goats had scared off those bad people.

I averted my eyes from Lois's speedometer while

she drove because it felt as if the car was going very fast. At the same time, I wanted to reach the fairgrounds as quickly as possible.

The drive that would have taken me over an hour in a buggy was done in less than thirty minutes. Lois parked by the front gate, and Sal met us under a lamppost just outside the fence. "I'm so glad you're here. And I'm so sorry I completely lost track of them. They are fast." Sweat ran down both sides of his face and dampened the collar of his shirt.

Lois patted him on the shoulder. "Don't blame yourself. Those goats are wild."

"That's true, but if I'd kept a better eye on the goat tent, this never would have happened. I knew they were trouble. I knew they were the ones I had to watch. It's just been such a long, tiring day. These hours are harder on me than I anticipated."

"That's no surprise, Sal. Working from six in the morning until midnight doesn't seem right. You need to rest sometime in that shift," I said.

"What kind of hours are those?" Lois asked. "You need to unionize, man!"

He shook his head. "It's just for one week."

Under the light of the lamppost, there was a yellow hue to his skin and his skin sagged into deep wrinkles around his chin and under his eyes. It might be just one week, but it was taking a toll on him. He was clearly exhausted.

"I do appreciate your calling me, Sal," I said, deciding I would deal with the goats first and then try to convince Sal to talk to the fair board about his ridiculous hours. "And I have to apologize for my goats' behavior. I never should have let Micah enter them in the fair. He was just so excited to have a livestock entry this year. At the greenhouse, all they have are cats."

He nodded. "I didn't know what else to do but call you."

"And I'm glad you did," I said. "I think we should start by looking at how they escaped."

He nodded and led us through the fairground, guided by the strong beam of his flashlight. "I should have looked at this before," he admitted. "I was just trying so hard to catch them that I didn't even check how they got out."

"I would guess they jumped the fence again," I said. "Micah and I made it twice as high after they jumped it this afternoon, but perhaps not high enough for a pair of excitable goats. I hope they weren't cut when leaping over it. The pair of them are too curious for their own *gut*."

"How high did you make it?" Lois asked.

"Nearly seven feet."

Lois whistled. "And they still were able to break out?"

"With enough determination, it is amazing what those goats can do," I answered. "That is something I had to learn the hard way. Do you know that I once found Peter on the roof of my buggy? I had to repaint the roof because the hoof prints marred the wood. Even now you can see the depression in the roof where he landed, if you look hard enough."

Lois shook her head.

Between Sal's flashlight, the floodlights scattered around the grounds, and the full moon, there was plenty of light. Lois pointed at the moon. "I can't remember if a full moon is a good sign or a bad sign."

"It's just a full moon," I told her. "It's nature. It's neither good nor bad, and not a sign at all."

"Oh, Millie, sometimes you are just so practically Amish."

I didn't bother to reply because it was a fact.

In the goat tent, large fans buzzed to help keep the animals cool in the humid night air. The young goats blinked at us. They weren't nocturnal creatures as a rule, so we were certainly interrupting their beauty sleep, something they would need for the next day of judging.

Scooter, the small baby goat I'd met earlier that day, shivered in one corner of his pen. He was wet and far too close to the fan.

"The poor thing," I said, and without a second thought, I stepped over the fence into the pen and picked the little goat up. I gathered him up in my apron. "He's soaked through. We have to warm him up."

Lois reached into her tote bag and pulled out a bright pink beach towel. I stared at it. In all the time I had known Lois, she had pulled a myriad of things out of that bag, but an entire beach towel was almost too much to believe.

"We can wrap him in this." She held out the towel and waited to receive the little goat.

I handed him over, and she wrapped him up and then snuggled him against her chest. He didn't fight her at all. "Oh, he's just a little darling."

"How did he get wet?" I asked.

Sal pointed at the water trough in one corner of

the pen, which was knocked over. "He must have fallen in there or the water splashed out on him."

I nodded. "Well, we will have to keep an eye on him tonight. He should be fine with something to eat and a dry bed. He's so young; I imagine he's still on a bottle." I looked around his pen and spotted a dirty cooler in the corner. I opened it, and sure enough there were full bottles of milk inside. I held one out to him, and he drank eagerly.

"I can keep him in the security office," Sal said. "He's just a little bit. I don't think he will be much trouble at all, and I can feed him every few hours too."

"Thank you, Sal," I said and then frowned. "Just make sure you put him back before Zach Troyer arrives at the fair. He will be in a panic if he can't find his goat. I'm surprised he didn't make provisions to feed Scooter during the night." I remembered how sad the boy looked when he tried to sell the goat. I was clear to me that he'd much rather keep it if that was an option. Apparently, it was not. I moved on to the far end of the tent where Phillip and Peter's stall was located.

Lois took the bottle from my hand and continued to feed Scooter, so I could take a close look at Phillip and Peter's pen.

I reached the stall and noticed the problem right away. Glancing back at Sal and Lois with the baby goat in her arms, I said, "Phillip and Peter didn't jump the fence. They were let out. Someone cut the wires. Do you see the gap here?"

Sal placed a hand to his chest as if his heart skipped a beat. "How did I miss that?"

Lois patted his arm with her free hand. "Don't

blame yourself. You had two wild goats running around. That would distract anyone."

"Can I borrow your flashlight?" I asked Sal.

His hand shook as he passed the flashlight to me.

"Don't worry, Sal," I said. "Truly. I'm sure the goats are fine and having the time of their lives running around the fairgrounds."

"Thanks, Millie. That is kind of you to say, but I messed up. I just wanted a quiet easy job in retirement. This one is more than I expected. I should have turned it down as soon as they said I wouldn't have any help until Friday." His voice wavered. "Clearly, there ought to be more eyes on this place than just my two."

I shone the light on the fencing. The wires had most definitely been cut. There were no bite marks to indicate the goats had chewed their way out. The cuts were clean and precise. It had been intentional. I guessed that wire cutters had been used.

I straightened my back and felt a slight twinge. At my age, these late-night adventures weren't as easy as they once had been. "Let's see if we can find them. When we do, we can come back and investigate further here."

Lois snuggled Scooter to her chest now that he'd finished his bottle. "If someone let the goats out, why yours? They could have let out any or all of them. Why were Phillip and Peter singled out?"

"I'm guessing because they would be the most distracting, and they had already escaped before . . ." I trailed off as my suspicions stirred.

"Distraction from what?" Sal asked, looking about.

"We don't know that yet," I said. "Let's find the goats. It would be easiest to split up. Sal, you take the east side of the grounds where the rides and games are. Lois and I will check the west side where the pole barns are."

We all agreed and set off. As soon as Sal was out of earshot, Lois said, "I think you're right, Millie. Letting your goats free was a distraction. Or I would even say a diversion."

I didn't like the sound of that one bit, but I had thought the same thing.

"You don't think they were goat-napped, do you?" Lois asked.

My chest tightened at the very idea. Was it possible someone had tried to steal my goats and they'd managed to escape? I prayed they were okay. I had missed them terribly on the farm this evening.

"I don't actually think that's likely," Lois said, backtracking as she'd seen my visible reaction to the idea. "No one would want to take them—they are way too much trouble." She held up Scooter. "They would have taken this little cutie first."

That didn't make me feel much better. I put my fingers in my mouth and gave a shrill whistle, the one I used to call the goats in at night.

I heard nothing other than Scooter whimpering in Lois's arms. I whistled again, and there came the sound of a far-off goat cry.

"Why do they sound so far away?" Lois asked. "It's almost like they're at a neighboring farm, or in the woods on the other side of the parking lot."

I bent my neck and listened. "It sounded like it was coming from this way," I said.

We walked toward the pole barns, all the while on the lookout for any signs of the two goats.

"Whistle again," Lois said.

I did as she asked. The response from the goats came from the quilt barn.

I grimaced. This was very bad news. If Phillip and Peter were inside the quilt barn eating the quilts, I would never again be able to show my face in a single quilt shop in the county, if not the state.

There were rapid footsteps behind us as Sal's flashlight beam bounced on the path. "Is everything okay? I heard whistling."

"That was Millie," Lois explained. "She was calling the goats, and I think we've found them." With her free hand, she pointed at the quilt barn.

"How'd they get inside there?" Sal wanted to know. "The door to the quilt barn is locked at night. I locked it myself. The last time I made my rounds, I checked the door and it was still locked."

"What time was that?" I asked.

He frowned. "Eleven or thereabouts."

Lois put her hand on the doorknob, and it turned easily. "It's not locked now. A shame because I always like a chance to use my lock picks."

"You wouldn't have to, Lois, even if the door was locked. Sal has a key."

"Millie, let a girl dream, will you?"

Sal stepped in front of us. "I had better go in first. You know, for safety reasons."

Lois arched her brow at him. "You want to go in there first with those two rascal goats leaping about? You're a braver man than I thought."

He stepped back. "On second thought, maybe you should go in first."

I stepped into the pole barn with Lois right behind me. It was pitch-black inside.

"Where are the lights?" Lois asked, and she ran her hand along the wall looking for the light switch.

A moment later, the entire barn lit up in bright white light. It was so bright, I had to hold up a hand to shade my eyes.

"Sheesh, I should put on my sunglasses," Lois said. "Did they put ultra-brights in here or something?"

"Our eyes will adjust in a moment." I squinted.

"I see spots," she complained.

I saw spots too. Instead of saying that, I called the goats. "Phillip, Peter, come here."

As I expected, nothing happened. It had been worth a try, but they were smarter than that. They knew they were in trouble.

Sal stepped into the quilt barn and looked around with fear in his eyes, as if he thought one of the goats would jump out from behind a quilt to pounce on him.

"Umm, Millie, I think I found out why Phillip and Peter were used as a diversion." Lois pointed to a pile of fabric at the far end of the pole barn.

Head quilt judge and fair board president, Tara Barron, lay facedown in the middle of a shredded quilt on the dusty concrete floor with a dent in the back of her head.

Sal went down like a felled tree.

Chapter Seven

"Is he dead?" Lois leaned over his body, taking care not to drop Scooter in the process. "Two dead people are way more than I bargained for tonight."

I gave her a look. "I think he just passed out from the shock."

"I have a water bottle." Lois handed Scooter to me and reached into her bag. A moment later, she pulled out a metal water bottle, decorated with bright yellow lemons. She opened it and dashed the contents onto Sal's face. The water was brown.

"What did you throw on him?" I asked, aghast.

"Whoops, that was iced tea, not water. He'll be fine. The antioxidants will do him some good." She gave me a sheepish smile.

I shook my head. Just then, Peter and Phillip appeared from behind one of the quilts. They approached the fallen security guard and began licking the iced tea off his face.

Sal groaned and opened his eyes.

"Don't get up so fast. You fell," I said. "I don't think you hit your head, but we can never be too careful."

"My head doesn't hurt. I'm just a little woozy." He glanced at Tara's body, but then quickly averted his eyes. "I've never seen anything like this." He wiped at his face, then noticed the goats standing nearby. "Why am a wet?" He paused. "And sticky?"

"I threw iced tea on your face to bring you back. The caffeine is probably good for you," Lois said as she was tapping a text message out on her phone. I noticed she made no mention of the goats licking his face. She then rifled through her purse and came up with a small roll of paper towels. "Here. This will help you get cleaned up."

Sal accepted the paper towel and cleaned his face. "Thank you."

"We have to call the police," he said. "I'm not equipped for something like this. I'm little more than a mall cop. The most serious things I've dealt with are shoplifters and rowdy teenagers."

"And goats," Lois said. "Don't forget the goats."

He looked like he might pass out again. He removed his phone from his pocket and fumbled with it. "We have to call the police."

"Already done," Lois said. "I texted Deputy Little while you were on the floor. He's in my favorites on my phone. We go way back."

Sweat gathered on his upper lip. "I need to let the fair board know. Tara was the board president. She did everything. What will happen to the fair now? Will we have to close? I think we should close." He took a furtive glance at the body.

"Let's wait until the deputies and the ambulance arrive. You can ask Deputy Little what he wants you to do," I said. "He's a very level-headed young man and will have good advice under these circumstances."

Lois glanced at me as if she were surprised that I'd discouraged him from telling his employers about Tara's death, but if she took the time to think on it, she would understand. Tara was on the fair board. It was very likely that the other members of the board would be suspects. Deputy Little would want to control the way they were informed of her tragic death.

"All right," Sal said as if he was relieved at the idea of postponing that uncomfortable conversation. He took a step back and stumbled over his own two feet.

Lois threw out her arm as if to catch him. "Steady there."

He really was in no condition to deal with the gruesome sight in front of us. To be honest, neither were Lois and I, but we were a bit more experienced in this regard than Sal.

"Sal, why don't you take Scooter outside and wait for the police? This is no place for a baby goat." I settled the little bundle in his arms. It was no place for a woozy security guard either, but I saw no reason to increase his embarrassment.

"Yes, that's a good idea." He accepted Scooter.

"And take the other goats with you," Lois said. "Millie, do you have their leads?"

I nodded and pulled the two leashes from my apron pocket. I clipped one on Phillip's collar and then the other on Peter's. They didn't fight me. I suspected the pair was spooked by being stuck inside the quilt barn with Tara's body for so long. I put the end of the leashes in Sal's free hand. With two Boer goats to lead him, he went out the door.

"Poor old sod," Lois said. "He didn't sign up for this mess. I hope he's being paid well."

I murmured an agreement and then inched closer to the body, trying to make out the pattern on the quilt. I knew right away it wasn't mine, because my quilt was hanging where I'd put it that morning. I couldn't help feeling a bit of relief after spending so many painstaking hours on that quilt. In fact, I wasn't sure it was a quilt from the fair at all. Every inch of wall space still had a quilt hanging in front of it.

It might not have been my quilt, but it only took a moment to realize whose work it was. Even with the fabric nearly torn to bits, I knew right away.

I glanced back at Lois. "This is Ruth Yoder's quilt."

"No!" Lois exclaimed. "Are you sure? Please tell me that you're wrong."

"It's her quilt, all right," I said with conviction.

Lois placed a hand on her face, and her large rings and bright orange nail polish shone in the fluorescent lights. "Why is her quilt even here? Didn't she storm out with it under her arm when Tara said she couldn't enter it into the competition?"

I nodded.

"Do you think Ruth's quilt being here has significance?"

"I'm afraid it does. As you said, the quilt shouldn't even be here."

Far off, there came the sound of a siren approaching the fairgrounds. It wouldn't be long before deputies and emergency personnel descended on the quilt barn.

"Do you think Ruth knows where her quilt is?" Lois asked.

"I'm certain she doesn't know it's in shreds and under a dead body, but she might know that it's here. After all, how would it get here without her knowledge?"

"I can't imagine that she brought it back in after she was turned away. Ruth is nothing if not a rule follower," Lois said. "Even if she didn't like the fact that Tara turned her away, she wouldn't defy the rules. Sure, she would complain about it until the end of time, but I can't see her foisting her quilt on the competition."

The sound of sirens was almost deafening now as it reverberated off the pole barn's aluminum sides. Lois covered her ears. "Let's get out of here. I don't want to lose my hearing at this point in my life. Besides, it's like an oven in here. We should at least open the door for some airflow. How did you sit in here all day? I feel as if I'm being cooked like a rotisserie chicken."

I winced at the image. It was very warm in the pole barn, but I wished Lois had said so in a less graphic way.

We got outside just as the driver-side door of a deputy SUV opened, and I recognized the short stocky deputy who got out as Deputy Luke Little. Recently married to his beautiful bride, Charlotte Weaver Little, Deputy Little moved with a new confidence that I hadn't noticed in him before.

Since the appointment of the interim sheriff earlier in the summer, Deputy Little had a spring in his step. I supposed after working for years under the previous sheriff—a grouchy and unpleasant man—his new boss was a breath of fresh air. It didn't hurt that Sheriff Aiden Brody was one of Deputy Little's closest friends either.

Sheriff Brody had been the top deputy in the department for years. He'd left nearly two years ago to work for the state investigation bureau and had come back to Holmes County just a few months before the old sheriff was caught red-handed up to no good. Aiden was the county commissioners' first choice for sheriff and was appointed to complete the old sheriff's term. After that, he could run for election in the fall.

One might have thought that Deputy Little would be upset that the advisory board had chosen Sheriff Brody over him. Sheriff Brody had left the department, after all. Some people might have thought that Deputy Little, who had stayed to the end of Sheriff Marshall's turbulent reign, should have been given the job; he was second-in-command in the department. However that wasn't the case at all. Deputy Little was thrilled to have his friend Aiden Brody back in the department and that was evident in his newfound self-assuredness.

Lois stood with me watching as Deputy Little approached us. "Should we tell him it's Ruth's quilt?" Lois whispered.

"*Nee,* not unless we are asked directly. Let's keep that little nugget of information to ourselves. I would like to talk to Ruth before the police get involved."

"Good idea," Lois agreed. "Because there were a lot of people who saw her argument with Tara. It wasn't a good look. The bishop's wife could be in some hot water."

Before I could respond, Deputy Little stopped in front of us. "Lois, I wish I could say I was surprised to get your text in the middle of the night letting me know that you and Millie had discovered yet another dead body, but I wasn't."

Lois smiled at him. "I should think at this point you would expect this sort of thing from Millie and me."

"Unfortunately, I do." He sighed. "Why were the two of you here in the middle of the night in the first place?"

"The goats," I said.

He looked at me. "Your goats?"

"Do we ever speak of any other goats, Deputy?" Lois asked. "I really think Phillip and Peter are more than enough."

I had to admit, it was a fair statement.

He rubbed the back of his neck. "Well, I see a security guard over there with your goats. What is that he's holding?"

"Another goat," I said. "It's not mine."

He moved his hand to his forehead as if he might already be getting a headache. "Maybe you should start from the beginning . . ."

"We would be happy to, Deputy," Lois said with a smile.

Chapter Eight

The next morning, I woke up with a start. Peaches was washing himself at the end of my bed. He glared at me with his left hind leg suspended in the air and his toes spread. How dare I interrupt his bath time?

Light poured in through my window. It was after seven in the morning. I hadn't slept so late in ages.

I sat up. "The goats must be beside themselves to get out of the barn. And poor Bessie has to put up with their ruckus." Just as I finished saying this, I realized the goats weren't at the farm. They were at the fairgrounds, and last night's events came rushing back into my mind. The goats, the quilt, Tara.

I slumped back into the bed. It was as if the weight of the memory pushed me back down.

As much as I'd wanted to take the goats home with me last night, I'd decided to leave them at the fair. I couldn't disappoint Micah. He'd worked too hard preparing them for judging.

With Sal's help, Lois and I were able to find an empty stall in the horse stables to put them in until the fencing of their pen could be repaired. Sal insisted that he would keep a close eye on them, and I believed him after last night's ordeal. As for little Scooter, Sal planned to keep the young goat in his trailer for the rest of the night now that he was no longer on duty. I thought worrying over the goats was a *gut* thing for Sal. I hoped it would keep his mind off Tara's death, and her possible murder.

In my mind, there was no doubt Tara Barron had been murdered. It was true she could have fallen and hit her head. The floor was a concrete slab after all. But that didn't explain the shredded quilt. Ruth's quilt.

I sat up in bed again. It was best to get on with it and face the day. An old Amish proverb came to my mind, *"The secret to getting ahead is getting started."* Keeping that in mind, I decided it was best to get on with my most difficult task for the day.

The first thing I planned to do was best achieved early in the morning, when Lois would be occupied with the breakfast rush at the Sunbeam Café. Lois hated it when I did any detecting without her, but this time it couldn't be helped. If I wanted Ruth to talk to me, Lois needed to be out of the picture.

I fed Peaches and Bessie, and then prepared for my day. Bessie seemed excited when I told her we were going for a ride. Lately, I had been depending more on Lois and her car to get me places. But

Bessie still needed to get out for exercise and to see things.

I scratched her cheek while I hooked her up to my small buggy. The buggy was over thirty years old and still in great working condition. I had heard of buggies lasting even longer than that. With all the bells and whistles that automobiles had, there were just more ways for them to break down. Buggies didn't have those issues. Wood and iron were much more easily replaced than all the electronic gadgets that seemed to be in cars today. I'd bought the buggy secondhand.

The Yoder farm was close by; only a few miles away. A thirty-minute ride by buggy. It was still too early in the morning for many of the summer tourists to be out, so Bessie and I had the road all to ourselves.

As I listened to the clip-clop of Bessie's hooves on the asphalt and the familiar rattle of the buggy, I thought over the events of last night. Why would anyone want to kill Tara Barron? True, I had only met her once, and she had been rude to me. However, at the time I had shrugged it off, thinking that she must be anxious with the fair about to begin. She was the fair board president after all. A lot of the event's success rested on her shoulders. I know if I had been in her position, I would have been nervous.

A more pressing question was what did Ruth have to do with the murder? I didn't for a second believe that Ruth would kill anyone. Reprimand and criticize, absolutely, but kill, never.

The Yoder farm came into view. It was a beautiful piece of property tucked high on one of the county's many rolling hills. Holmes County was just on the edge of Ohio's Appalachian foothills, so our rolling hills became more dramatic peaks farther south. The Yoders were dairy farmers, and black-and-white Holstein cows dotted the bright green grass of the hillsides. It was like looking at a real-life version of a postcard in one of the gift shops in town.

There were two large barns behind the house: one for the cows and one for the other barnyard animals, like horses, sheep, and mules. The house itself was huge even by Amish standards. The home and property had been in Bishop Yoder's family for five generations. Each generation seemed to be more numerous than the last. As a result, each generation added a wing for a bigger kitchen, living space, and more and more bedrooms.

Ruth had added on to the front of the house, tripling the living room in size and adding a massive wraparound porch that circumnavigated the entire house. The addition had been made when her husband became bishop of the district so as to accommodate Sunday services.

We Amish didn't have church buildings. Instead, we met every other week at a member's home. The off Sundays were for private devotions and fellowship with a member's immediate family. If Ruth had her way, we would meet every single time at the Yoder farm. As it was, she had the services at her home at least once a month, sometimes twice.

The long drive had recently been paved, so Bessie and my buggy traveled smoothly along it.

The front door opened before I could even climb out of the buggy.

"Millie Fisher, you had better be here because you want to apologize," Ruth said.

I sighed. Ruth was in one of *those* moods. It was difficult to reason with her when she was stirred up like this. Her greeting did not bode well for the conversation that I had planned.

I grabbed the plate of treats I had made earlier. In truth, they'd been for our quilting meeting that afternoon, but I would have to make something else. I knew better than to go to Ruth's house empty-handed, especially when I wanted information.

"I have date-nut bars dipped in white chocolate," I said. "I know they are one of your favorites." Standing at the foot of the porch steps, I held the plate out in front of me like an offering.

Ruth studied my plate with suspicion. I guessed she knew in her heart that I wanted something from her, and by taking the date-nut bars she was silently agreeing to whatever that might be. At least, I hoped that was the case, because I really wanted her to answer my questions.

She loved date-nut bars. Maybe not as much as I loved blueberries, but she liked them enough that it seemed she was willing to risk finding out what I wanted.

"You might as well come inside." She walked up the porch steps, obviously expecting me to follow.

The living room of the Yoder home was the size of the entire main floor of my little farmhouse. Actually, it was likely a touch bigger. At the moment, it contained a cold fireplace, two large sofas, several comfy chairs, and side tables sprinkled about. Everything was spotless and there was a faint scent of lemon and vinegar in the air. Ruth prided herself on keeping an immaculate home.

When church meetings occurred at the Yoder farm, all of this furniture was moved out, while rows and rows of wooden folding chairs were set in its place.

"Let's go to the kitchen," Ruth said. "You got here so early, I haven't even finished my coffee yet."

I followed Ruth through a door that led into a very large eat-in kitchen. A long oak table and chairs were on one side of the room with places for twelve to sit. I knew from church meetings that the table could be expanded to seat twenty if the need arose.

Ruth went to the percolator on the stovetop and poured a mug of coffee. She set it on the table. "That is for you."

I perched on my assigned seat.

She then collected her own coffee, two small plates, and my small platter of treats, adding them to the tabletop.

Ruth sat across from me, and after taking one of the date-nut bars, she slid them in my direction. I took two, believing I would need the fortification of both for this conversation.

Ruth eyed the number of bars I'd taken and wrapped her hands around her warm mug. "As much as I enjoy a visit from any of the church ladies, I must ask why you're here. We can speak freely. The bishop is visiting Grandma Leah, who is feeling poorly."

"I didn't know that. Will she be all right?" I

couldn't keep the worry from my voice. Grandma Leah—who was close to one hundred years of age—was the oldest member in the district. However, if one saw her, it would be hard to believe. She still actively helped out on her family's Christmas tree farm. She could be found in the orchard, pruning trees and collecting all the fallen pinecones, which the family also sold for holiday decorations.

"She thinks so. It's just a few aches and pains according to her, but then again, I don't know if Grandma Leah would even admit it if she were to take ill. In any case, she is ready to go home to the Lord when her time comes."

I sipped my coffee. Ruth's words weren't an uncommon notion in the Amish community when a member reached a certain age. Grandma Leah, a faithful servant, was confident of where she was headed when she died.

"Why are you here, Millie?" Ruth asked, getting right to the point.

A virtue of Amish life was our tendency not to dance around a subject. Because of this, I wasn't the least bit surprised by Ruth's direct question.

"When was the last time you saw your quilt?" I asked.

Ruth wrinkled her nose. "My quilt? What are you talking about? I really wish you wouldn't answer *my* questions with another question. It is an annoying trait you have."

"I apologize," I said. "I'm speaking about the quilt you brought to the fair yesterday."

Ruth scowled. "If you are going to tell me that you didn't approve of how I acted yesterday or any such thing, you can stand up right now and march out the door. I had every right to enter my quilt in that competition. That Tara person was being completely unreasonable."

I pressed my lips together and stared down at my mug. It took all of my might not to remind Ruth that the rules and deadline of the quilt competition had been given to her well in advance. Normally, I would just say it, but it was best to keep my mouth shut on the matter for the time being if I wanted answers to my questions.

"This is not at all what I thought you wanted to discuss." She sipped her coffee and then set the mug down on the small table beside her.

I frowned. "We are in a quilting circle together," I said. "The majority of the conversations we have are about quilts. Why did you think I came here?"

"I thought it was about Uriah, of course."

I stared at the date-nut bars on my plate and the pair of them seemed to have lost all their appeal. I had suddenly lost my appetite. "Uriah? Why would I come to your house to speak to you about him?"

"Well, he was here to visit the bishop just last night about *you*."

"*Me*? Why would he be speaking to the bishop about me?"

She cocked her head. "Millie, you know why. He's been back for six months. By this time, we all expected you to be married. It was about time he came to the bishop and had the conversation."

"The conversation? About marriage?" I kept parroting everything she said, but I couldn't help it. Uriah and I hadn't even had a conversation about marriage yet. It was traditional for a man to go to the district bishop for a blessing on the match before asking for a woman's hand, but not before the bride-to-be knew about it!

"Are you certain that's why he was here?" I asked. "There could have been many reasons why he might need counsel from the bishop. And I don't believe it is right for you to eavesdrop on those conversations."

Ruth bristled. "Eavesdrop? I do not eavesdrop! I happened to go by the door to my husband's study and heard them speaking. The bishop asked Uriah plainly if he intended to marry you, and Uriah said *ya*." She scrunched up her nose. "I wasn't out looking for this information. I just happened to be in the right place at the right time."

While moments ago I'd been prepared to drink my coffee and eat the two date-nut bars, suddenly I was queasy.

"Well, I can assure you, this is all news to me, and not the reason I'm here." It was time to get the conversation back on track. I would worry about Uriah later. "Do you know where your quilt is?" I asked for a second time.

She sniffed. "I marched out of that fair with it and brought it home. The truth is, I should have known better than to enter it in the first place. Winning such a competition would be prideful. I would never be prideful."

Nope, never, I thought. It took all my willpower not to roll my eyes. It was a terrible habit I had picked up from Lois, and I was trying to quit.

"It's interesting that you say you took it from the fair, because it was found in the quilt barn last night."

She threw up her hands. "If you knew where it was, why did you ask me in the first place?"

"I just wanted to make certain it was your quilt," I said.

"It either is or it isn't," Ruth said. "My quilt is distinctive. You should have been able to recognize it right away. Double Stitch worked on it."

She was right, but under the dire circumstance I had seen the quilt, it wasn't as distinctive as it had once been. Had I been wrong about its being Ruth's quilt? Why would someone come all the way to her house to steal the quilt, only to shred it and leave the scraps around Tara Barron after killing her? The notion seemed ridiculous and morbid.

"I didn't take it back into the quilt barn," Ruth said. "I would never. Not after I had been so horribly insulted. How dare that woman turn me away? I know she is *Englisch*, but even she should know the status I hold in this county as the wife of one of the most prominent bishops. It was disrespectful, if you ask me."

"Where is the quilt now? Is it here somewhere? Can I see it?"

She narrowed her eyes. "I left it in the buggy. I was just so upset yesterday; I came right into the house and told Bishop Yoder what had happened. After that, I didn't go back out to get it because my daughter and grandchildren were here."

I bit my lip. "Can I see the quilt?"

She studied me. "Why?"

"Just indulge me this one time, Ruth."

"I have never known you to play games, Millie. Lois is the one for that. But if you insist, we can go retrieve the quilt." She stood up and set off, and I quickly got to my feet to follow her out of the house.

The Yoders were a big family and had more than one buggy. The one Ruth most often drove was a much newer model than mine. I knew most *Englischers* wouldn't notice the difference, but I did right away. Even Amish transportation changes a bit over the decades, but just a very tiny bit.

There was a wooden trunk on the back of her buggy. "It's right in here." She opened the trunk.

It was empty.

Chapter Nine

When I explained to Ruth what I believed had happened to her quilt, she insisted we head straight to the fairgrounds. I offered to drive us there in my buggy, as it seemed Ruth was far too upset to hitch up her horse properly. I knew her nerves had gotten the better of her when I saw her hands were shaking, causing her to fold them in her lap.

She left Bishop Yoder a scribbled note on the large kitchen table, but I wished we'd used the shed phone to called Grandma Leah's place and tell him what had happened. Ruth needed his calming presence more than ever, and I did too. I had never seen her so on edge and it was unnerving. She was silent during the ride to the fairgrounds. Ruth always had something to say.

As Bessie turned into the parking lot adjacent to the fairgrounds, Ruth leaned forward, as if she could urge the horse to go faster. I drove Bessie to the hitching post and pulled back on the reins. Ruth was out of her seat almost immediately and stomping in the direction of the entrance gate. As quickly as I could, I tied up the horse and hurried after her.

Sal was at the front gate again. The poor man had dark bags under his eyes. I wondered if he'd gotten a single wink of sleep the night before. By the looks of it, he had not.

"If you're not presenting, you can't go in without a ticket," Sal said to Ruth as she marched by the ticket booth.

Ruth shook her finger at him. "I'm not buying a ticket for this. I have been treated terribly from start to finish by the organizers of this fair, and now I hear that my quilt has been stolen. Step aside."

Sal's eyes rolled in his head, reminding me of Bessie when she spotted a mouse in the barn. The horse really hated mice. Thankfully, Peaches had taken it upon himself to remedy that issue. Bessie had been much happier with her living quarters since I had adopted the cat.

"Sal," I said, "can Ruth come into the fair with me? It's about what happened here last night." I gave him a meaningful look. "She might be of some help."

"Oh." He paused. "*Oh.* Yes, of course, you both can go in."

"*Danki,*" I said, but Ruth stomped away without saying thank you.

The fair was just beginning to open for the day. I could already smell the fat bubbling in the deep fryers. My stomach turned at the distinctive scent.

I wasn't completely recovered from my reckless eating the day before. I wanted nothing more than a strong cup of tea. However, that would have to wait as I hurried through the fairgrounds behind Ruth, who was a *gut* five inches taller than I and three times as upset.

As we rushed past the axe-throwing booth, Ruth shot the operator an angry look as if she blamed her for our current predicament. The closer we came to the quilt barn, the less likely I thought it was that we would be able to go inside. Crime scene tape crisscrossed the door, and Deputy Little and Sheriff Aiden Brody stood outside the quilt barn speaking in hushed tones.

This would be a time for Ruth to approach the two men politely and endear herself to them. However, Ruth used a different technique. We were still a good five yards away from them when she waved her arms. "Is it true? Is it true that my quilt was found with a dead body? Sheriff Brody, what are you going to do about this? You were appointed interim sheriff to keep us safe in this county. There has been no change in the crime rate since you took the position. And now there is a dead body on my quilt?"

Sheriff Brody removed his departmental ball cap and scratched the top of his blond head as he studied Ruth with tired yet kind brown eyes. "Your quilt, Ruth?"

"That's what Millie told me. I don't for a minute believe it's true." She shot me a dirty look. "But I had to come and see for myself just in case."

Deputy Little shot me a look over Ruth's shoulder because he knew as well as I did that I hadn't shared that bit of information with him. I didn't believe it would help my case if I confessed I hadn't mentioned this detail because I'd wanted to check with Ruth first. A favor that had completely backfired on me since she'd outed me the first chance she got. Honestly, I should have expected as much from Ruth.

A woman stepped out from behind Deputy Little. I hadn't noticed she was standing with the two men, perhaps because she was so small. If she'd told me she was five feet tall, I wouldn't have believed her. She almost looked like a child until I saw her face. Then it was clear to me she was an adult, an adult who had been worn down by hardship and too much sun and who wasn't much younger than Ruth and I.

"Please. I need an answer," the small woman stammered. "The fair must go on as scheduled. We want as little disruption as possible. We can't let this unfortunate event derail us."

I glanced around. It appeared to me that the fair *was* going on as scheduled. People were in growing lines to buy food and drinks. Children screamed on the fair rides and vendors shouted at passersby to come give their games a try. Other than the crime scene tape on the quilt barn, it was business as usual at the Holmes County Fair.

When Sheriff Brody didn't immediately answer her, she said, "The quilt judging must go on!"

"The sheriff's department has the right to hold the quilts or anything else in the barn as evidence," Sheriff Brody answered. "However, we will keep only those items that we need for the investigation."

"I need my quilt," Ruth interjected.

The woman adjusted the wire-rimmed glasses on her nose. "Who are you?"

Ruth placed a hand on her chest as if offended that anyone in Holmes County would fail to recognize her on sight. "I'm Ruth Yoder."

When the woman's face remained blank, Ruth went on to say, "I am the wife of the bishop of the largest Amish district in Harvest."

"Oh, Harvest," the woman said. "I rarely go over there. It's all the way on the other side of the county."

I was relieved that Margot Rawlings—the community planner for Harvest—wasn't around to hear that. Her life's goal was to make Harvest *the* place to visit in Holmes County, if not all of Ohio. She would have been completely insulted by someone's claiming they never went there.

I smiled at the woman before Ruth could say something else rude. I gave Ruth the benefit of the doubt for her unkindness because she was fretting over her quilt, a project she had spent months and months on.

"I'm Millie Fisher, a member of Ruth's district," I said, more for Ruth's benefit than to inform the woman. "What is your name?"

"I'm Star Paley. I'm a member of the fair board. I was overseeing the games this year. You know, going through vendor applications and the like. But since Tara d—Since there has been an accident, I've now been put in charge of the quilt barn and craft judging. I was just asking that we continue with the quilt judging," Star said. "Tara would want the program to go on. She put so much work into the fair, and especially into the quilting competition. She wouldn't want it to be canceled."

"I understand that," Sheriff Brody said. "However, it's my job to make sure everyone is safe and the person responsible for Tara Barron's death is brought to justice."

Star swallowed hard. "Do you really think she was murdered? That is just so difficult to believe."

"We can't rule anything out at this point," Sheriff Brody said. "Which is why we need to keep the quilt barn closed and secure. There might be more evidence to be found. We can't have people going in and out of there."

"I understand." She wrung her hands. "I'll find a new place for the quilts. When do you think they'll be released?"

"I can't give you an exact time frame, but I assure you, we're working as quickly and diligently as we can," the young sheriff said.

Star opened her mouth as if she wanted to say more and then snapped it closed.

"I want to see my quilt," Ruth insisted. She wasn't taking the news about the quilt barn being closed quite as well as Star.

Sheriff Brody's brown eyes slid in my direction. "I think I would like to speak to Millie alone before we discuss your quilt, Ruth."

Ruth put her hands on her hips. "That is not acceptable! I am the bishop's wife. What I need should take precedence over whatever it is you want to say to Millie."

"I need to talk to Millie about the quilt and what she saw last night," he said. "I will be brief."

Before Ruth or Star could protest, the sheriff ushered me over to his SUV a few yards away. He folded his arms. "As soon as I heard that Lois had called in the incident last night, I expected you to show up sometime this morning, Millie," Sheriff Brody said. "But I would have thought Lois would be with you now, not Ruth."

"Lois is working the breakfast shift at the Sunbeam Café this morning."

He arched his brow. "Does she know you're here without her?"

I smoothed an imaginary wrinkle in my dress sleeve. "*Nee*. She is not going to be happy with me when she finds out either, but I needed to speak to Ruth alone. Ruth and Lois are always just like cats and dogs. Ruth wasn't going to tell me anything with Lois there."

He nodded as this was common knowledge throughout Harvest. "And what did you want to tell Ruth?"

I smoothed that wrinkle in my sleeve again. "I wanted to be sure the quilt she made for the competition was still with her. When I saw Tara's body, I took note of the quilt. It looked much like the one Ruth had made, but I needed to ask her to be sure. The quilt I saw late last night was in such poor condition, I might have been mistaken."

"You didn't tell Deputy Little your suspicions?" he asked.

"*Nee*, I wanted to speak to Ruth first. If I was wrong about the quilt, she would be angry with me for sending the police to her home."

"What else didn't you tell Deputy Little?"

"I can't think of anything," I said.

"You also neglected to tell him that Ruth's quilt wasn't accepted in the quilt competition, and she argued with Tara Barron in front of a barn full of people."

"You are right. I didn't tell him that either," I said. "And it seems I didn't need to, as you have found out on your own. But, Sheriff, I will remind you that we both know Ruth Yoder would never kill anyone. She may be bossy and rude at times, but she is not a killer."

"I wish I could dismiss her from the suspect list, but we have both dealt with suspicious death long enough to know that's not how it works. I have to consider everyone."

"So it is murder?" I asked.

"The coroner hasn't filed his final report yet, but the preliminaries point to murder, yes. She didn't hurt her head from falling on the concrete slab. The coroner believes she was struck from behind. Considering the positioning of the impact, she could not have done that to herself."

I shivered. It was what I'd suspected when I'd seen Tara lying on that shredded quilt, but that didn't make it any easier to hear.

Sheriff Brody put the ball cap back on his head. "Am I wasting my breath telling you and Lois to stay out of this?"

"Most likely," I replied.

Chapter Ten

After my conversation with Sheriff Brody, he showed Ruth a photograph of the shredded quilt. Thankfully, the picture on his phone didn't feature Tara's dead body. Ruth confirmed what I already knew. It was her quilt. She took the news harder than I expected. She rushed off, saying that she needed to call the bishop at Grandma Leah's. It made me wish even more that we'd called him earlier. The bishop should be with his wife at a time like this.

I was uncertain whether I needed to take Ruth back home, or whether her husband would ride to the rescue, but I thought it best if I stayed at the fair until that determination was made.

I thought I should use my time wisely and go check in on the goats. Sheriff Brody didn't ask me much about how the goats got out the night before, or what they were doing when we heard them inside the quilt barn. I supposed Deputy Little had filled him in on the pertinent bits of information.

I was unsure if the goats were back inside the goat tent or in the stables where we'd left them last night. I decided to start with the goat tent as there was a possibility Sal had taken them back in time for the judging this morning.

I started down the line of pole barns arranged one after another, side by side. The largest one was where the indoor races and judging would be. Just as soon as I walked by the gap between the indoor arena and the neighboring pole barn, I heard crying. And not soft crying either. This was loud and heart-wrenching.

I stopped and poked my head into the gap, "Hello, are you all right?"

A sniffle was my reply.

"Can I help? You sound like you could use some help."

"I'm fine," the stuffy-sounding female voice said.

She didn't seem to be fine at all. I stepped into the gap between the buildings in order to escape the glare of the hot sun. Its blinding light was keeping me from see who or what was in that space.

When my eyes cleared, I found Star standing there, dabbing a tissue under her eyes. "I told you I was fine. You needn't come in here. Can't I just have one moment to myself? I can't wait until this fair is over. It has been a nightmare from start to finish."

"I'm so sorry I bothered you, but I can assure you I only peeked in here to make sure you were all right. You sounded very upset," I said.

She shoved the crumpled tissue into her neon-green fanny pack. "I am upset! I have every right to be upset. A fair board member is dead, and I'm supposed to pick up the pieces. I'm just the secretary on the board. I shouldn't be the one to run to the rescue. Everyone knows a person volunteers to be a secretary of an organization because they want to sit in the background, take notes, and not speak. Now, I'm supposed to run this whole fair. And I don't know how to!"

"That does sound very stressful," I said soothingly.

"It is. Tara did *everything*. You know the type, the ultra-organized woman who can do it all and still have perfect hair." She looked like she might cry. "I have to keep an extra pair of shoes in my car because I leave the house in my bedroom slippers so often." She held up her foot to show me her pink slipper. "I did it again today and couldn't even remember to put on my shoes from the car. It's little wonder though after I heard that Tara was dead. How am I going to run the entire fair? I'm not equipped for this."

"Is there no one else who could take your place? Another board member perhaps? It couldn't be just you and Tara on the board."

"The vice president could, but he is uninterested and completely incompetent. When Tara put him in his place weeks ago, he completely checked out from all his commitments and responsibilities in regard to the fair. Meanwhile, the treasurer is terrible. He can't even do math! Who elects a treasurer who can't do math? The truth is, no one wanted to work with Tara, so the people we did get to help are from the bottom of the barrel."

"When you say the vice president checked out, what do you mean?"

Star stared at me as if I had antlers growing out of the top of my head. "It means exactly what I said. He was done with the fair. He stopped doing anything. Tara wanted him to step down from his position so another person could take the spot. He refused out of spite. He just wanted to make Tara's tenure as board president as painful as possible."

All the bells and whistles went off in my head. It seemed Star had just introduced me to my first viable suspect. In fact, she had given me more than one, because it sounded like the fair board was just dysfunctional enough to have a killer in its ranks.

She shook out her hands as if she'd touched something that gave her the creepy-crawlies. "I have to find a new venue for the quilting competition." She tried to move around me. We were both small women, but the space was tight. I backed out of the spot so she could step past me.

"I entered my quilt in the competition. Perhaps I could help you find a new place for the judging. I would know the best place for the quilts to be hung," I said.

She stared at me. "You would help me? Why?"

She didn't even try to keep the suspicion out of her voice.

I smiled. "Because you could use the help."

She blinked as if she'd never expected someone to say something like that. "All right."

"What about the arena?" I suggested. "It's temperature controlled and would be a better place for the quilts than even the quilt barn."

"But there are farm animals going in and out of there. Surely, the quilts and other handicrafts will be soiled."

I shook my head. "Not if we set it up right. Let's take a look."

The arena was just on the other side of the quilt barn, so it was a few feet away, making it a *gut* choice for sheer proximity's sake. The quilts were almost all queen- or king-size and their giant hanging frames were extremely heavy. The shorter the distance we had to move them, the better.

As we stepped into the arena, the smell of animals and hay was heavy in the air. I could certainly understand Star's reluctance to use this place for a backup venue.

"This is never going to work," Star said. "The quilts would absorb the barnyard smell. None of the quilters will want their quilts going home smelling of a horse stall."

She had a valid point. As if we needed further proof this wasn't the best location, the goat judging was happening in the middle of the area. At least two dozen Boer goats waited to be judged, my two goats among them, handled by Micah.

"Next up we have Sir Lancelot. Lance, as he is called, is a three-year-old Boer goat, and is being showed today by his owner and handler, Suzy Keim. Suzy says that Lance has a bubbly personality—his personal mission is to make you smile."

Suzy Keim marched around the show ring with her brown goat, which had one white hind leg. Both girl and goat looked quite pleased with themselves as they stopped before the judge. In front of the elderly *Englisch* judge, the goat planted his hooves into the dirt arena floor and stood perfectly still.

Meanwhile my goats, Phillip and Peter, were tugging so hard on their leads that my great-nephew Micah had to wrap his free arm around a cedar post to keep the goats from springing away.

I patted Star on the arm. "If you will excuse me just for a moment." I didn't give her time to answer as I hurried as fast as I dared to the other side of the show ring.

"Micah," I said in a hushed voice.

He looked at me, his arm still wrapped around the cedar post. "Hi, Aenti! I have everything under control here."

It didn't look like it.

"Maam, Jacob, and Ginny are in the stands!" He turned and waved at his *maam* and siblings. Edith and Ginny, both very fair with pale skin and light blond hair, waved back. Jacob was also blond like Edith and all three children, but his hair was sandier and he didn't wave. He had his arms folded across his chest. Even though Micah and Jacob were close in age, there was tension between the brothers. For years, Jacob had felt he had to be the man of the house after his *daed* died, while Micah allowed himself to just be a kid.

"Phillip is up next. Peter was already judged."

"How did he do?" I asked.

"Well, he ate the judge's notepad, so I don't think he's a contender for a ribbon. Since all of the judge's notes about the goat entries were on the pad, I'm not sure even he knows who will win.

Peter can really eat fast. Phillip should do better," he said brightly. "There is no notepad left to eat, and the judge is having another person take notes now."

I wasn't so sure that Phillip would do much better. He was the more ornery of the two goats and the ringleader when it came to getting the pair of them into trouble.

"Next up, Phillip, presented by Micah Hochstetler," the judge announced. His voice wavered a tad when he read Micah's name. Possibly because he was remembering the last time Micah had brought a goat into the show ring. I hoped it wasn't a favorite notepad of his that Peter had eaten.

"Aenti, will you hold on to Peter's leash while I show Phillip?"

I nodded and took the leash from his hand. As soon as Micah entered the arena, Peter looked up at me with his round yellow eyes. I shook my head. "Don't you give me those puppy-dog eyes! I know what you did, and it is unacceptable." I put a hand on my hip. "You can't go around eating people's notes."

He hung his head. He was truly sorry, but I didn't have high hopes that he wouldn't do it again if given a chance. Peter had a taste for paper.

I watched as Micah and Phillip made their way around the ring. The goat was on his best behavior and stood perfectly still as the judge looked him over. I was astounded. I had never been able to make the goats be still in my life. I would have to ask Micah what his secret was.

The judge told Micah he was done, and the next handler and goat were called.

As Micah approached Peter and me, he was beaming. "Aenti Millie, did you see that? Did you see how well Phillip did?"

"I did," I said in shock. "What is your trick?"

"Well, I told him if we won, he'd get two carrots every day forever."

I smiled. "And I suppose that I'm the one who will supply the carrots to make *gut* on that promise."

"He does live at your farm . . ." Micah trailed off.

I handed him Peter's lead as I saw Star about to leave the arena. I had a murder to solve. I'd gotten off track. Goats will do that to a person. "I'm glad I got to see you show them. I'm impressed."

Star went out the door. I might have missed my chance to ask her more about the surly fair board members, but I had one more question for my nephew. "Where were the goats when you got here this morning?"

He blinked at me. "What do you mean?"

"Were they in their pen?"

"Of course, they were. They were just where I left them yesterday."

"And the fence around their pen was repaired?"

"Repaired? Why do you ask that? There was nothing wrong with it."

"Oh, I must have been mistaken," I said, not wanting to tell my young great-nephew about the murder.

But I wasn't mistaken.

Chapter Eleven

Someone had fixed Phillip and Peter's pen before Micah arrived at the fair at eight that morning. I guessed it had been the security guard Sal. I hoped that also meant he had returned Scooter, the little pygmy goat, to his pen before Zach Troyer returned to the fair. The poor child seemed to have too many worries for one so young. Stress on a child was something I hated to see.

"Millie Fisher, there you are!" Lois cried. She walked up to me carrying a pig, and it wasn't just any pig. It was Jethro, the black and white polka-dotted pot-bellied pig who had become a bit of a mascot for the village of Harvest. I wasn't the least surprised to see either of them at the fair, but I was surprised to see them together with no sign of Juliet Brook, the pastor's wife, or Bailey King, Juliet's regular pig-sitter, nearby.

Lois hurried over to me. Her large purse slapped against her hip and the pig's head bobbed up and down like one of those bobblehead dolls that an elderly *Englischer* sold from the back of his pickup truck at the flea market. Lois and I went to the flea market often because she was always looking for another piece of furniture to refinish.

"Lois, I thought you were at the café working the breakfast shift," I said. "And why is Jethro with you?"

"I was," she said. "But that was before I was told you were at the fair investigating without me." She stuck her lower lip out in a pout.

I grimaced. "How did you hear that?"

"Charlotte Little was on the phone with her husband while she was at the café getting coffee for the crew at Swissmen Sweets, and he told her you were at the fair with Ruth. Ruth! Mildred Fisher, how could you have Ruth Yoder be Watson to your Sherlock Holmes? I thought we were a team."

Lois knew how much I hated my given name Mildred. She only used it when she was under extreme duress, so she was obviously very upset.

"Lois, I was not investigating with Ruth."

"That's not what Charlotte said."

"Charlotte was just repeating what she heard from her husband. Deputy Little will hear from me on that point. I came to the fair with Ruth because of her quilt. I wanted to confirm it was hers before I shared the information with the sheriff's department."

"Oh," Lois said, mollified. "I suppose I should have thought of that."

One the characteristics I loved most about Lois was her ability to get over disagreements quickly. Sadly, I can't say that I was the same way.

"So was it her quilt?" Lois asked, shifting the pig in her arms.

I nodded.

"Oh dear." She shook her head and her long dangly earrings bounced off her cheeks. "I'm sure she had a few choice words to say about that."

"More than a few," I assured her. I nodded at Jethro. "Why do you have him?"

"Well, it's a long story . . ."

It always was when it came to Jethro.

"But," she went on, "when Charlotte came to the Sunbeam Café this morning for that coffee, she had Jethro with her. It seems Juliet is at some sort of pastors' wives retreat this week and couldn't take the pig with her, so—"

"She left Jethro with Bailey," I finished for her.

She nodded. "Right, and Bailey is beside herself working to open her big candy factory before Christmas, so she left Jethro at the candy shop with Charlotte. Apparently, he got into the peppermint jar and made a huge mess. Charlotte was close to tears when she told me all this. I think she's still getting used to managing Swissmen Sweets while Bailey is so caught up in the factory. The peppermint jar was the straw that broken the camel—er—pig's back."

"So you offered to watch him," I said, knowing that was exactly what Lois would do. I would have done the same under similar circumstances. No one wanted to see sweet newlywed Charlotte Little in tears.

"Just for the day," Lois said.

I hoped that was true. I wasn't up for any pig sleepovers and neither was Peaches.

"This pig is getting heavy." She set Jethro on the ground, removed a blue and white polka-dotted leash from her purse, and attached it to his collar. "Now, tell me what else you learned. I can't believe you didn't poke your nose in around here, gathering leads while you had the time."

She knew me well.

"Let's go over to the goat tent, and I will tell you on the way," I said.

After I filled Lois in and just before we entered the goat tent, Lois whistled. "Sounds to me like the fair board is a mess. We definitely want to find the other members and learn what they know."

I agreed, but before we did that, I wanted to see for myself how Phillip and Peter's pen had been fixed.

As soon as we stepped into the tent, I heard an angry voice.

"You're just like your mother," Hezekiah said to Zach in Pennsylvania Dutch. "Why don't you leave now and become an *Englischer* like her? At least then, you won't be my responsibility any longer. I didn't ask for this burden."

Zach's lower lip wobbled and he held tight to Scooter, who was snuggled so deeply in his arms, I couldn't see the small goat's face.

"I'm sorry, Grossdaadi. I will do better. I promise."

"You should be sorry," Hezekiah growled. "Now, get out of my face. I told you my decision already and it's not up for discussion."

In tears that he could no longer hold back, Zach ran from the tent with Scooter in his arms.

"I have no idea what that man just said to that child," Lois said. "All I know is I want to slap that old coot across the face."

I felt the same way, and I was Amish. I walked over to Zach's *grossdaadi*. "Hezekiah, is Zach all right? I just saw him run out of the tent in tears."

He spun around and glared at me. "That is none of your concern."

"A hurting child is *always* my concern," I said sharply. "It should be yours as well."

He stomped away without another word.

"What an awful man," Lois declared. "If I didn't have Jethro with me, I would have smacked him with my purse, and it would have hurt. You know I have a brick in there."

I did know.

"I think we need to talk to Zach and make sure he's okay," I said. "I don't like the way his *grossdaadi* spoke to him."

"What will you do if he's not okay?" Lois asked.

"Then we will have to go to his bishop or my bishop to intervene."

I stepped out of the tent and scanned he grounds for Zach. He was nowhere to be seen. I prayed he was all right. The next time I saw him, I planned to ask him what was going on between him and his *grossdaadi* and how could I help. Some Amish men, just like *Englisch* ones, could be gruff and have a sour disposition, but it seemed to me that Hezekiah Troyer was downright cruel to his young grandson.

The goat tent was mostly empty. There were just

a handful of small goats napping in the corners of their pens. Most of the goats were at the judging in the arena. I walked over to Phillip and Peter's pen, and sure enough, it looked as if it had never been cut.

I wasn't sure why this bothered me so much. Maybe the fencing couldn't be securely repaired, and someone had just put in new fencing altogether, but it seemed to me there was another reason for the replacement. It smelled like a cover-up.

I said as much to Lois and she wholeheartedly agreed, but then again, Lois loved nothing more than a *gut* conspiracy theory.

She picked up Jethro. "So what's the plan now?"

"A couple of things," I said. "We find these other board members and talk to them, and we learn who fixed this fence. It could have been Sal."

"Well, you are in luck about finding the board members. There is about to be a presentation in the grandstand involving every last one of them."

I blinked at her.

"I looked at the schedule online, Millie. I'm in the know, you know," she replied.

Jethro lifted his snout as if he was in full agreement with Lois.

Lois and I left the goat tent just as all the children showing goats came back with their charges on leads. Micah, Phillip, and Peter were among them, and Micah was grinning from ear to ear. "Aenti! Aenti! Phillip won the blue ribbon!" He waved the bright blue ribbon in the air. "He's the best goat at the fair!"

For his part, Phillip was beaming, and I knew there was no chance he was going to let us ever forget his victory. It seemed to me that Peter knew this too, since his head hung low as he stared at his brother goat.

"That is *wunderbar*, Micah! Many congratulations to you and Phillip. Of all the goats here, I can hardly believe Phillip came in first place."

"The judge said he was a perfect example of a Boer goat."

Phillip lifted his chin as if he were absorbing this praise. The goat did love to be praised.

"That is something," Lois said. "I thought at first he got the blue ribbon for being the most disobedient goat. He would be a shoo-in for that."

Chapter Twelve

The grandstand was the one part of the fair-grounds that I'd never been to before. I wasn't much for the tractor pulls or motorbike races usually hosted there. Lois, on the other hand, was very familiar with it.

"Do you smell that?" she asked as she inhaled the air. "I love the scent of diesel in the morning. Some of the motorbikes must have been here early to practice."

We went through the opening under the grand-stand and found ourselves standing just on the edge of the course that the trucks, tractors, motor-bikes, and who knew what else would race on every evening at the fair.

It was a design of manmade earthen mounds in groups of two and three, and even one of four. My jaw hurt at the very idea of riding over those bumps. I hoped the young men and women who drove over them didn't have fillings in their teeth because they were sure to fall out.

At the moment the course was empty, and in one corner to our right there was a cluster of people, perhaps a few dozen in total.

They stood on a small, paved area in front of a riser with a podium on it, including a microphone.

"We could not be more grateful to the county for dedicating these funds to upcoming fairs and events on the fairgrounds. With this money, we can enhance the fairgrounds and make the area usable for a number of events, not just the fair," the man at the podium said. He was tan, bald, and wore a button-down blue shirt that was unfortunately already showing dampness under his arms. It was a very warm day.

Next to the bald man was Star, the fair board's secretary, who had a fake smile plastered on her face as she held a giant cardboard check made out to the fair board for the amount of one hundred thousand dollars.

"Wow," Lois said. "That's a lot of money for the county to be giving them."

I agreed, and it was the first I had heard about this appropriation. However, as an Amish woman, I didn't keep up with county politics unless Lois was filling me in on the latest gossip.

"County Commissioner Hawthorne would like to say a few words," the bald man said and then stepped back from the podium.

The second man to step up onto the platform had thick gray hair and black-rimmed glasses. "We are so pleased to be giving this gift to the fair board. The Holmes County Fair is a paramount event in the county every year, but let us be honest, in the last few years attendance has declined, especially among young people. It is our hope that this money will be used to bring people back to the fair and to start other events on the grounds to engage the young people of the county. We have full trust in the fair board that this will happen." He took a breath. "However, I would be remiss if I didn't share my sadness and the sadness of the county at the loss of Tara Barron. Ms. Barron was a force to be reckoned with on the board. If she had not been in leadership of the fair board, this gift would have never happened. She was able to make the case that the fairgrounds needed a refresh and how the renovation would benefit all members of the county, young and old, Amish and English. We are heartbroken to hear of her passing, but we trust that the board members and new president, Rein Pierce, will do an excellent job of carrying the mantle of the fairgrounds going forward."

Applause erupted from the small audience, and the bald man who had been speaking when Lois and I entered the grandstand waved both arms over his head and smiled.

"Why do I feel like I just heard a campaign speech?" Lois asked.

I was wondering the same.

The bald man dropped his arms to his sides, though he was still beaming. He was obviously the former vice president, now president. He was also the man that Star, the secretary, had said didn't want anything to do with the fair because Tara had downgraded his responsibilities.

He was an excellent suspect indeed.

Rein stepped forward to the podium again. "Thank you all for coming to this small presentation. Your support means the world to me. Now please go and enjoy the fair!"

The crowd dispersed quickly. The county commissioners and officials scuttled out of the grandstand as if they couldn't get away from it fast enough. They left behind Star, Rein, and three young Amish men who were folding up the chairs used for the presentation.

"That man is the one we want to talk to," I said to Lois.

She rubbed her hands together. "Then let's go get him!"

Before I could reply, Lois hiked her purse strap high on her shoulder and marched over to the podium.

Rein stepped down from the riser and went to speak with Star. He had the large cardboard check under his arm. "The fair has to be put back on track. I was afraid the county was going to revoke this gift after Tara's death."

"She was the driving force behind it," Star said.

"Well, it's too bad for her that something is finally out of her control. I will be the one to decide how the funds are spent, not her."

Lois and I shared a look.

I cleared my throat.

Rein spun around. "Can I help you?"

"Yes," Lois said. "We would like to talk to you about Tara Barron."

He scowled. "And who are you?"

Lois rose to her full five-foot-six-inch height. Well, actually she was five-five and a half, according to her last physical, so she had lost a half inch, but you didn't hear that from me. "I'm Lois Henry, and this is Millie Fisher. We were friends of Tara and would like to know what the fair board is going to do about her untimely death."

I think *friends* was a huge stretch on Lois's part. Even if she'd said *acquaintances*, it would have been a stretch.

He narrowed his eyes. "You're *friends* of hers?"

Lois nodded. "We are. Millie is a quilter and she is entered in the quilting competition at the fair."

Star nodded to me. "She's the woman whose quilt was with Tara's b—er—was with Tara when she died."

I shook my head. "*Nee*, it wasn't my quilt. It was my friend Ruth Yoder's quilt. However, Lois and I found the body."

Star nodded. "You're right. I'm sorry. It's been a difficult morning."

And it was showing. Dark circles hung under Star's eyes, and her cheeks were drawn. She was wrung out. I wondered how she'd looked before Tara's death. Was she always this anxious or had the murder put her over the edge?

"I don't care whose quilt it was," Rein said. "All I care about is salvaging what we have left of the fair and turning the fairgrounds into a focal point of the community again. They have been neglected for too long."

I wrinkled my brow. This seemed like a turn-around involvement for Rein. Star had told me that the former vice president of the board had done nothing to prepare for the fair. I could only assume with Tara gone, he was attempting to take over the fairgrounds planning going forward, and that also included the rather large check the board had just received from the county commissioners.

"Tara wanted the same things," Star said, and then she winced as if she knew she had said something that would set Rein off.

Rein's face turned an even deeper shape of red. "She wanted to do it all on her own," he said. "She wanted to do it for the praise and accolades, and look where it got her."

"Are you implying she was killed because of her involvement with the fair board?" I asked with a slight cock of my head.

He spun in my direction. "I'm implying nothing of the kind, and I do not appreciate your saying that!"

He stomped away, still holding the giant check. Star ran after him.

Lois folded her arms. "If I was looking for a killer, he'd be on the top of my list. He clearly didn't like Tara and has some anger issues. I can see him flinging something at the back of her head."

I had to agree, but I also felt that Rein was too obvious to be the killer. If he were, I thought he would have said something rash by now to turn the police's attention onto him. He wasn't the type to watch his words.

Lois sighed. "Detecting makes me hungry. Let's go get an elephant ear."

I groaned at the thought of the massive piece of fried dough blanketed in powdered sugar.

While Lois and I were waiting in line for an elephant ear for her, Ruth Yoder marched over to me. "Millie Fisher, I have been looking for you every-where. I would have thought you, of all people, would not be standing in this long line for an ele-phant ear. You always gave me the impression of being a healthy eater except for your love of blue-berry pie."

"Oh, it's not for Millie," Lois said. "It's for me."

"I *never* thought of you as a healthy eater. Do you really think that is a good idea at your age?" Ruth asked as she wrinkled her nose. "You could have a heart attack. It's dripping with cholesterol."

Lois rolled her eyes. "Ruth, an elephant ear is a terrible idea at any age, but so is sky diving. You only live once, right?"

Ruth snorted and turned back to me. "I'm ready to go home. I have no intention of staying a mo-ment longer at this fair. In fact, I don't ever plan to come back, and you had better believe I will be hav-ing a conversation with the bishop as to whether or not this is a secular event that our district should be a part of. I have my doubts. People are being killed around here and Amish quilts destroyed."

Lois opened her mouth—and I had little doubt in my mind whatever Lois was about to say wouldn't be taken well by the bishop's wife—so I spoke first. "Why don't you take my buggy? We have a quilting meeting at your home later this af-ternoon. I can pick it up then. Lois can drop me off for the meeting, and I can return home in my buggy." I glanced at Lois. "Is that agreeable to you?"

"Sure! I'd love to see your home, Ruth. For whatever reason, you have never invited me over," Lois said.

I stopped just short of stepping on her toes. At this point, Lois was simply trying to get a rise out of Ruth. I couldn't say I blamed Lois. Ruth often did the same to her. They had an irritate/hate relationship that wasn't helpful to me because I was inevitably the one stuck in the middle. Even though my loyalty would always go to Lois first, I still had to respect Ruth Yoder as my bishop's spouse.

"I don't often invite *Englischers* to my home," Ruth said primly.

"Even old childhood friends?" Lois asked.

I interrupted this argument. "Ruth, do you remember where I parked Bessie and my buggy this morning?"

"*Ya,*" Ruth said, making a point of ignoring Lois. "I suppose this will work, but you can't visit too long when you come to my house, Lois. Double Stitch has much to discuss."

"Oh, I know," Lois said. "Murder."

Chapter Thirteen

Lois got her elephant ear, and with her first bite created a giant powdered-sugar cloud in the air that covered her, a young man who was in the wrong place at the wrong time, and me.

I tried to brush the powdered sugar off the front of my navy-blue dress, but my efforts only made it worse. It appeared as if my whole body had been dusted for fingerprints. The fact that fingerprinting dust was my first thought would be particularly worrisome to Sheriff Brody and Deputy Little.

Some of the powdered sugar, I was able to brush from my dress fell on Jethro at my feet. He licked it off his snout and gave Lois woeful eye to beg for a piece. She ignored him.

"I can feel my arteries seizing up, but it is delicious," Lois declared. "How'd you get covered with sugar? You really should be more careful, Millie." She took another bite.

I scowled at her.

Lois cleared her throat, perhaps sensing it would be wise to change the subject. "We agree that Rein is a major suspect, but we cannot forget that there is an even bigger one out there."

I frowned. "Who?"

"Tara's ex-husband, of course. An ex-husband who was also her business partner. Having a few ex-husbands myself, I can tell you it's very unusual that you'd want to go into business with the man you fought over the china set with."

"So it isn't normal among divorced *Englischers* that the former spouses stay in touch through business?"

"No, but it does happen. It never would have worked for me. When I am done with a marriage, I am done and ready to move on to the next relationship. My ex can keep the china as far as I'm concerned."

How well I knew that. Lois had an uncanny ability to allow herself to love over and over again. That was a struggle for me. The perfect example being my friendship with Uriah Schrock. I cared for him very much, and I knew he cared for me. At times, I thought it could be more. I knew as a matchmaker that we were a *gut* fit for each other, but anything more than friendship seemed like a betrayal of Kip, my late husband.

"I say we go check out the husband."

"That sounds like a *gut* plan, but how do we find him? I don't even know his name."

"Oh, Millie, it's easy as can be to find out on the Internet. You'd be so much more in the know if you used a computer."

"That wouldn't be very Amish of me."

"I suppose not. In any case, I found him earlier. His name is Tyce Barron and he is a real estate investor."

"What kind of real estate?"

She grinned. "I'm so glad you asked. Apparently, he buys up struggling small businesses in Holmes and Wayne Counties and reopens them. Sometimes the original owners stay on to manage the business, and sometimes he cleans house and hires new people. In the case of Tara's quilt shop, it had once been an antique store, but he closed that business completely and put Tara's quilt shop in its place. Here's the real kicker."

I raised my brow and waited.

"It was part of their divorce settlement."

"What was?" I asked.

"The store," she said. "Apparently, he agreed to buy her the store instead of paying alimony."

"How do you know all of that?"

"Well, that little bit I got from some gossip at the café. Two of my customers were talking *all* about it. They agreed that Tyce and Tara had a rocky marriage. One thought Tara should have taken the alimony instead of the shop. She believed Tara would have gotten more over time if she'd done that. Tyce is very wealthy."

I considered this. "Who were these women?"

"Their names are Bernadette and Patsy. They come into the café just about every day for coffee and a scone. I can ask them more about it tomorrow. I'd be surprised if they weren't there. I wished I had their phone numbers. I could ask them sooner!"

"Tomorrow will be soon enough," I said. "But it will be interesting to hear how well they know Tara and her husband."

"I do have another interesting tidbit I learned from the Internet."

I raised my brow.

"Tyce was on the fair board with Tara."

"He was?"

She nodded.

"But he wasn't at that presentation of the check from the county."

"You're right! I wonder why."

"You learned a lot, but I wish we could find out more about her husband," I said.

"We can just go to his office and ask him." She waved her phone at me. "I have his address right here."

"If we are going, we should go now," I said. "I can't miss the Double Stitch meeting this afternoon. You know Ruth will never let me forget it if I do."

"I can't miss the meeting either," Lois said. "It will be my first chance to see her house. I've been waiting for this day my whole life."

I chuckled and shook my head.

As Lois and I went out through the gate, Sal waved at us. We waved back. I really hoped his job at the fairgrounds improved. He'd had more than a rocky start. If I were he, I don't know whether I would have agreed to work the day after I'd come upon a murder victim. I wanted to stop to ask him how the goat pen had been repaired, but Lois wasn't stopping for anything. She really wanted to see the inside of Ruth's house.

When we got into Lois's sedan, I settled Jethro on my lap and she handed her cell phone to me. "Hold this," she said.

Not knowing what else to do, I held it in my hands with the same disdain I felt when I picked up a dead mouse that Peaches had left by the back door as a gift.

"The GPS will tell us how to get there," Lois said. "But his office is in downtown Millersburg, so it won't be hard to find. Even though it's the biggest town in Holmes County, it's still tiny by any other measure."

The phone spoke, "Turn left in four hundred feet."

I set it on my lap next to Jethro as Lois made the turn.

Before too long, we were in Millersburg. The fairgrounds were just five minutes from downtown by car. Lois drove down State Route 39, and the massive county courthouse with its cupola came into view. Just across Route 62 from the courthouse was a crumbling building. Through the car's open windows, we could still smell the faint scent of the burnt fabric. I shivered at the thought of all the quilts that must have been lost inside that building. I said a quick prayer of thanks that no one had been hurt, and that the *gut* Lord had protected the businesses on either side of what had been Tara's quilt shop.

Lois whistled through her teeth. "My land! That place went up like a tinderbox, didn't it? If the Fire District hadn't been just down the street less than a minute away, I think a whole lot more buildings would have burnt to the ground." She parked her car across the street from what had once been the quilt shop. "You can see there how the next building over is singed from exposure to the flames. It must have burned hot and fast."

I looked at her. "You seem to know a lot about fire."

She nodded. "Well, ever since the flea market burned up a couple years back, I have been reading up on fires. I want to be able to help if something like that happens again."

I could understand why. Because unlike this fire, when the flea market burned, a very kind, well-meaning Amish man had been killed. I never wanted to see anything like that again.

Lois removed her car key from the ignition. "I know we are here to look for Tyce's office, but we might as well check out the crime scene." She paused. "The original crime scene. I'm willing to bet my granddaughter's piecrust recipe that the fire and Tara's death are related."

I had to agree with her on that.

Lois got out of the car, and I did the same. As soon as I stood, the oppressive August heat hit me like a bag of flour. It was getting into the afternoon and the hottest part of the day. Normally, this was the time of day I would retreat to the shade with my quilting if I were home. With a murder on our hands, that wasn't an option.

There were times I thought the air conditioning in Lois's car, as well as all the shops and businesses in town, made the heat that much more difficult to bear because I wasn't as used to it as I had been before. In an Amish home, we deal with the heat by staying in the shade near a propane-powered fan, sipping a tall glass of cold lemonade.

Jethro seemed to be in agreement, and it took some doing to convince him to hop out of the car and snap on his leash.

Lois shook her finger at him. "You get out of there. The car might be cool now, but it's not a safe place for a little pig in the summer without the air on."

He sighed and hopped out.

Two people stood outside the remnants of the former quilt shop. One was an older *Englisch* man with silver hair and the other was a blond *Englischer*. I guessed he was in his forties from the laugh lines around his mouth and eyes.

"Rusty Bellwether?" Lois asked.

The silver-haired man turned. "Lois Henry. Even in this small county, I haven't seen you for ages."

Lois folded her arms. "That might be because you never come to Harvest anymore. I'm not a hard one to find. I'm sure you've heard that my granddaughter Darcy opened the Sunbeam Café, and I help her out when I can. All you need to do is look there."

He blushed. "Congratulations to Darcy. She always was a sweet kid."

I stood a foot or so behind Lois, wondering if I should interrupt.

The younger man didn't have the same qualms I did. "We're conducting business here. I would suggest you move along."

"Tyce, that is no way to speak to these ladies," Rusty said, aghast.

Tyce clenched his jaw.

Lois looked back at me and widened her eyes. We had to be thinking the same thing. This wasn't just any Tyce. It was Tyce Barron, Tara's ex-husband, and he was standing in front of her burnt-down quilt shop.

I studied Tyce with renewed interest. He had a full head of blond hair that was combed back from his forehead and looked as if it had some sort of styling product in it because it never wavered when he turned his head. I couldn't say what the product was. Being Amish, I was not up on those sorts of things. His skin was tan and he wore a tan suit, which almost washed him out completely, and a pair of sunglasses had been artfully tucked into the breast pocket of his suit jacket.

Lois placed a hand on her chest. "You wouldn't be Tyce Barron, would you?"

Tyce turned to Lois. "Who are you?"

"I'm Lois Henry. As you may have guessed, Rusty and I are old friends. I'm just out for a summer stroll with my dear friend Millie Fisher." She gestured in my direction and then pointed toward Jethro at the end of his leash. "And Jethro the pig."

Tyce curled his lip when he looked down at the pig, as if he wanted to turn the sweet creature into a row of sausage links right then and there. Jethro was no dummy and must have sensed the real estate investor's animosity. He hid behind Lois's leg. I couldn't say I blamed him.

"Millie is a quilter, and we're so sorry for the destruction of your store here," Lois said. "Rusty, you must be here for the insurance adjustment. I suppose it's a complete loss. You know with fires, what the flames don't get, the water will. It's a shame. I was really looking forward to seeing what Tara had to offer here." She paused. "I was so very sorry to hear about your wife's passing. You've had so much adversity of late."

"She was my ex-wife," Tyce said. He said this as if it was an automatic response.

"Even so," Lois said. "She was an important person to you, or you would not have been in business together."

"We weren't in business together," he said through gritted teeth.

"Oh, my mistake."

Rusty cleared his throat. "Lois, I have to say, it's a real pleasure seeing you again, and you are as direct as ever. However, Tyce is right. He and I have to get back to work here. I will look you up at the Sunbeam Café."

"You can have a piece of pie on me." Lois looked over her shoulder. "Millie, are you ready to go?"

Ready to go? We hadn't learned anything from Tyce except for the fact he had an insurance adjustor looking at the burned-down quilt shop and he claimed not to be in business with Tara after all. If that was true, what was he doing here?

Lois started to walk away, but then she stopped suddenly and looked over her shoulder. "Tyce, excuse me for asking, but you wouldn't know anyone who might have wanted to hurt your wife, would you?"

"Ex-wife, and no. We were divorced for over a year. We weren't in each other's lives any longer."

"Oh, my mistake, I had heard you were on the fair board with her. Is that not true?"

"I resigned," he said in a clipped voice.

"And when was what?" She smiled at him.

"This conversation is over." Tyce stomped away.

After waving one last time at Lois, Rusty ran after him.

Chapter Fourteen

Lois shook her head. "I'm parched after that. Let's stop at the ice cream shop for some refreshment."

"I don't think ice cream helps with thirst," I said.

"Millie, ice cream helps with everything. All sweets do. Have I taught you nothing in the last sixty-eight years?"

Shaking my head, Jethro and I walked with Lois to the Malt Shoppe, two doors down from the remains of the quilt shop. A bell rang over the door as we stepped inside. The interior was like an old-fashioned soda shop with a jukebox in one corner and black and white checkerboard tile on the floor. The chairs and tables were bright red with a silver canister of napkins in the middle of each tabletop, and the ice cream counter gleamed as if it had been freshly polished.

I glanced down at Jethro and whispered to Lois. "I'm not sure he can come in here."

She arched her brow. "Are you suggesting we should leave him outside in the heat?"

"*Nee*, but . . ."

"I have an idea." She picked up Jethro and the little pig's eyes became huge as she tucked him into her giant bag. Really, I didn't know how she carried the thing without injuring her shoulder.

The little pig popped his head out, and Lois gently tucked him back inside the bag. "If you're a good little pig, I will share my ice cream with you."

He buried his head in the bag.

"Are pigs allowed ice cream?" I asked.

"I'm sure once in a blue moon is fine."

I wasn't as sure about that. The last thing I wanted was for the pastor's wife's pig to become ill on my watch.

"Good afternoon," a young woman behind the counter said. She had long curly brown hair that was pulled back into a ponytail on the top her head. "Would you like to try a sample?"

"That question is music to my ears," Lois said. "I'll try the double brownie and the butter pecan."

The young woman removed a tiny wooden spoon no bigger than my thumb from the box on her counter and scooped a little bit of ice cream on the end. "This is the double brownie." She handed it to Lois and went back into the box for another little spoon. "And here is the butter pecan."

Lois tasted both. "They are both perfect, but the butter pecan is to die for. I will take two scoops of that in a waffle cone."

The woman smiled and scooped the ice cream.

When she handed the cone to Lois, she turned to me. "Is there anything that you'd like to try?"

I looked up and down the counter. It was overwhelming. There had to be thirty flavors there, including some that were dairy-free or sugar-free.

"Oh look, Millie, she has blueberry ice cream!" Lois cried.

The shopworker smiled. "It's a new recipe. Blueberry and lavender. Would you like a sample?"

I nodded, and she removed another tiny wooden spoon and scooped a little bit of the blueberry lavender ice cream onto the tip. She reached over the counter and handed me the spoon.

Apparently the smell of sweets was too much for Jethro to bear any longer, and his head popped out of Lois's bag, almost causing her to drop the ice cream cone. Before Lois could stop him, he took a huge bite out of the mound of ice cream in her cone. It smeared all over his snout.

"Oh my heavens!" Lois cried.

I grabbed the ice cream from her hand before she could drop it or the bag.

Lois set her bag on the ground, and Jethro jumped out, licking the butter pecan from his lips all the while.

Lois's ice cream dripped on my wrist. We were all a sticky mess.

"You have Jethro with you!" The woman behind the counter gasped. "I'm a huge fan of *Bailey's Amish Sweets.* I watch the episodes over and over again on streaming. Her show is a big reason I opened my own shop! It's the goal I've had since I was a girl, and she inspired me. I'm forty and finally living my dream!"

"That's wonderful to hear," I said as the ice cream dripped.

The shop owner held out her hand. "Oh, give me that. I'll throw it away and get you a new cone."

"*Danki.*" I grabbed a fistful of napkins from the canister on the counter and did my best to clean my hands. However, the napkins weren't doing the job. I excused myself and went to the bathroom to wash my hands.

When I came back, the shop owner and Lois were talking excitedly together.

"Millie," Lois said. "This is Ellen Packer. I was just telling her that we are friends with Bailey King."

"I still can't believe you know her," Ellen said. "She's like a celebrity."

"She doesn't act that way," Lois assured her. "Have you met her in person?"

Ellen shook her head. "I've been to Swissmen Sweets many times and have seen her there, but I've never had the nerve to say anything to her."

"You should," Lois said. "She would love to talk to you. She's very encouraging about small businesses. My granddaughter owns the Sunbeam Café across the square from Swissmen Sweets, and Bailey has been so kind about giving her advice to grow her business. Bailey is just as sweet as the candy she makes."

Ellen smiled. "I will say something the next time I'm there."

I smiled. "We will be sure to tell her about your business too. I see her just about every day she is in town and not filming her show in New York."

"I would be so flattered if you did," Ellen said.

She started to scoop the blueberry ice cream for me. I had asked for one scoop in a dish. I took the dish, and she handed me a scoop of vanilla in another dish. "For Jethro."

At my feet, the little pig's tail wiggled with anticipation. I set the dish in front of him, and he dove into it, snout first. We were going to have to hose him down after this visit to the ice cream shop.

Lois handed Ellen her debit card.

"Lois, you don't have to pay for my ice cream," I said.

She waved me away. "You can get it next time."

I sighed. Lois always insisted on paying if we were out. Had I not gone to the bathroom to wash my hands, I would have beaten her to the cash register.

As Ellen printed her receipt, Lois said, "It's a shame about what happened to that shop on the corner."

The glow that had been on Ellen's face since she saw Jethro the pig faded. "It's just terrible, and the whole experience has been terrifying. I had my place professionally cleaned afterward, but there are times I swear I can still smell the smoke from the fire. I don't know if it's in my head or I'm actually smelling it."

"You were here during the fire?" I asked. "Wasn't it in the middle of the night?"

"It was. It was close to two in the morning." She nodded. "My apartment is over the shop, and I live alone with my guinea pig." She smiled down at Jethro. "I love pigs, but the guinea is the best I can do in a one-bedroom apartment, and it seems at times even that is too much for me."

"What happened that night?" I asked and then added, "If you don't mind me asking."

She smiled. "I don't mind. I believe with stress-ful and adversarial events, the more you talk about them, the more power you have over what happened to you. Ask my friends. I talk about my terrible ex-husband all the time." She smiled to take the bite out of her words. "When I smelled the smoke, I thought my shop was on fire. So I grabbed Sundae and ran down the back escape stairs from my apartment."

"Sundae?" Lois asked.

"That's my guinea pig."

"Aww," Lois replied.

"The smoke was so much worse outside, but I couldn't see any evidence of fire in my shop. That was when I heard a large cracking noise coming from down the street. I ran along the alleyway to the front of the building and saw the quilt shop ablaze! Flames were licking the sky. It was like something out of a movie. Thank heavens the fire department was already on the scene and was fighting the fire. But I have to say, at first it didn't look like they were having much luck combating it."

"How long did it take for the fire department to get it under control?" Lois asked.

"It seemed like a very long time. Several hours at least. They evacuated the whole block within minutes. A friend of mine owns a photography studio the next block over. She's out of town right now, and I have a key to the studio so I can go over and water her plants and that sort of thing. Since it was outside the evacuation zone, I took Sundae and myself there. I guess we were there three or four hours. By the time the firefighters and police were walking up the street saying it was all clear, dawn had broken. I left my friend's studio and ran back to my ice cream shop. There were still so many firefighters and police officers about. I had never seen anything like it in Millersburg. I told them to spread the word that there was free ice cream for everyone who had helped. I was scooping ice cream for the next hour."

"That was so kind of you," I said.

"It was the least I could do. They saved my livelihood and my home. A little bit of ice cream would never be enough to repay them for everything they'd done."

"There was no damage to your property?"

She shook her head. "Nothing serious. The only real issue I had was the smell. I wish I'd thought to close all the windows in my apartment before I ran out, but Sundae and I thought we were running for our lives at that point. When I went back into the ice cream shop, the smell wasn't too bad, but the windows were open in my apartment and the smell was terrible up there. Sundae and I had to sleep downstairs until it was professionally cleaned. I hired a company to clean the shop and my apartment. This is my first day fully open after the incident. Being closed for three days was a hit to my business. It is summer after all, and ice cream season. However, it could have been so much worse. I thank God that the firemen came so quickly."

I considered this. Did the person who started the fire take into account that the fire department would be on the scene in no time at all and save the surrounding buildings?

Lois licked her ice cream, and then said, "If the fire spread so quickly, could it have been arson?"

Ellen looked around as if she was afraid someone would overhear her, but she, Lois, and I were the only ones in the store.

Lois and I, sensing this would be some *gut* information, leaned in too. "Have you heard that it is arson?"

Ellen scrunched up her face. "No one said that to me directly, nor would I have asked."

"But you heard something," Lois suggested.

"When the officers were getting their ice cream, I overheard that there was evidence of kerosene all over the quilt shop. That's why the blaze burned so fast."

Kerosene? That wasn't oil used often by *Englischers* like Tara, but it was commonly used by the Amish. Did that mean the arsonist was Amish? I shivered at the very idea. It wasn't as though I believed that everyone in my community was perfect. But even so, I didn't want another murder in this county to be attributed to a member of my faith.

"When did this all happen?" Lois asked. "I'm not sure about the date."

"It was last Friday," Ellen said. "It seems like it was so much longer ago than that and yet more recent too. It's just been a nightmare." Her face reddened. "I know it is much worse for Tara Barron. She is the one who lost her shop."

"You know Tara?" I asked.

She shook her head. "Not well. In fact, I've only spoken to her once. I walked over one morning before opening my shop to introduce myself. I was excited that there was another woman entrepreneur on the street. In my mind, I was already making plans of how we could work together to help each other's businesses." She sighed.

"And was Tara receptive?" I asked, believing I already knew the answer from her expression.

She shook her head. "Not in the least. She was rude and told me to get out of the store unless I planned to buy something. I would never buy anything from her after the way I was treated."

"That *was* rude of her," Lois said.

Ellen nodded. "I tried to remind myself that she had just opened the shop, and those first few months after opening a new business can be so stressful. Even so, I kept my distance from her after that. If I saw her on the street, I would wave and say hello. I can't say she always did the same."

"What was her shop like?" I asked. "I'm a quilter and was hoping I could visit to see her materials, but I never got a chance."

"It was just like mine except for the ice cream. It had the same number of rooms and general layout. It also had an apartment on the second floor. That's where Tara was living. On this side of the street, the interior of all the buildings have been redone with businesses on the ground floor and apartments overhead. I rent my space. I would love to buy it from the owner someday, but I just don't have the funds yet. I'll get there eventually."

"I'm sure you will," Lois said. "Where was Tara the night of the fire? She wasn't home, I gather."

"I don't think she was. She wasn't on the street when the police were evacuating the block. I saw her the next day in front of the remains of her building, talking to a sheriff's deputy."

"Which deputy?" Lois asked.

She shook her head. "I don't know."

I knew Lois and I were both hoping it was Deputy Little. We'd have better luck getting information from our friend than another person in the department.

The bell over the door rang and a group of school children in baseball uniforms poured into the shop. The one adult with them looked as if he might pass out from heat stroke.

The children began immediately shouting flavors of ice cream to Ellen. Lois picked up Jethro before he could get trampled. We waved goodbye to Ellen and hurried out the door.

When we were in the safety of Lois's car, I let out a sigh and took a bite of my ice cream, which was half melted at this point. I licked the spoon. "Why wasn't Tara Barron home the night of the fire?"

Lois licked her new ice cream cone while Jethro watched forlornly from the back seat of her car. "You think she wasn't home on purpose."

"Maybe. I'm not sure that it matters, but I wonder if the person who started the fire knew she wasn't home. In that case, the arson was only destroying property."

Lois stared at me. "But if the arsonist thought she was home in her apartment, it might have been attempted murder."

I nodded. "A failed attempt. But the killer was successful the second time."

Lois's eyes went wide. "I think you are really on to something here. If we can find that out, we might just be able to piece this mystery together.

And I am one hundred percent confident you can do that, Amish Marple."

I sighed. "I wish you would stop calling me that."

Her eyes twinkled. "Stop solving murders, and I will."

With the number of crimes I had solved lately, it wasn't looking very likely. So it seemed that I was Amish Marple for *gut*.

Chapter Fifteen

Before Lois and I could go to the Ruth Yoder's home for the Double Stitch meeting, we needed to return the pig to Juliet Brody or Swissmen Sweets. Ruth would not be pleased if Jethro made an appearance on her farm.

The drive between Millersburg and Harvest was close to thirty minutes due to summer traffic in Berlin, which was a major tourist stop between the county seat and our village. When we finally parked at the square, I gave a sigh of relief. I was never comfortable in a car in traffic. I felt trapped. At least if I was in a buggy, I was higher up and it felt more open.

Lois parked in front of the Sunbeam Café. It was close to the church were Juliet Brook served as the pastor's wife. The church itself looked like it came straight from a New England postcard. It was white with a tall, straight steeple, complete with a bell that rang every Sunday morning when services were about to begin, and a bright purple front door reached by a steep set of concrete steps. For those with mobility issues, there was a second entrance near the bottom of the stairs that led to an elevator in the lower level of the building. I had to admit, I much preferred the second entrance when my knees were stiff.

Thankfully, we didn't have to walk up those steps because Juliet came down them. She waved to Lois and me and met us in the church parking lot. "Jethro! Oh, my sweet boy. I'm so glad to see you."

The little pig pulled at his leash, and Lois let it go. He bolted to his mistress. Juliet picked him up and held him to her chest. By the way the pair of them acted, you would have thought they had been away from each other for years, not just the morning. "When Charlotte told me Jethro wasn't at the candy shop, I was beside myself. However, then she told me that he was with you, Lois, and I felt so much better. I have just returned from my retreat and was headed to your café to collect him. Now, here he is. You must be a mind reader to know I was looking for him."

Lois smiled. "We were happy to help."

I noted that Lois hadn't told Juliet all of the adventures Jethro had gone on throughout the morning with us. Perhaps she decided it was better for Juliet to believe her little pig was tucked in a safe, cozy corner of the café with a piece of pie. In fact, that didn't sound too bad a fate to me either.

Juliet sighed. "Now that I'm home for the rest of the summer, I hope to work on wedding plans."

"For Bailey and Aiden?" I asked.

"Of course!" Juliet said excitedly. "I'm beside

myself that they are finally getting married. When I was at this spiritual retreat, I'm ashamed to admit it was difficult for me to focus on the lessons. I'm just so excited about the wedding."

"Have they picked a date?" I asked.

Her face fell. "They have not. All I know is it's supposed to be next year sometime." She sighed. "Bailey says she can't think about it until the candy factory is up and running." She sighed again, more loudly this time. "It's so difficult to wait when I have waited so long already. I've waited years! Years!"

"They have waited a long time too," I said. "Sometimes these things come down to timing. They will set a date when the time is right. You just have to trust in them."

"They could elope," Lois suggested. "Then it will be over and done with at little cost. I've eloped a couple of times. It was quick and easy. The marriages, however, were not so quick and not so easy."

Juliet placed a hand on her chest and gasped. "Please don't breathe a word of this to Bailey or Aiden. I would never survive it if they didn't have a wedding right here at the church."

"Does Bailey want a church wedding?" I asked.

She turned to me this time. "Why wouldn't she?"

I said nothing. I knew Bailey attended services at Juliet's church now and again, but she wasn't religious in general. At least, I had never heard her speak of her faith. I did know that she was raised outside of any church. When her father left the

Amish over thirty years ago to marry Bailey's mother, who is *Englisch*, he rejected his faith.

Juliet clutched her pig closer to her chest. "Aiden is my only child. I deserve to see his wedding, and Bailey is an only child as well. Her parents deserve to see her get married. I can assure you that this will not be an elopement." She said it with so much certainty that I wondered if it had been discussed in the past, and if so with whom. I kept my mouth shut, as those were questions I was not in a position to ask.

Juliet glanced back at the church. "I should go inside. I haven't seen Reverend Brook since I got home, and I have much to do to get ready for Sunday. There is always a lot to do at the church. I imagine you need to return to the fair, Millie?"

I shook my head. "We aren't going back to the fair today. I will be there tomorrow. That's when the quilt judging will be held."

Juliet set Jethro on the pavement. The pig shook his head as he marched around her feet as if he was trying to shake the cobwebs loose. Not for the first time, I wondered what Jethro thought about all the time. He appeared to be perpetually confused, but I supposed if I were a pet pig and my owner wanted to make me a movie star, I would be confused too.

"They are still holding the quilt judging?" She cleared her throat. "After *that* incident?"

"You heard about the murder."

"Of course," she said. "It was all anyone was talking about at the women's retreat. It's a terrible shame. It hit close to home for us because Tara had been a church member for so many years. She left about a year ago when she went through that horrible divorce."

"Did her husband Tyce attend your church?"

"Not often. He might be there on Christmas, Easter, or another holiday, but Tara Barron was very involved. She was organized too. She was one of the ladies I leaned on heavily to plan big events at the church. No matter how well-meaning some church ladies are, not all of them are organized enough to take on that level of responsibility. Tara was." She sighed. "Reverend Brook has reached out to her family to see about funeral arrangements. He is hoping he will be permitted to preside over her burial as she was such an important member of the church for so long."

"And what did the family say?" Lois asked.

"He left a message. That was the last I heard."

"Who did he reach out to?"

"Her ex-husband. He is the only family we know of. They didn't have any children. From what Tara said, they tried for many years. It was something that Tyce wanted too. In the end, she said that was what had ended their marriage, her inability to give him a child."

"That's so sad," Lois murmured.

I could feel Lois watching me. As my dearest friend, she knew my own troubles with infertility.

My heart ached for Tara, who must have yearned so badly for a child. I knew what that pain felt like, as my husband Kip and I wanted so much to have children of our own. We'd never been able to conceive. At a point, we had accepted the life Gott had given us and the knowledge that we could be loving adults in the lives of our nieces and nephews and other children in the district. Even so, that pain had remained for a long time, and at times, it showed up on days like today. I could see how a woman who wanted children and could not have them would feel rejected by Gott. However, I knew in my heart that Gott had not rejected Tara Barron or me. His plans had just been different for us. I prayed Tara, too, realized that before she passed.

Lois cleared her throat. "It takes two to tango. It wasn't just her fault that she couldn't have a child. It burns me up that women are still the ones who take most of the blame in these circumstances." She folded her arms. "So, what happened? He ran off and found another woman who could give him children? Ridiculous."

"I don't believe he's remarried yet." Juliet lowered her voice. "Tyce had money." She said it in the same tone someone might say that a person was an ex-convict.

Lois seemed to notice this too because she said, "Just because someone has money doesn't make them bad. It's how they use the money, or how they acquire it that might be questionable. Although having met Tyce Barron, I didn't like him."

"You're right," Juliet said. "I visited Tara once to see if she would be interested in coming back to the church."

"Oh," Lois said. "And what did she say to that?"

"She refused." Juliet fiddled with the plastic polka-dotted bracelet on her wrist. "She said that God had abandoned her, and she'd abandoned Him. It was the last thing I wanted to hear. I feel our church failed her in some way if that was her conclusion."

My heart hurt hearing those words, and I said a silent prayer, hoping that Tara had made peace with God before she was killed.

"I'm glad to hear that the judging of the quilts will go on," Juliet continued. "There is so much work put into the event, not just by the quilters, but by everyone who plans and organizes the fair. I used to be on the fair board, you know. I was a member for years and years, even before I married Reverend Brook. It is a lot of work."

"Was Tara on the board when you were there?" I asked.

She shook her head. "I think she took all the energy she used to put into the church into her new quilt shop. I have to say, I was surprised when she opened the shop. I didn't even know she could sew. Why she decided to open that quilt shop is a complete mystery to me."

And now it was a mystery to Lois and me as well.

Chapter Sixteen

"I can't believe that I'm finally going to be able to see Ruth Yoder's home. It's a dream come true," Lois said. "I love old farmhouses, and hers is one of the oldest in the county. I bet she has old furniture in there that goes back generations. I can't wait!"

"Parts of the farmhouse are old," I said. "Other parts are much newer. It's been added onto so many times, it can be tricky to know where the old house ends and the new parts begin."

"I'll be able to tell," Lois said. "I have an eye for these sorts of things."

It was true, she did. Lois always knew what things were worth at the flea markets.

"Can you do me one favor?" I asked.

"I'll give it a whirl," Lois said.

It was the best I could hope for. "Please try not to upset Ruth. She's already so upset about her quilt."

"And rightfully so. I would be upset too if something I made was shredded and left with a dead woman. No amount of mending is going to fix that quilt."

I winced.

Lois turned her car up the long driveway of the Yoder dairy farm. Black-and-white cows gathered in little clusters around the pasture. Their tails whipped back and forth as they tried to shoo the large, late summer horse flies from their backs.

Lois shook her head. "Summer is my favorite season, or it would be if it weren't for the heat and bugs."

I eyed her. "You complain about winter too."

"I sure do. I'm an Ohioan, aren't I? Complaining about winter is required. In summer, I like not having to drive in the snow."

I agreed with her on that point. I hated to drive my buggy in the snow, even though I trusted Bessie implicitly to get me from point A to point B. The issue was not all drivers on the narrow country byways of Holmes County were as careful, and many times underneath the snow was a sheet of ice from the freezing rain that often preceded the snow. On days like that, I stayed warm and dry, tucked away on my little farm with my horse, cat, and goats.

A pang of sadness hit me as I thought of the goats. I didn't think I would miss them as much as I did. And I still didn't know who'd cut them out of their pen the night of the murder. Lois had been right—I believed it had been a diversion. One to distract Sal so the killer could escape the fairgrounds unnoticed.

At the moment, the idea of being cozy on the

farm was very appealing. Much more so than getting into a debate with Ruth Yoder as to whether or not I was responsible for the ruin of her gorgeous quilt.

Bessie and my buggy stood to the right of the house in front of the large barn, which meant I had a ride home. However, I didn't have much hope I would be able to convince Lois to leave before the quilting meeting was over.

"This is a real hodgepodge house," Lois said. "It grew out in all directions except for up. It reminds me of a Revolutionary fort designed to keep the British out."

"Don't say that to Ruth," I warned. The last thing a pacifist wanted to be compared to was the military.

"I know better than that," she said. "For the most part. What I don't understand is why they didn't just add a second story so the home would look less like a school and more like a house."

"It would have been harder to live there during construction if they had."

"That is a good point," Lois replied. "This is why you are Amish Marple, and I'm your charming and amusing sidekick, a role I was born to play." She parked the car.

"I don't think anyone would look at you, Lois, and say you were a sidekick," I observed as I unbuckled my seat belt.

Before we reached Ruth's front door, it opened. Ruth filled the doorway, and she didn't look happy to see us. "I thought you were just dropping Millie off." Ruth directed her comment to Lois.

Lois waved at her, and the colorful bangles on

her wrist knocked together. "Ruth, it's so nice to finally be invited to your home. Your house is so *unique.*"

Ruth narrowed her eyes as if she suspected that Lois's assessment of her home wasn't a compliment. She would be right, but I wasn't going to confirm her suspicions.

"You have brought Millie here to my home safely. You can be on your way. There is nothing for you here. We're just a bunch of women quilting. You would be bored."

"Oh, Ruth." Lois laughed. "You and I both know you are much more than a quilting circle. You ladies have been involved in many of our investigations in the past. I'm excited to hear what you might know about Tara Barron."

Ruth scowled. "I know nothing about her other than she wouldn't let me into the quilt competition and destroyed my quilt. What else is there to say?"

I was looking around Ruth's shoulder at the other women in Double Stitch. It appeared Lois and I were the last ones here. Typically, I was the first to arrive at these sorts of meetings.

"You think Tara was the one who destroyed your quilt?" I asked. "Why would you say that?"

"It's not like she shredded the quilt in a blind rage and then killed herself," Lois said. "From what Sheriff Brody told us, it looks like murder. She couldn't have inflicted the injury to the back of her own head."

"Maybe she fell. She shredded the quilt and tripped," said Ruth, who appeared not quite ready to give up on her theory.

I made a face.

"You might as well come in," Ruth said grudgingly. "All the other ladies are here and eager to discuss this *situation.*"

Lois grinned. "I would love to."

Ruth held the door open wide to let Lois and me inside. I watched as Lois took in the room. I had been here countless times. It was a big space that featured ten-foot-high walls and groupings of chairs for conversation. As there would be no church this coming Sunday, the furniture in the room was arranged as the Yoders used it for day-to-day life.

"This room is huge," Lois said.

Ruth looked around. "It is big. It used to be four smaller rooms, but we made it one large one to accommodate church services. I keep telling my husband we should really have church here every service weekend because we have the space. There are too many times we end up uncomfortably cramped in a district member's house."

"Ruth, you should be glad there are members of the district who are willing to have services at their homes," Leah Bontrager said. "You'll never see me doing such a thing, but I don't begrudge members who will."

"Let's all sit down," Ruth said grumpily. She hated it when anyone corrected her, and Leah was just about the only woman in the district who could do it and not receive an instant reprimand in reply.

Lois leaned in my direction. "Have you ever wondered what Leah has on Ruth?" she asked in a whisper. "It has to be something good if she can talk to her that way."

I had never thought of it like that, but it was possible Lois was right.

I saw that Ruth had brought my quilting basket in from my buggy and placed it next to a comfy-looking armchair. The quilting circle was set up in a cluster of chairs near the door to the kitchen. Through the kitchen door, the aroma of the Yoders' dinner wafted into the room, and it smelled wonderful. Ruth was a lot of things, and one of them was an excellent cook.

It smelled like pot roast to me. Before going to my seat, I went to the small table next to the large fireplace. Taking a plate in hand, I piled it high with fruit, cheese, crackers, and two cookies. Lois did the same.

Raellen eyed our plates as we joined the circle. "The two of you must be hungry."

"We are," Lois said after swallowing a bite of cookie. "We didn't have lunch. This spread is more impressive than I expected. It's like a whole meal. Who made the cookies?" She held up a sugar cookie. "They are perfection."

"I did," Iris said with a shy smile.

"Iris, I didn't know you could bake. You will have to share this recipe with Darcy. She will want you to make these for the café."

Iris, who worked a few hours every week at the café as a waitress, blushed. "Do you really think so?"

"I know so, and if you don't tell her, I will." She polished off her cookie.

Iris smiled down at her quilting. Everyone was working on their own projects that day. Last week, we had finished quilting a queen-sized bed quilt for Leah, and no one else in the group had a project ready to be quilted just yet. Typically when we met, it was around a large quilt frame and we all worked on the same piece.

After eating some of the cheese and crackers, I set my plate on the small table to my right and opened my quilting basket. Inside there was ladybug-printed fabric with black and red ribbon for embellishment. I was working on a quilt for a friend of Darcy's who was having a baby. The mother-to-be adored ladybugs and that was the theme of the nursery. It was much flashier than my usual work.

I set the pieces on my lap.

"Millie Fisher, what on earth are you making with that outlandish fabric?" Lois wanted to know.

"It is for a new baby."

"Not an Amish baby, I gather?"

I shook my head. "*Nee.*"

"Is that a *gut* idea to be taking so much work from the non-Amish?" Ruth asked.

I studied her. "We have to make money somehow. It was a *gut* commission to receive. If you are offended by the fabric, you don't have to help me quilt it when the time comes."

She sniffed. "We all have to make a living."

"This is true," Leah said. "I'm so sorry to hear about the loss of your quilt, Ruth."

"What about the loss of Tara Barron?" Iris asked.

Everyone looked at her. Iris wasn't one to contradict an older member of the district.

Raellen winced as she waited for Leah to snap at Iris.

Thankfully, Leah relaxed. "You're right. The

loss of life is so much worse. I pray for her family and friends during this time. I just made a comment about the quilt because we were talking about work. We all know if Ruth's quilt had not been destroyed, she would have easily gotten a thousand dollars for it at market. That is a loss too."

"You're right. I'm sorry if I was short with you," Iris said. "I worked with Tara in the past, so I suppose I am extra sensitive when it comes to the matter."

"You worked for her?" Ruth asked.

"She hired me to set up the quilt barn. Well, I suppose it was actually the fair board that hired me, but I never spoke to anyone else."

"I didn't know you were doing that," Ruth said. It was impossible for her to hide the irritation in her voice. "Does your husband know about this?"

Iris's face grew even redder. Ruth's question chafed because Iris had gotten work at the Sunbeam Café over a year ago behind her husband's back. Her one son was all but grown, and she wanted to contribute financially to the family so that Carter Sr. didn't have to travel to roofing jobs all over the state.

"He knows. He doesn't like it, but I told him. He understands that we need the money considering . . ."

We all knew what she meant. Carter Sr. had fallen a month ago from a second-story roof. He'd hurt his back, bruising several discs, but overall was fine. It could have been much, much worse. Even so, he was in a lot of pain and couldn't go back to roofing anytime soon. Iris had confided in me that the doctor advised her husband not to go back at all and to find different work. If he fell or hurt himself again, he could end up paralyzed. To tell an Amish man that he couldn't work with his hands was a type of death sentence. I knew Carter Sr. felt that way. My Kip would have felt the same.

"I'm sure we could give you extra shifts at the café if you need more work," Lois said. "Summer is a busy season, and it will become even busier in fall when all the leaf peepers come out to see the fall foliage."

Ruth sat in an old wooden rocker and folded her hands on her lap. "Carter has not spoken to the bishop about his struggles with work. That is what the community is for, to help members during life's trials."

Iris looked down. "He wouldn't. He knows pride is a sin, but it does not change how he feels. He wouldn't want a handout from the community to get by. Carter would want those funds to go to someone who was really struggling."

"What exactly is really struggling?" Lois asked. "Because I would think his injury was a real struggle."

"My husband doesn't feel that way. Please, Ruth, don't say anything to the bishop about this. Carter would be so embarrassed." She looked at Lois. "And if I can pick up extra shifts at the café, I will gratefully take them. Anything at this time will be a help. My son is old enough to work now too, and he's contributing to the family. We will be fine."

I reached over the arm of my chair and squeezed her hand. "Of course, you will be. Gott is always there for you, and we are too."

She gave me a wobbly smile.

"*Danki*," she murmured.

I cleared my throat. I didn't want to make Iris any more uncomfortable than she already was, but I did want to get back to the topic of her working for Tara. However, I decided to give her a moment before I questioned her further. "I'm sorry I didn't bring a snack or a dessert to share," I said. "Lois and I haven't been home since we left the fair. I didn't have time to make something." I didn't add that I had already given Ruth the date-nut bars I'd made specifically for the meeting.

"There is more than enough to eat," Raellen said. "We always have too much food. There will be plenty to give your family tonight, Ruth."

She nodded. "That is a *gut* thing. My husband has been so busy the last few days. So many people in the community need his guidance and comfort."

My Amish friends nodded. We knew that it wasn't our place to ask who was in need of the bishop's guidance. Lois, however, didn't play by Amish rules and never had. "Who needs so much extra attention from the bishop?"

Ruth frowned at her. "I can't tell you that."

"You mean that you know but won't say." Lois arched her brow.

If I was closer to Lois, I would have stepped on her foot at that very moment to encourage her to be quiet. If she kept this up, Ruth was going to kick her out the door. She wasn't welcome in the Yoder home as it was.

Thankfully, Leah interjected, "You know, Iris. I know another way that you can earn extra money for your family, and it's something you're already doing."

"What's that?" Lois asked.

Ruth shot her an irritated glance for butting into the conversation.

Leah folded a swatch of navy-blue cotton on her lap. "Go to a quilt broker. She will sell your quilt for top dollar. I've used one before, and my quilts sold well."

"What's your broker's name?" Raellen asked as she held a peanut butter cookie in her hand.

"Sondra," she said. "But you can't use her. She's dead."

Chapter Seventeen

We all stared at Leah, who sipped her coffee as calm as can be. She wrinkled her brow. "What is it? Do I have powdered sugar on my face? Those snowball cookies were delicious but messy."

"How can you say a woman is dead just like that?" Raellen asked.

"Like what? It's a fact. You don't know her, so there's no reason to become emotional in my delivery."

"It just seemed a little cold," Raellen said and set her cookie plate down as if she'd lost her appetite.

"It's not cold," Leah argued. "It's how I speak. I don't talk about people dying unless we are helping Millie with one of her murder investigations."

"They aren't *my* murder investigations," I argued.

"That's right," Lois said. "They are both of ours. Millie can't do this job alone. She needs her loyal sidekick." Lois pointed at herself with one of her long orange nails just in case they didn't know who that loyal sidekick was.

I sighed. That hadn't been what I'd meant either.

Iris turned a spool of thread over and over again in her hand. "What does a quilt broker do, and how will it help me?"

Leah folded another swatch. "The quilt broker finds a buyer for your quilts at top dollar. Using one, I have sold many of my quilts for twice as much as I would have sold them myself. The broker has a fee for her services, of course, but you still come away with a higher profit because of her connections."

"How much is the fee?" Raellen asked.

"It's a percentage of the price of the quilt. My broker took ten percent."

Ruth narrowed her eyes. "Making more money should not be the goal of an Amish woman."

Leah frowned at her. "By making more for my family, I'm also making more for the district because I will be better able to contribute when other church members need support."

Ruth didn't have an answer for that.

Lois wiped her mouth with a napkin before saying, "What happened to your broker?"

"It was sad. She died of a heart attack. It was so sudden too. She was a nice lady, but she had seemed stressed lately over something. Usually, I could stop by anytime with a new quilt, but last time I was there, she wouldn't answer the door. I knew she was home. Her car was in the driveway, and I could hear the TV blaring."

"Do you think she was already dead?" Raellen asked just above a whisper.

"*Nee*, she died a month after that. She might have been sleeping, but I don't know how she could have been with the television on so loud."

"If she only took ten percent of the sale price of the quilt," Lois said, "she must have been working with a lot of quilters to make a living."

"She did, and she worked with quilt shops too. I think she had fifty or so quilters in Holmes and Wayne Counties. There was a waiting list to work with her. I was on it for months."

"How did you learn about her?" I asked. "I've been quilting forever and never heard of a quilt broker before."

"My sister in Wayne County worked with her first, and I got on the waiting list just as soon as I saw how well she was doing. I was on the list for six months before there was an opening, and there was a tryout to be one of her quilters."

"Tryout?" I asked.

Leah nodded. "She had to inspect your work to make sure you were up her standards. She wouldn't sell quilts made by careless workers."

"And there are many buyers calling such brokers for quilts?" Raellen asked dubiously.

"You know *Englischers.* They love to collect things, including quilts and just about everything else under the sun."

Ruth folded her arms. "And this is the first time you're telling us about this? When we are all quilters here? Is there a reason you kept this information to yourself?"

Leah leveled a look back at her. "I knew that you wouldn't have approved, Ruth. I am telling Iris now to help her while her husband isn't able to work."

I frowned. I was just as surprised as Ruth that Leah hadn't mentioned this before. It wasn't the Amish way to be secretive among friends. I could not help but wonder what else we didn't know about her. Leah had always been the most guarded in our group.

"Will it be difficult to find a new broker?" I asked. "It seems to me that all those quilters will be looking for a new one right now if Sondra was so sought after."

Leah shrugged. "Some *Englischer* will come up out of the woodwork to take the job. One always does."

"Just like some *Englischer* will step forward to take Tara Barron's place on the fair board," Iris said sadly. "They always do."

Later that afternoon when I drove home in my buggy with Bessie, I thought over everything I had learned in the last twenty-four hours. My goats had escaped, I'd found a dead body, and Ruth Yoder was a murder suspect. It was a lot to take in.

Part of me thought that Sheriff Brody couldn't possibly think Ruth was the killer. He knew her. She could be hard to deal with, of course, but she wouldn't kill someone over a quilt. Who would? But why was the quilt there? How did the killer take it from Ruth's buggy and why? And did the quilt have anything at all to do with the murder, or was the quilt simply in the wrong place at the wrong time?

It was just after four in the afternoon when I returned to the farm, and Peaches ran up to the buggy. When he saw the goats weren't with me, he turned up his tail and marched away.

"Well, I suppose he told us how he feels, didn't he?" I said to Bessie.

She curled back her horsey lips.

I was unhitching her from the buggy when I heard the familiar clip-clop and rattle of a horse and buggy on the road. It wasn't an unusual sound this far out in the country, but when the sound slowed as it neared my driveway, I looked up from my task.

A buggy rolled toward me, and just like a schoolgirl, I felt a fluttering in my stomach.

"You're a mature, grown woman, Millie Fisher. You don't get butterflies."

But the butterflies bounced around in my middle all the same.

My butterflies might be happy, but Uriah Schrock, the buggy's driver, wasn't smiling, and the butterflies changed into pieces of lead in my stomach. I finished unhooking Bessie from the buggy and led her to my small pasture. It was a nice evening, not too terribly hot, and I thought it would be good for her to have some sunshine and fresh air.

By the time I returned to the driveway, Uriah was out of his buggy and had tethered his own horse to the hitching post.

"Millie, where have you been all day?" His tone was as harsh as I had ever heard it.

I took a step back. "What do you mean?"

"This is the third time I've driven to your house today looking for you. I also went to the café four times and the fairgrounds where you were supposed to be with your quilt and couldn't find you."

"I didn't know that you were looking for me. If I had, I would have told you where to find me. I was with Lois."

He frowned. "I know you were with her. You're always with her."

I clenched my jaw. I didn't like the way he was speaking to me in the least. "She is my friend. My friend, and I have known her longer than just about anyone else in my life, including you."

He put his hands over his eyes. "I know. I know. I am sorry. I have just been so worried about you. I heard about the murder in the quilt barn at the fair. I've been a mess ever since I learned of it. How do you get into these predicaments over and over again?"

"I don't go out looking for them, if that's what you think."

"You need to be more careful. I can't always be there to protect you. It seems that I am never there when you need protecting."

"I do not require your protection." My body tensed. "Lois and I can take care of ourselves."

"I know this too, but it is difficult for me to hear you are in any danger because I care about you so much."

My anger dissipated somewhat. Even though I still didn't like the idea of Uriah Schrock scouring the county for me, I knew his heart was in the right place. Perhaps I had been a widow for too long and had become too accustomed to doing what I wanted when I wanted to do it. I didn't have a husband or children to answer to.

Uriah was my friend, and I knew very well that he wanted to be something more than that if I agreed. However, I wasn't certain I could.

"I do appreciate that you worried about me," I said. "And I'm sorry you had so much difficulty finding me."

He tugged on his grizzled beard. "Darcy told me you and Lois were out detecting again. It made me worry even more. I overreacted, and apologize for that. I know you and Lois can take care of yourselves. I'd wanted to offer my help, and then when I couldn't find you, I began to worry."

I nodded. "I do understand that, but as you can see, I am fine. Lois and I were at the Double Stitch meeting at the Yoder farm, and then I came home." I decided not to tell him we had also gone to Millersburg to see the quilt shop that had burned to the ground. He was already worried enough as it was.

He chuckled and began to relax. "Ruth allowed Lois at the meeting? I'm shocked."

I smiled. "It was a surprise, but I think they made a breakthrough in tolerating each other better, which is all I can ask for after sixty years."

He laughed at this.

"Would you like to come in for some coffee? Or maybe lemonade? It is still quite warm."

He shook his head. "I have to get back to the village square. Margot Rawlings is beside herself because so many visitors are skipping Harvest to go to the fair. She asked me to make sure the square is pristine for the square dance later this week, and she wants me to walk around town and ask merchants to hang posters about it in their windows."

"Square dance? She can't be expecting Amish to attend that."

"She's not. She knows very well that people of our faith don't dance, but she hopes the event will attract *Englischers* in the county for the fair. Apparently, *Englischers* like to dance or so Margot tells me."

"The fair is only one week a year," I said. "Margot shouldn't be upset that it's popular for just a few days."

"That doesn't matter to Margot. She wants Harvest to be the top destination in Harvest year-round."

"Do you need help preparing for the square dance?" I asked. "It's the least I can do since I caused you to run around the county looking for me all day."

He smiled. "*Nee.* I have Leon to help me. Now that I have laid my eyes on you, I feel better and can go about my work. The only thing I ask is that if something like this happens again, you get a message to me to say you are safe."

I blinked at him. After twenty years as a widow, I was used to not being checked up on. I thought that I would chafe at the idea, but in truth, it was nice to know that someone was looking out for me. Well, someone other than Lois, who tended to be right there with me finding trouble.

He looked me in the eye. "You're very special to me, Millie Fisher, and if something happened to you, I don't know what I would do."

My heart tightened in my chest. I cared for Uriah too, but fear kept me from saying it aloud. I was afraid if I said it, then the life I had built over these last many years would be gone. I wasn't certain I was prepared to give that up for something else even if that something else might be better.

I fought the urge to push Uriah completely away. However, I still didn't know whether that was what I really wanted to do. An old proverb came to my mind. *It is better to give others a piece of your heart than a piece of your mind.* Would I ever be ready to give Uriah a piece of my heart?

Uriah shoved his hands in his pockets and rocked back on his heels. "I'll be at the quilt judging tomorrow to cheer you on and keep an eye out for you. It's clear that someone has to. I can't leave it up to Lois alone. I know she will be there though. She is a very *gut* friend to you. I appreciate her for that."

"It will be nice to see you there, and Micah and the goats will be happy to see you too. He's showing them at the fair. Phillip came away with the blue ribbon today."

He shook his head as if in disbelief. "The world is full of wonders, is it not? I can't imagine that goat stood still long enough to be judged, but I am happy for him and Micah."

"I am too, but I will be even happier when the goats are back on the farm. I didn't realize that I would miss them this much."

He smiled. "They do have a talent for making their way into our hearts, don't they? But then again, I could say the same of you." He strode back to his buggy.

As he drove away, I couldn't shake his last words from my head no matter how I tried.

Chapter Eighteen

The next morning as I walked into the fair-grounds, I was still mulling over my last conversation with Uriah. I knew that he wanted me to marry him, but would I ever be open to that? I was a different person than I had been when I was happily married to Kip. It was difficult to know what Kip would think of the woman I am now. I am so much more confident than the wife he had known. I have done so many things alone without him and things he would not approve of, including solving murders. What if I missed the life I'd been forced to create when my husband died? It was a life I had grown to love despite my terrible loss at a young age.

"Millie," Sal said as I reached the gate. "Boy, I'm glad to see you. Yesterday, the fair was packed by afternoon. I have never seen anything like it before. My feet ached from the number of times I had to walk across the grounds because of some kind of disturbance, which was usually kids roughhousing or being too loud. Come night, it got even worse."

"I'm sorry to hear that. Did Phillip and Peter behave themselves last night?"

He nodded. "If they had their way, they would have been outside of their pen running around with all the young people, but they didn't try to escape, and no one let them out. I still wish I knew who let them out of their pen last night."

"Me too," I said. "Did you get any sleep at all?"

"A little, but I slept here in the guard house so I could keep a better eye on things. My trailer is behind the stables and too far away to see what's going on. Things were better too, because I had support. Two deputies from the sheriff department were on the grounds all night, and knowing they were there let me relax a bit."

"Who were the deputies?"

"Deputy Pickle and Deputy Whaler."

I frowned. I didn't know either one of those names, but I had heard since taking over the sheriff's department, Sheriff Brody had made a lot of changes to the staff. Deputies Pickle and Whaler had to be the newer deputies on the force. I would be lying if I didn't admit I wished that Deputy Little had been one of the men on the grounds at night. If he had, Lois and I would have a better chance of getting information about what was going on. However, Deputies Pickle and Whaler might be willing to share more since they were new and might not know better.

"Have the deputies mentioned any suspects for the murder?" I asked. I knew it was unlikely I would be able to get this information from Sal, but he was law enforcement—sort of—so it was possible Deputy Little or some of the other deputies had been a little more candid with him than they were with me.

He shook his head. "They said they didn't know much at all and that Sheriff Brody was taking over the case. It's the first big case he's had since he became sheriff, and he knows everyone in the county has their eyes on him."

"I'm sure that's true since he was appointed to the position by the county commissioners. In the fall, he will have to run for reelection on his own merit." I adjusted my basket over my arm. It had needles, thread, and fabric in it. I didn't know how long the quilt judging would take, so I had come prepared with something to do. "Where is the quilt judging to be? They hadn't picked a new location before I left the fair yesterday."

"It will be in the show arena."

"Oh *gut*. The show arena isn't ideal with the animals moving through it, but at least it is protected from the weather. Star chose the best spot available."

"I don't know if they had any other options. All of the quilts were moved in there yesterday afternoon. Last I saw, Star was still making adjustments to the display."

"Oh my. I should go over and help her."

He nodded. "Don't find any dead bodies today."

I glanced back at him. "I never plan to do such a thing."

With my basket hitting my side, I hurried through the grounds. The games and rides were just start-

ing up for the day. The two young people I had noticed the first day at the axe-throwing booth were
standing there alone, and by their stance, they
weren't too happy with each other.

"Where did you find it? It's been missing for two
days," the young man said.

"I didn't find it. It was just in the bin with the
others," the young woman said.

"Are you sure it was missing in the first place?
Could you have miscounted?"

She put her hands on her hips. "You saw it was
missing too! And you counted the hatchets just as
many times as I did."

He made a face. "Let's just be happy it's back.
Now we don't have to tell Virgil it disappeared."

"Fine. I'm going to get a coffee." She stomped
away.

I was continually surprised how young *Englischers* were willing to fight so loudly and openly even
though they knew others were around to see and
hear them. The two employees from the axe-
throwing booth didn't seem to care they made a
scene.

I needed to get to the arena to help with the
quilt-judging setup, but the young woman's mention of coffee got my attention. I was dragging that
morning, and a cup of coffee was just what I
needed. After which, I would be much more helpful to Star.

The coffee stand was just outside the arena,
which was the perfect spot for me to watch who
came and went through the building. There was a
line at the stand, four people deep, and I joined

the queue just after the young woman from the axe-throwing booth. She had her arms folded around her chest, and she glared at the sky.

I adjusted my basket on my arm. "Are you all right?"

Her neck snapped in my direction, and she scowled at me. Almost immediately the scowl on her face disappeared. I believed it was because I was old enough to be her *grossmaami*. I tended to disarm people in that way.

"I'm fine," she said.

In my experience anytime a young woman said she was fine, she wasn't. I decided to risk saying more. "I happened to see you arguing with a young man. Was he upsetting you?"

"You mean Jordan. Yes, he was upsetting me. He was telling me I wasn't remembering the fact that one of the hatchets in our booth went missing. He suggested I miscounted them, but he counted them too! We're dating. He can't be gaslighting me like this if he wants us to stay together for the rest of the summer."

I wasn't sure what gaslighting meant. It wasn't an *Englisch* phrase I had heard before. I would ask Lois about it later. However, it seemed to me that the young man was questioning his girlfriend's memory.

"That is not kind of him if he thought one was missing too."

"Exactly! It was missing for a whole day. He saw it was gone, and then when it came back, he said I was seeing things. The nerve!"

"If he doubts you now, how do you think he will

act in the future?" I asked, putting on my caring-matchmaker hat. I couldn't keep from helping a young couple in a bad spot. "If he's your intended, you may want to reconsider the match."

She stared at me as if my prayer cap had suddenly burst into flame. "Intended? You mean like to get married?"

I nodded.

"No way. We're so far off from that. It's just a summer fling. But I might end it early because he's being such a jerk."

"I am relieved to hear it. From what I observed, I don't believe he is your perfect match."

She blinked at me. "Are you some kind of Amish witch to know that? Can you see the future or something? Because I have a few questions for you if you do."

"I'm not a witch," I said calmly, understanding the young woman couldn't know how insulting it was to say such a thing to an Amish woman. "But I do have a sense when people are right for each other. It's just a gift I have."

Her shoulders sagged. "I already knew it wouldn't last beyond the summer. He blames me for everything that goes wrong in the booth, including one of the hatchets going missing. He almost acts like I hid it just to mess with him." She flipped her long hair over her shoulder. "I would never do that. If one of the axes went missing, Virgil and the whole company could be in a lot of trouble. Virgil went through so much to get this booth at the fair. He had to go through more safety protocols than any other vendor, including the rides, which are basically metal death traps. People are much more likely to be hurt by one of those than an axe thrown in a cage."

"Next," the man at the coffee stand called.

The young woman moved forward and placed her order. Her coffee order was so complicated, it wasn't something I would even try to repeat, and who knew something called oat milk even existed?

She paid the man and accepted her beverage masquerading as coffee.

When she turned around, she smiled at me. "I'm Amber Lyn, by the way."

I nodded at her. "Millie."

"It was nice talking to you, Millie. You gave me some clarity about Jordan. You should stop by and throw a few hatchets. I bet from all the farmwork, you have a great arm on you. It would be an awesome social media post for the company if we had video of an Amish woman throwing an axe. What a juxtaposition! It would go viral. I work as an influencer on the side. I know what works." She waved and walked away.

Influencer? Truly the girl spoke in riddles.

As much as I wanted to ask about her employer, Virgil Rinaldi, I stopped myself. Something told me that I shouldn't let her know yet my connection to Lois and therefore Virgil.

I watched her walk back in the direction of the axe-throwing booth. If I did only one thing that day, at least I'd made Amber Lyn feel a bit better, but I wouldn't be running to the axe-throwing booth anytime soon for those pictures. It was clear to me Amber Lyn didn't know much about the

Amish or the fact that we didn't want our photos taken. We certainly wouldn't want them on the Internet.

I walked up to the stand and ordered a small coffee, black. He handed me a paper cup. "No charge. You were a saint to listen to that young woman for so long."

"*Danki,*" I said and tucked my two dollars into his tip jar.

Chapter Nineteen

I was looking forward to seeing the arena and what Star had put together for the quilt judging. I had full confidence in her. The issue was Star didn't have very much confidence in herself.

The sun beat down on my head, my sewing basket was heavy on my arm, and I regretted the hot coffee that was burning the inside of my palm. I stepped inside and squinted in the dim lighting. The sound of oinking and snorting echoed off the metal walls and ceiling.

In the middle of the arena, a line of enormous pigs were walking in a circle around the show-ring. Their teenaged handlers jogged before them. By the look of it, it was a group of sows, and the smallest one could not have been under a hundred and fifty pounds. The largest one had to be close to two hundred. Seeing the sows prance around the ring, Jethro came to mind. The little pig was no bigger than a toaster. What would he have thought of these giant sows?

As if I'd beckoned him, I heard someone crow, "Jethro, look at all the pretty ladies in the ring!"

I turned around to see Juliet Brook walking into the area in a bright orange and yellow polka-dotted sundress and strappy high-heeled sandals, which were just about the worst footwear she could have chosen for the fair. The chance of stepping into something unsavory on the grounds was about eighty percent if not ninety. I tried not to think what might be on the bottom of my black sneakers.

Reverend Brook followed a few steps behind his wife. He was a plain and mild-mannered man with glasses, and I had never seen him in anything but a buttoned-up long-sleeve dress shirt and dark slacks. One time, I happened to be driving my buggy by the church on the way to the Sunbeam Café, and he had been trimming the church's hedges in the same outfit.

"Oh, Millie." Juliet waved the arm that wasn't wrapped around Jethro's torso. "I'm so glad to see you here."

I walked over to them. "I didn't know you were coming to the fair today. You didn't mention it yesterday."

She placed a hand on her cheek. "I know. That was awful of me. My only excuse is that when we last spoke, I didn't know I was coming. However when the reverend said he had some free time to spend with Jethro and me this morning and I checked the schedule and saw the pig judging was going on, I knew this was the perfect family outing. Jethro is just thrilled."

I glanced down at Jethro, and his eyes just about bugged out of his head as he stared at the giant hogs in the ring. It was quite clear to me that he had never seen a pig quite as big as those sows.

"Jethro, are you ready to meet some of the ladies? Maybe we can get you married just like Aiden!" She nuzzled her face into the top of his head.

His face said, "*Nee!*"

Reverend Brook smiled at me. "Hello, Millie, it is nice to see you. I am sorry about what happened to Tara Barron." He looked around as if to check whether anyone had overheard him. When he seemed confident that no one was listening to us, he said, "She was a very active member of our church at one time. It's always difficult when a pillar of the church leaves the congregation abruptly like that."

I nodded. "Juliet mentioned to me that she left a year ago."

He nodded. "Yes, she was in the middle of a very difficult divorce and told me that she felt she couldn't do everything she had committed to at the church. She said she was leaving. I told her that was no reason to leave. She was welcome to take a break from her obligations, but we didn't want her or any member of the church just to do tasks. We are there to support our members through the good times and bad." He sighed. "I don't believe my message got through to her because she never came back to the church after that conversation. I reached out to her many times over the last year, trying to convince her to return. I even went to her quilt shop, but she wouldn't speak to me."

I felt my back straighten. Reverend Brook had been to Tara's shop before it burnt down. "Do you know what her ex-husband's involvement was in the quilt shop?"

Reverend Brook rubbed his clean-shaven chin. "No. He was there the last time I visited."

"When was that?" I asked.

"A month ago, shortly after the shop opened. He had come to the church a handful of times, so I knew who he was. To be honest, she didn't look very happy with him."

"Why was that?"

He frowned. "When I came in, he was saying that her inventory wasn't going to make any profit because she had the same things in the shop as every other quilt shop in the county."

What had Tyce Barron wanted his ex-wife to sell in her shop, and if they weren't in business together, why did he care?

Juliet hiked Jethro up onto her shoulder. "Let us go, dear," she said to the reverend. "Jethro doesn't want to miss his chance to see other pigs in action. You see, this is a teachable moment for him."

Jethro appeared stricken at the very idea.

Reverend Brook nodded. "It was nice to see you again, Millie. Please know you are welcome in the church at any time."

I thanked him. Tyce Barron remained at the very top of my suspect list.

Chapter Twenty

As Reverend Brook, Juliet, and poor Jethro walked away from me, an announcement was broadcast over the loudspeaker. "We have grand champion, Lulu La Oink of Holmesville. Lulu likes to spend her time sleeping in the sun and eating as many apples as she can get under her snout!" a man in a top hat and suspenders was announcing from his perch on a wooden platform five feet off the ground.

In the ring, a slim young girl walked up to the judge with the biggest pig I had ever seen on a leash. This must be the one and only Lulu La Oink. The pig was so big, her eyes were just black dots behind folds of fat.

"That is some pig!" someone said behind me.

I jumped. I had been so caught up in the drama of the ring that I hadn't heard Lois approach. Hot coffee sloshed out of my paper cup and onto my hand. I moved the cup from one hand to the other and blew on my slightly burned wrist. "Lois! Don't scare me like that."

"I'm sorry. You're not burned, are you?" She took the paper cup from me and gave me a paper towel from her purse while she inspected my hand for burns.

I wiped at my skin. "I'm fine. You startled me is all."

"I can see I did. You were so enthralled with the pig judging. I would say if they judge on sheer size, Lulu is a shoo-in."

She just might be right. Lulu La Oink was enormous.

"What are you doing here? I thought you had to help Darcy out at the café this morning."

"I picked up Iris so she could take my shift. As she told us at the Double Stitch meeting, she and her husband could use the extra money, and I could use the extra time to help you solve this latest murder. It's a win-win for everyone."

I nodded. "I'm glad you were able to help her out."

"Darcy and I are doing what we can. I also advised her to look into that quilt broker idea Leah shared with her. Ruth might be against it, but what is Ruth Yoder not against? Iris is the best quilter in the county. If she can make even more money for her family with her gift, I see nothing wrong with that."

Neither did I.

Lois and I skirted around the judging ring to the back of the arena. Star stood in the middle of the space chewing her fingernails down to the quick. "Please, please be careful with those quilt

racks. They can't fall on the dirty floor," she called
to the group of Amish men who were setting up
the giant quilt frames that would vertically display
all twenty-four quilts to be judged.

I gave a sigh of relief when I saw my quilt was already up and attached to a rack. It looked a bit
rumpled, but all the quilts did from being so
abruptly moved from the quilt barn. A young *Englisch* woman was going from quilt to quilt with a
portable steamer to get the worst of the wrinkles
out of the fabric.

By the looks of it, there were only three more
quilts to be clamped up on the frames, and everything would be ready for the judging to begin. My
nerves were strung taut. I'd never entered a competition like this before. In fact, I had never entered a competition at all. I had decided to do it
because it was a challenge that kept me occupied.
And because I had wanted to make a quilt for Bailey and Sheriff Brody's upcoming wedding, it
seemed like the perfect opportunity. After the fair,
I would fold it up and tuck it away in my hope
chest until their wedding, whenever that was to be.

Lois put her hand on her hip and looked around.
"Star was able to pull this off. I had my doubts. She
must be made of stronger stuff than I gave her
credit for."

I had felt the same way, and I was relieved Star
had conquered her fear and moved the quilt judging so successfully. Even so, I knew there was still a
lot of responsibility weighing on her shoulders
now that Tara was gone. She could use support.
"Let's go see if we can offer some help."

Star had her hands clasped together so tightly,

her knuckles had turned white. "Careful. Careful. Treat it like you would a child. These quilts are like babies to the crafters. Many of the women have spent a year or more creating them."

The two Amish men on the ladders who were clamping the quilts in place looked at each other as if Star was speaking in riddles. I supposed to them she was. It wasn't often that an Amish person compared an inanimate object to a child. It wasn't a comparison we would make.

With the quilt they were working on successfully clamped in place, they climbed down from their ladders to hang the next one. They moved quickly and with confidence. It seemed to me that Star was worried for no reason.

Star bounced back and forth on the balls of her feet. "The judging starts in fifteen minutes. The quilts have to be up and ready to go before the judges see them. They all must be displayed to their best advantage so that it is a level playing field."

The Amish young men kept working without a word, as if perhaps they had stopped acknowledging Star's string of worries at some point.

"You've done an amazing job, Star," Lois said when we joined her. "In fact, I think the quilts are much better displayed here. The judges can see them all at once and really make a comparison. Although, I personally think Millie's is the best."

Star stared at Lois for a long moment. "Have we met?"

I stepped forward. "The two of you met briefly yesterday after the presentation in the arena."

Her eyes cleared when she recognized me. "Oh yes, now that I see you with Millie I remember."

She placed a palm on her cheek. "The last twenty-four hours have been a complete whirlwind. I don't know if I'm coming or going, to be honest. Your suggestion about moving the quilts here was a good idea. It was at least one decision I didn't have to make."

"I'm happy I was able to help. I am only sorry I was distracted by my nephew at the goat judging when we came into the arena."

She smiled. "I understand. You must be very proud of him."

"I am, and the goats too." I glanced around. "Is the new board president, Rein Pierce, not here?"

She pressed her lips together. "He's a very busy man with responsibilities all over the county. He should be here later."

She made this statement with little confidence.

"What are those responsibilities?" Lois asked.

"I—I don't know for sure. He works in insurance and is in very high demand, or so he says."

Her last comment made it known how she really felt about his not being at the fair.

"Is there anything we can do to help before the judging begins?"

She glanced around the room. "I don't believe so. I don't expect a big audience of spectators for the quilt judging. It's not like the horses or cows."

"I think the quilts are beautiful," Lois said.

"I do too," Star said quickly. "However, interest in them tends to be from a specific audience."

We didn't have a chance to say anything else because Deputy Little appeared at our side.

"Good morning, Deputy," Lois said with a bright smile.

He nodded to us and said to Star, "I have to leave on another call, but we still have one deputy here working with your security guard Sal for the rest of the day. Two others will be here through the night again."

Star clasped her small hands together. "Thank you. We really appreciate how seriously the sheriff's department has taken everything."

"We always take murder seriously," he replied.

"Yes, of course," she murmured and then cleared her throat. "I should go over my introductions of the judges. If you will excuse me . . ." And with that, she all but ran away from us.

"Deputy Little, you chased her off," Lois accused.

He eyed her. "How can you say I chased her off? It could have been the two of you."

"Bah," Lois scoffed. "She was talking to us just fine until you came around."

"About what exactly?" He arched his brow.

"Quilts," I said. "I do have one entered in the competition."

Deputy Little scrunched up his brow as if he didn't quite believe that.

"So," Lois asked in a deliberately casual way. "Who do you think did it?"

Leave it to Lois to just jump in with the question she most wanted answered.

"I knew you weren't just here about the quilts," he grumbled.

"We're multitaskers, Deputy," Lois said. "Do you still have Ruth Yoder on the suspect list? Because if she was going to kill someone, it would have been a long time ago and not over a quilt."

He squinted at her. "What do you mean by that?"

"Just that she is a bossy, grumpy person, and if she hasn't snapped in the last sixty-something years, she's probably good to the end."

"Lois," I groaned.

"Hey." She held her hands aloft. "I'm just keeping it real, like the kids say."

"No, Ruth is no longer a suspect," he said. "And I can tell you that because I just told her myself an hour ago. According to the coroner, Tara was hit on the back of the head sometime between ten at night and three in the morning. Ruth's husband vouched that she was home with him during that time."

"And you don't think he's lying," Lois said.

"Should I?" he asked. "I thought Bishop Yoder was considered to be a very honest and upstanding man."

"He is," I interjected and gave Lois a withering look.

"Just playing devil's advocate here. Every detective needs to do that now and again. It keeps us from getting soft, right, Deputy?" Ruth smiled at him.

He groaned in reply. "I do hope now that your friend has been cleared, you'll give up this idea of finding Tara Barron's killer. Her death really has no connection to you."

"Her death does have a connection to us. Tara was a woman who lost her life. We can't just ignore what happened, and we found the body. We will always be connected to that memory."

"Oh yeah," Lois said. "It's burned into my retinas forever. I'll never look at a wedding-ring quilt the same way again."

Deputy Little pressed his lips together. "You know I had to say you need to butt out of the investigation. I fully expected you to ignore me," he said. "However, Sheriff Brody will insist that you stop. He's taking the lead in the investigation now with my help and the help of the rest of the team."

"We can handle the sheriff," Lois said. "We take care of his mother's pig from time to time. He owes us some grace."

I completely ignored Deputy Little's suggestion about butting out of the case and asked, "Did the coroner have any idea what the murder weapon was? Or was it found in the quilt barn?" I asked.

He eyed me and stopped just short of rolling his eyes. "Nothing that could be the murder weapon was found in the quilt barn. The coroner believes something was thrown at Tara that hit the back of her head. Now, the question remains, did the person throwing the item mean to hit her or even kill her? Hopefully, we will be able to determine that when we find the perpetrator. Intent is a huge piece when it comes to charging an individual."

"Because if it was an accident, it would be manslaughter, not murder," Lois said.

He rubbed his clean-shaven chin. "That's right."

"I watch a lot of crime shows." She beamed.

The deputy shook his head. The radio on his utility belt began to crackle.

"I have to go. Please stay out of trouble. Charlotte would never forgive me if I let something happen to either of you."

"We will be perfectly behaved," Lois promised.

He sighed and walked away.

"Sheesh." Lois patted her spikey hair as if to check it was still upright. "You would think after all this time that Deputy Little would cut us some slack. He knows we always get our man."

"I think that's his concern," I replied.

Chapter Twenty-one

Star held the microphone in her hand. "Good morning, ladies and gentlemen." Her voice quavered, and no one paid her any attention.

Lois and I sat in the first bleacher facing the quilts and the small podium where Star stood. I had my quilting basket next to me on the bleacher seat. Without the quilt it was no longer heavy, and as of yet, I hadn't started working on a new project. I was more nervous about this competition than I'd expected I would be.

I glanced over my shoulder and saw there were at least forty people scattered around the bleachers ready to watch the quilt judging. I thought that was a respectable number for a competition that didn't have any live animals that could break loose and careen through the crowd.

"Good morning, and welcome," Star tried again.

"This is never going to work. No one is paying her any mind," Lois said as she got out of her seat and then walked up to Star. She took the microphone from Star's hand. "Listen up! The judging is about to begin. Star will introduce our judges." She handed the microphone back to Star and returned to the seat next to me on the bleachers.

The space was silent. Even the pigs on the other side of the arena were quiet.

Lois folded her arms over her chest. "And that's how it's done," she whispered to me.

"Yes," Star stammered. "Thank you, Lois." She licked her lips. "I'm very pleased to introduce our panel of esteemed judges. First, we have Paula Lee Kiplinger. Ms. Kiplinger is a quilt and handicraft broker working out of Charm."

Lois nudged me in the side. "We need to talk to her for Iris. If Iris were here, I would make her talk to Paula Lee, but since she is working in the café, it's only fitting I make the first contact with the quilt broker."

I knew the second person Star introduced as a judge. It was Netty Dienner, an Amish woman who owned a quilt shop in Charm. She worked there with her granddaughter Faith. I felt a little better seeing Netty among the judges. I knew she would be fair when it came to evaluating the quilts, and in her work she had seen every level of quilter from novice to master of the craft. Netty would be firm but fair, and that's all I could ask for when it came to the judging.

However, the judge who really surprised me was the last one.

"Finally, we have quilt shop owner Tyce Barron. Tyce recently opened a new quilt shop, the Thread Spool, in Millersburg, and has been working with the best quilters in the county to bring topnotch quilts to the public. The shop is currently closed . . ."

And she ended there. What else could she say? That his quilt shop had burned to the ground and his ex-wife and business partner had been murdered in the next building over? The most interesting part of the introduction was that he was the owner of the Thread Spool. This meant that Tara and Tyce *were* in the business together.

"Don't you think it's weird that she didn't say anything about the fact that the quilt shop burned down or that his ex-wife and partner was just murdered?" Lois asked.

"I'm sure she didn't want to alarm anyone," I whispered back.

"Alarm anyone? This murder is what everyone at the fair and the county at large is talking about. If the people here were truly alarmed by it, they wouldn't be at the fair today."

"I suppose you're right, but I think the fair board wants to keep up the pretense that everything is just fine."

Lois shook her head. She didn't care much for pretention of any kind. "More people are here *because* of the murder. Since I suffer from morbid curiosity as well, I know it when I see it."

She was probably right.

"And why is Tyce a judge?" Lois asked again in a hoarse whisper. "What does he know about quilts? He just wrote the check for the quilt shop, didn't he? Did he ever work there? How deeply was he involved?"

"We don't know that. He might know more

about quilts than we thought. Maybe he was more involved in the shop than we imagined."

She shook her head. "I'm not buying it. They needed a judge quick after Tara died. He was available. Though the ex-husband, who has to be a suspect in the arson case and her murder, would not be my first choice for a replacement judge. Star is just asking everyone to focus on what happened to Tara by having him here. They'll recognize his last name. A quick Internet search shows you who he is, and there are even photos of him with Tara."

She held up her phone to show me.

It baffled my mind how much information Lois could find on the little phone in her hand. I understood the temptation of the convenience, which was the exact reason the Amish weren't allowed to have them.

"Nor would he have been mine."

She gave me a look. I knew that expression. It was her you-have-got-to-be-kidding-me look.

"All of the judges will have an hour to look at the quilts, and winners will be announced at eleven thirty this morning. For those of you who placed a quilt in the competition, thank you so much for your submission." Star appeared to be much more composed now that she was through the introductions. "We have the most beautiful group of quilts ever submitted to the fair. I know the judges have a difficult decision in front of them. We wish you all the best of luck."

The audience clapped, and the judges, each holding a clipboard, walked up to the first quilt.

Lois folded her arms. "Now, what are we supposed to do for an hour?"

Before I could answer, she elbowed me in the side again. "I know what you could be doing."

I rubbed the spot on my side. "I wish you'd stop poking me. There are so many other ways to get my attention."

"Sorry," she murmured. "But look who just walked in."

I glanced at the other side of the arena and saw Uriah making his way around the show ring that now was populated with a group of small yearling pigs.

A blush crept onto my cheeks, and I busied myself with the contents of my sewing basket so that Lois wouldn't see. It was difficult to admit even to myself that I was delighted to see Uriah. He had said he was coming and though I had no reason to doubt him, I was so happy he was there for me.

"Uriah!" Lois waved at him.

"Shh," a woman close by said.

"Is quilt judging like golf or something?" Lois asked.

Uriah waved back and made his way through the arena to the bleachers where Lois and I sat.

"*Gude mariye,*" Uriah said. "I'm so very glad I made it here before the judging began. Margot has been keeping me busy on the square. Have they made it to your quilt yet, Millie?"

"Margot will always keep you busy if you let her," Lois said. "She means well, but you have to learn how to stand up to that woman or she will walk all over you. Look at the number of times she's convinced Bailey King to do something outrageous."

He laughed. "I know you're right, but she's my employer. I am required to do what she asks."

Feeling that my blush was finally under control, I looked up and smiled at Uriah. "You didn't miss anything at all. They just started and are only on the first quilt. I think mine is the last in line."

"And I have to say that it's not the most exciting thing in the world to watch. Maybe this is what Star meant when she said it wasn't a big crowd draw," Lois said. "At least if you are watching animal judging, there is a chance that one of them will break loose and there will be a chase scene."

Uriah chuckled. "Millie, I just have to say I'm so proud of you for joining this competition. I know it takes a great deal of dedication and skill to create a quilt that you would feel was *gut* enough to enter. I know you have very high standards for your work."

"The quilt is perfect," Lois said. "All the other quilts are lovely, but I think this is the best one she's ever made. It's intended for Bailey King and Sheriff Brody, but I wish she'd keep it for herself and her own hope chest." She winked.

I wanted to elbow Lois in the side. I forced a laugh. "You two are going to give me a big head if you keep on talking like that. As for the hope chest, I am far too old for such a thing, Lois, and you know that."

"Bah," Lois said. "Age is just a number. That's always been my mantra. You're much more fun now than you were when you were twenty."

I shook my head but knew what she said was likely true, at least according to Lois's standards of fun. I certainly wasn't traipsing all over the county solving murders at twenty.

"And perhaps you *should* keep the quilt," Uriah said with a smile.

I stood up and dusted off my skirts. "I think I will stretch my legs for a little while. They grow stiff if I sit in the same position for very long."

"I can walk with you," Uriah said eagerly.

"That's very kind of you, but I'd just like a few moments to myself."

Lois's face scrunched up as if she realized that she had pushed me a bit too much. She had, but I knew our friendship would withstand it. It had survived so many more difficult events in the past. I just needed a moment.

Uriah nodded. "Lois and I will wait here until you return."

I smiled at him and left my quilting basket on the bleacher seat. Quickly, I walked through the arena. The young pigs were racing around the show-ring. It seemed these small pigs were in a physical race, not a show for looks. The crowd watching cheered them on. I smiled as I spotted Juliet, Reverend Brook, and Jethro standing on the sidelines. Jethro stared at the running pigs as if the race was the most outrageous thing he had ever seen.

By the time I reached the outdoors, I was already feeling better. I had probably overreacted to Uriah and Lois's comments. I knew they both cared about me and didn't mean any harm. A little *gut*-natured teasing wouldn't hurt me. Since I was still sorting out my feelings about Uriah, their comments just stung a little bit. No matter what he claimed, I wasn't sure he would wait forever while I made up my mind.

The events of the last few days had definitely put me off balance. It wasn't often that I found a dead body, no matter what Deputy Little might say.

Across from the arena, I could see the goat tent. I knew Micah would be inside chatting with visitors about Phillip's big win. Phillip would bask in the praise, and Peter would be pouting. After the week they were having, I knew there would be a lot of re-training to be done when the goats returned home. Even so, I couldn't wait until they came back to my little farm. I'd never imagined I would miss them so much, and I had to admit I felt more secure when they were there. They always let me know when someone was coming up the driveway or if something wasn't quite right on the farm.

I was about to return to the arena and give my apologies to Uriah and Lois for leaving so abruptly when I saw Zach Troyer run out of the goat tent. I only saw his face for a split second, but it appeared he was crying.

Even though I knew I would never be able to catch him, I went after him as quickly as I could. As long as I could keep him in sight, I could follow. He wove in and around people moving through the fair and seemed intent on reaching the stables.

After a little while, I did lose sight of him, but I was at the far end of the fairgrounds now. The only building in front of me was the horse stable. I might miss the judging of my quilt, but I couldn't walk away if I could comfort the young boy.

I stepped into the stables. Most of the horses were in the back pasture or being worked in the practice paddock. A lone draft horse stood in one stall. He had a feed bag around his neck and occasionally dipped his muzzle in it to take a mouthful of grain.

There wasn't another soul in the place. There were so many ways Zach could have gotten out of the stable. All the windows were open to let in the fresh air, and the doors on all four sides of the stables were open too.

I didn't think it was a *gut* use of my time to search every single stall for Zach, so I did the next best thing: I just called out to him. "Zach Troyer? Are you in here? It's Millie Fisher. I'm Micah's *aenti.*"

I heard no response except the chewing of the draft horse. I had expected that. At ten years old, Zach was coming to the age when crying in front of people might be embarrassing. That might explain why he'd run away from the goat tent.

But what had made him cry? His *grossdaadi* came directly to my mind. He didn't even try to hide how poorly he treated his grandson. Listening to Hezekiah speak so badly about Zach hurt my heart.

The draft horse batted his long eyelashes at me.

Even though I didn't plan to search every corner and every stall, I decided that the least I could do was walk the full length of the stables to see if anything jumped out at me as a clue to where the boy had gone.

I made my way down the long aisle between the stalls; at the very end was a ladder that led up into the hayloft overhead. I stared at the unstable-looking loft ladder. If I were a child who wanted to hide, the loft was the place I would run.

I set a hand on the ladder and shook it. It creaked but held. It was sturdy enough, and I wasn't a large woman. It could hold my weight.

I put my foot on the first rung. Lois would be so mad at me if she knew I was doing this. Not because she would be afraid I might fall, but because I was doing it without her. She loved a rescue mission, as she would have called it.

I let out a breath. It was best to get this over with. As quickly as I dared, I made my way up the ladder. The wooden rungs whined and moaned with every step. By the time I made it to the fifth rung, I was questioning the wisdom of making this climb. If I fell, I would surely break something, and at my age, there were no minor broken bones.

By the eighth rung I was high enough to peek my head over the side. I'd decided that if I didn't see Zach right away, I would make my way back down the ladder and return to the quilt judging. By now, I knew Lois and Uriah would be wondering what had become of me. They might even be searching the fairgrounds for me.

I blinked in the darkness of the loft. There was very little light here. When my eyes adjusted, I saw Zach sitting cross-legged on a canvas tarp that was draped over several of the hay bales. A flashlight and box of crackers were at his side.

"Zach, what are you doing up here?" I asked.

He looked at me with his big brown eyes. "I live here."

Chapter Twenty-two

"You *live* here?" I asked.

He nodded and picked up the flashlight. He held it tightly in his pale hands, but he didn't turn it on. There was enough light coming from below, as well as from the small window at the end of the loft. The window—which didn't have a screen—was wide-open, and I could smell the air warming up the hay bales all around us.

I climbed the rest of the way up to the loft.

Zach set the flashlight on the hay bale next to him and jumped out of his seat to lend me a hand.

"*Danki*," I said and perched on a hay bale across from where he was sitting.

The scent of hay and dust brought memories from my childhood flying back in a rush. When we were children, Lois lived on the farm right next to mine, and as her home life was difficult, she came to my house every single day.

Even though she wasn't Amish, my parents welcomed her with open arms. Many times, my mother fed her breakfast, lunch, and dinner on summer days. Lois and I spent countless hours in my family's barn up in the hayloft, laughing and making up games. Those were some of my most cherished memories.

I rubbed my right knee, which was sore from the climb up the steep ladder. I could no longer run up and down loft ladders the way I had as a child.

Zach sat back on his hay bale and pulled his knees up to his chest as if he needed some sort of barrier between us. My heart broke for him while he searched for the words to tell his story. We sat like that for a few minutes.

As much as I wanted to know what he meant when he said that he lived there, I didn't want to pressure him or cause him to run away again. It was clear he was running away from something or someone. I had seen how Hezekiah treated him. It wasn't difficult to imagine he wanted to escape his *grossdaadi*'s harsh treatment. But could he really? Hezekiah was his guardian and his kin. In the Amish world, that was a tie that could not be broken. Family had to stay with family no matter what.

Families broke up, of course. Many times, but rarely was a child as young as Zach separated from his family. He could make that decision himself when it came to *rumspringa* in a few years, but not before. Not when he was still a little boy.

He finally lifted his head. "Are you going to tell my *grossdaadi* where I am?" he asked.

There was fear in his voice.

Despite his fear, I couldn't lie to him. "I will

have to tell him. He is your guardian, and he has a right to know."

He gave a great sigh that seemed to be that of a much older person with many more burdens than a child of ten should have. However, if Zach was willing to run away, his burdens were likely as heavy as those of some adults.

"He will not care when you tell him. He told me to leave. I don't plan to stay here long, just until the end of the fair, and then Scooter and I will leave the county."

"Where will you go?"

"I will find work. I've heard they need field workers in Wayne County. A man was speaking about that earlier." His face reddened. "He didn't know that I overheard. But I can pick vegetables and help with the harvest."

Fear gripped my heart as I thought of the young boy and little goat out in the world alone together. Zach wouldn't last long. As an Amish boy, he'd been sheltered from many of the terrible things that could happen to him. Even I was sheltered from knowing some of those things, but in the last several years, my eyes had been opened. "With your goat?" I asked. "It will be difficult enough to take care of yourself. With a baby animal, it will be that much harder to survive."

He picked up the flashlight again. It was as if he needed something to busy his hands so that he could continue to speak. "I can't leave him behind. My *grossdaadi* wants to sell him and he said that if he can't find anyone to buy Scooter, he will put him down."

I shivered. Hezekiah Troyer was sounding more

awful by the second. How could he call himself an Amish man if he treated his own flesh and blood this way?

"Where is Scooter now?"

"He's in his pen. I won't leave without him." He sniffled.

"Why did *your grossdaadi* tell you to leave?" I asked.

"He said that it wasn't his place to raise another child. When my mother left at the beginning of the summer, she said that she would send for me in two weeks' time, but she never did. She abandoned me and placed the burden of raising me on my *grossdaadi*. He said he wouldn't accept that, and I had to go. He said I had a black mark."

"A black mark?" I asked. I had never heard of such a thing.

"*Ya*, because my father is *Englisch*." He looked away from me. "And my mother wasn't married to my father when I was born."

My heart ached for Zach. Neither his parents' choices nor his *grossdaadi*'s were his fault.

"Did your mother leave the community to be with your *daed?*" I asked. "Perhaps if we found him, we could also find her."

He shook his head. "*Nee.* She has never told me who he was. She said he wasn't a *gut* man, so it was better not to know."

Zach's story was becoming more heartbreaking by the second. Although the *Englisch* world might accept children born out of wedlock, the Amish world still did not. I imagined that it had been quite difficult for Zach's mother over these last ten years. The people in her district would have looked

at her differently and looked at Zach differently
too. I wasn't surprised that she felt she had to leave
the community. What did surprise me was that
she'd lasted so long. However, none of this was
Zach's responsibility to address. "Does your *grossdaadi* know you plan to take Scooter?" I asked.

"*Nee*, but I have to take him. He's mine. He was
a gift from my *maam* before she left. She raised
goats and sold them. Before she left she sold all of
them but Scooter. She told me to keep him until
she came back, so we could start a new herd with
him. I promised her that I would. I can't go back
on my promise! I only tried to sell him during the
fair to keep him safe until my *maam* returned. I
knew he wouldn't be safe at my *grossdaadi's* home."

I was certain Hezekiah wouldn't see it that way.
"How many nights have your slept up here?"

He thought for a moment. "Three. My *grossdaadi* dropped me off at the fair the day before it
began and told me to stay here. He is in charge of
the goat tent but doesn't come every day. He said
it was my job to feed and water the goats since I
had so much experience from working with my
maam."

That meant Zach had been on the fairgrounds
at the time of Tara's murder. My pulse quickened
as I thought about it. He might have heard or seen
something. But then again, he might not have, as
the stables were at least two hundred yards from
the quilt barn, with many other outbuildings and
rides in between. It would be difficult to see much
more than the roof of the quilt barn from this loft.

Even so, I had to ask him what he knew about
that night. But it would have to wait. First, I had to

make sure he was safe and cared for. I would also have to talk to Hezekiah, much as I was dreading it. Anything I had to say to the churlish Amish man would not be well received.

"Did you go to your bishop or another member of your district for help?"

"We aren't in a district. We left after my *maam* left. My *grossdaadi* was angry at the bishop because he didn't convince my *maam* to stay. The bishop said every person has to make their own choice, and he wasn't going to force any of his people to stay in the community if they weren't happy. He said those who want to leave become bad seeds in the district and corrupt the other members. The bishop did ask Maam to leave me behind until she was settled. He thought it would be better if I had some security with my *grossdaadi* until my mother could provide a place for us to live. My *grossdaadi* blames the bishop for me still being here too."

I frowned. It seemed I would need to have a conversation with this bishop, or perhaps it would be better to ask Bishop Yoder to speak to him. *Ya*, that was the best idea. Some bishops were against speaking to women from other districts. "What was your bishop's name?"

"Bishop Klein. Our district is in Winesburg."

I had never heard of that district, but I was certain Bishop Yoder had. He had been a bishop for so long, he knew all the Amish leaders. He would have much more success speaking to the Troyers' bishop than I would.

"Why don't we climb down out of this loft and watch the quilt judging. My quilt has been entered."

He licked his lips. "I—I guess that I could do

that. My *grossdaadi* left for the day. Since the goat judging was yesterday, he doesn't have much left to do. He is also upset with the fair board and said he wasn't going to give them any extra time."

It sounded to me as if Hezekiah Troyer was upset with just about every person he met. "Why is he upset with the board?"

"I don't know. It has to do with the lady who died, I think. They got in a huge fight the first night of the fair."

I tried to hide my surprise. Zach was completely unaware that he'd just added his *grossdaadi* to my growing list of suspects in Tara's murder.

"Maybe I should stay out of sight. If my *grossdaadi* came back and saw me with you, he would be angry."

"Hogwash," I said. It was a favorite phrase of Lois's that I had inadvertently picked up. "Have you eaten anything today beside crackers?" I nodded at the box next to him on the hay bale.

He shook his head.

"Then we will get you a proper meal and watch the quilt judging." I stood up and dusted the hay from my skirt.

"What should I do after that?" he asked in a small voice.

"Everything will be decided in due time."

Chapter Twenty-three

At the food stands, Zach opted for two hot dogs, a root beer float, and curly French fries. As I paid for his meal, his face turned bright red. "Maybe I got too much. Are you sure this is all right?"

"Zach, it is fine. This is my treat. You have been in the same goat tent for the last few days with Phillip and Peter. I know that can't be easy."

The redness faded from his face. "They aren't that bad, and they are very distracting to my *gross-daadi*, which keeps him from reprimanding me all the time."

"You also helped Micah catch them once or twice when they ran away from the pen."

He accepted the two hotdogs from the vendor. "I did do that."

I took his French fries and drink from the man. "Let's go into the arena. You can eat your food there."

He nodded, but already half of one hot dog was gone.

Inside the arena, there were more pigs in the show-ring, and a large sow we walked by eyed Zach's French fries. I held them high, out of her reach.

Uriah and Lois were just where I had left them close to an hour before.

"Millie Fisher, where have you been?" Lois wanted to know. Her face was scrunched up in irritation. I could see why she was upset. If Lois had been gone so long, I would have worried too.

"I ran into my friend Zach here. He's the same age as Micah, and they are both showing goats at the fair."

"Are your goats anything like Phillip and Peter?" Uriah asked.

Zach slurped his root beer float through a straw that was a touch too narrow. He lowered the cup. "*Nee*, I just have one. He's a pygmy named Scooter."

Uriah nodded. "If you ask me, Scooter is a fine name for a pygmy goat."

Zach lowered his gaze. "*Danki.*"

"How did he do in the showing?" Lois asked.

Zach hung his head. "Not very well. He was nervous. He really is a very *gut* goat."

"I'm sure he is. The show ring doesn't appreciate goats for their sweetness. It's all flash and style," Lois said encouragingly. "That is how Phillip won his category. He's a showboat."

Zach wrinkled his brow. "Showboat?"

"We're glad you made it back, Millie," Lois said. "Your quilt is the next one to be judged."

"They are still doing the judging?" I asked.

She nodded. "They had to stop in the middle of the judging because Tyce Barron said he needed to rush out to make an urgent call." She gave me a meaningful look as she said that.

"Oh, and what was it about?" I knew Tyce wouldn't tell Lois, but I also knew Lois well enough to be sure she had tried to find out what pulled the quilt judge away from his work.

"I'm glad you asked." Her eyes sparkled with mischief. "I just so happened to run to the ladies' room at the same time he was called away."

Uriah snorted.

Lois squinted at him. "I needed to powder my nose. It is very warm in here, and I am far too old to have a naturally dewy complexion."

"What happened?" I asked before Lois could go into more detail about her makeup.

"He was standing behind the arena talking on his cell phone, and he was furious. He was pacing back and forth, and his face was as red as a cherry tomato fresh from the vine. He told the person on the other end of the call to 'fix it,' and then he added a few choice words that I shouldn't repeat in Amish company or in front of a child."

I grimaced. "Do you know anything more? What was he speaking to the person about?"

She shook her head. "Not exactly, but I do think it had something to do with his ex-wife."

"Why do you think that?"

"Because he called Tara a name, a very unkind name, at least four times."

Tyce just ticked up on my suspect list. As of right now, I had Tyce Barron, the victim's ex-husband but also her business partner in the quilt shop;

Hezekiah Troyer, Zach's unkind *grossdaadi*, who had argued with the fair board president; and Rein Pierce, the current president, who was angry that Tara had marginalized his position as vice president when she was alive, but now seemed to put all the work of managing the fair on Star, the fair secretary. Could the killer be one of these men? Or were Lois and I leaving the killer off our list completely?

Zach slurped up the last of his root beer float and moved on to his fries. It was interesting to me that it seemed he had to completely finish one item before he started the next one. It was as if he didn't want to mingle the different flavors in his mouth.

Lois gripped my arm. "Millie, they are on to your quilt now."

I turned my head in the direction of my quilt. Netty Dienner reached out and touched the quilt. She ran her index finger along the tiny stitches of the pattern. Even though she was my friend, the relationship was no advantage to me here. The quilts were judged blind. The judges didn't know which quilters made which quilts. It was the best way to keep the competition fair and unbiased.

The three judges conversed in front of my quilt, and Tyce Barron shook his head as if he wasn't in complete agreement with what the two female judges were saying.

He picked up the edge of the quilt and tested the fibers in his fingertips. He then promptly lifted the quilt to his nose and inhaled.

"Did he just smell your quilt?" Lois asked.

"I think he did."

"Does quilting have a smell?" Uriah asked.

"*Nee*," I said. "If my quilt has a smell at all, it is probably cookies from my baking."

Uriah grinned. "That just makes me want to buy your quilt on the spot for the scent of fresh-baked cookies. Your chocolate chip cookies with walnuts are my very favorite."

"I think he's just faking that he knows what he's doing, but is actually looking like a fool," Lois said.

The three judges made notes on their clipboards and appeared to come to some sort of agreement. Then, as my quilt was the very last to be judged, they walked over to Star and turned in their decision.

A hush fell on the arena. Lois clasped her hands on her lap. "I wish Iris was here for the judging. Her quilt is sure to win."

"There she is," Uriah said and nodded in the direction of the show ring, which was emptying as the pig judging was coming to an end. It would be another hour before the sheep entered the ring.

Iris hurried through the arena. Lois and I both waved at her. She slid into the seat next to me just as Star went back up to the podium.

"Thank you, ladies and gentlemen, for your patience as the judges deliberated over their decision. It was a very difficult one to make as we had so many wonderful quilts in the competition. This is really the best quilt show that the Holmes County Fair has ever put on, and that is because we have so many talented quilters in our community. This would not be possible without you." She paused. "Now, head judge Tyce Barron will announce our winners."

"Head judge," Lois whispered into my ear. "How much do you want to bet he refused to be a judge at all without that title?"

From what I knew of Tyce, I thought that wasn't much of a stretch on Lois's part.

"Thank you, Star," Tyce said and turned his attention to the audience, which I will admit, had dwindled quite a bit in the course of the judging. The only people who remained had a quilt in the competition or were friends or family of the competitors.

"I will announce the winners in reverse order, so the blue ribbon winner will be the last name you will hear." He cleared his throat. "In third place, with a vibrant wedding-ring quilt, is Millie Fisher of Harvest."

Lois grabbed my arm. "Millie, you won a prize."

"Millie, can you please come up by me at the podium and remain here until all the winners are called?"

At first, I didn't move, I just was so stunned to place at all in the competition. There were so many gorgeous quilts and talented quilters, many of whom were far better than I at the craft.

I still hadn't moved, so Lois poked me. "Go! Go! You don't want them to give your prize to someone else, do you?"

I got to my feet, and with a little shove from Lois, made my way to the podium. Star smiled at me, but her smile didn't quite reach her eyes. Tyce didn't even try to force a smile as he mumbled congratulations and handed me a white ribbon and an envelope. "You can stand there," he said, pointing to the other side of Netty.

"Well done, Millie," Netty whispered into my ear as I took my place beside her.

I nodded and faced the bleachers. The two-dozen people sitting on the bleachers all stared at me as if I was a fish in a bowl. I wasn't accustomed to standing in front of so many people. It was quite uncomfortable.

Thankfully, my discomfort didn't last long as Tyce announced the second-place winner, an *Englisch* quilter from Walnut Creek. The young woman stood next to me, grinning from ear to ear. In contrast to me, she seemed to be quite comfortable with her place in the spotlight.

I felt my body tense. There was just one more ribbon to be awarded. It had to go to Iris. It was impossible to me that she could return home empty-handed. She had made the most intricate Broken Star quilt in black, purple, teal, and navy. I had never seen anything else like it.

"And now," Tyce said, "it is time to announce our winner. The quilter who won this competition gave us a perfect example of an Amish Broken Star quilt. We looked over every inch of her quilt and could not find a single flaw. It is sheer perfection. The winner is Iris Young."

Iris clapped her hands over her mouth and tears came to her eyes. I saw Lois had to give her the same tough love she had given me to make Iris walk up to the podium.

Shaking, Iris finally made it to the spot in front of Tyce. He gave her a giant blue ribbon, an envelope, and a golden trophy. Iris's face was as red as I had ever seen it.

"*Danki*," she murmured as she received all the items.

"Congratulations to all the winners," Tyce said and abruptly walked away from the podium.

Star watched him go with alarm. She then jumped behind the podium. "Thank you all for being here. The quilts with their ribbons will be on display in the arena for the remainder of the fair." She swallowed and looked in the direction Tyce had gone. "I encourage you to come up and take a close look at each one of them. Each is more beautiful than the last." Her eyes darted in Tyce's direction again. "Thank you for coming."

And just as Tyce had done a moment ago, she abruptly left the podium and the arena.

Chapter Twenty-four

I wanted to follow them, but Iris put a hand on my arm. "Oh, Millie, I can't believe this. I have never won anything in my life."

"It's very much deserved, Iris. You're a wonderful quilter. It is truly your gift," I said.

"*Danki*, Millie. I am so grateful to you and all the women in Double Stitch. You have been such an encouragement to me. I spoke to my husband about contacting a quilt broker."

"You did?" I couldn't hide my surprise that she had come to a decision on the matter so quickly. "What did Carter say?"

She nodded. "I think it would be a *gut* decision for our family, but I cannot do it without Carter's approval."

"I understand that." Even though asking a man—husband or otherwise—for permission to do anything would rub Lois the wrong way, I understood Iris's position. In our community, the man of the house was the one making the decisions for the family, and that was especially true when it came to earning money for the family.

She swallowed. "At first, he didn't even want to discuss it, but I asked him to just let me say my piece on the matter. He agreed, and in the end, he saw the benefit of it. Now, I just need to find a broker."

"You are in the right place then," I said.

"Right place?" she asked.

"One of the judges, Paula Lee, is a quilt broker. She's right over there." Paula Lee was speaking to the second-place winner in front of her quilt. "You should talk to her."

"Oh." Her face was tight. "I should talk to her now?"

I smiled. "I believe so. If working with a quilt broker is really something you want—and it sounds like it is—I encourage you to do it now. You don't know when you will get another opportunity like this."

She put her hand to her prayer cap as if to check it was in the proper spot on the top of her head. "You are right."

I patted her arm and then watched as she walked across the concrete floor to introduce herself to Paula Lee. My heart was brimming with pride watching her speak to Paula Lee. By the looks of it, the quilt broker was very enthusiastic. And why wouldn't she be excited to work with Iris? Iris had just won the blue ribbon at the Holmes County Fair.

I glanced down at my ribbon. It might not be blue, but I cherished it all the same. I thought I would tuck it in my nightstand drawer when I returned home that day. It was not the Amish way to lavishly display awards around the home. That would be prideful. But I decided tucking it into the single drawer by my bed would be fine. I could open the drawer and look at it anytime I doubted myself or needed a little encouragement.

I couldn't keep my curiosity at bay any longer. I opened the envelope. I had expected a congratulatory card, but that was not what I found.

Inside the envelope was a gift certificate to Tara's quilt shop in Millersburg. The same quilt shop that had burned to the ground. I wrinkled my brow and tucked the gift certificate back into the envelope.

Lois, Zach, and Uriah were waiting for me in the same spot in the bleachers where they had been before the winners were announced.

"I'm so happy for Iris," Lois said. "She was a shoo-in to win, but you should have gotten second place. You were robbed." She narrowed her eyes in the direction of the podium.

I shook my head. "*Nee.* The *Englischer*'s quilt was lovely, and she deserved second place. I'm just shocked and happy that I placed at all."

Lois shook her head. "You're too nice, Millie."

Uriah smiled at me. "I am so pleased for you, Millie. I know how long you have worked for this. You have to continually practice your art to do so well."

I found myself blushing like a schoolgirl.

Zach was still sitting on the bleachers looking a bit lost. I had told him after the quilt judging was over, we would decide what to do next, and that time had come. However, I was unsure of the best thing to do.

I knew I needed to speak to Hezekiah, but I didn't want Zach to become upset and run away again. I doubted he would go back to the hayloft now, as I knew of that hiding spot.

Lois saved me from having to decide what to do next by acting. That was typically the case. Lois was a big proponent of acting first and giving reasons later. Sometimes it worked to her advantage, and sometimes it went horribly wrong.

"Oh look," Lois said. "Paula Lee is done speaking to Iris, and they both appear to be very happy. Now, Millie, let's go over there and speak to her about Tara's quilt broker who died. There could be a connection to the case."

Uriah sat back down on the bleachers with a sigh. "Zach and I will wait here until you are done."

Before I could argue, Lois ushered me across the room.

Paula Lee smiled at me. "You're Millie Fisher. I was hoping I would have a chance to speak to you before your left the arena. Iris just told me you were the one who encouraged her to talk with me. I have to thank you. She is unbelievably talented; working with a quilter like her is a once-in-a-life-time gift. I also wanted to speak to you because your quilt is exceptional as well. It was such a close call between places two and three." She set a hand on her chest. "I honestly wanted to give the second-place ribbon to you, but I was overruled."

Lois nodded in agreement with this.

"*Danki*," I said. "I'm grateful to place at all. There

were so many gorgeous quilts, I wasn't expecting to win anything at all."

"You should have," Paula Lee argued. "Yours was a cut above most of the quilts. That excludes Iris's quilt, of course, but I know you understand that. Iris tells me you are in the same quilt circle."

I nodded. "We have been for many years."

"Well, you must have a wonderfully gifted group of ladies. I would love to come to one of your meetings sometime and talk to all of you about what I have to offer."

I tried to keep my face neutral, but I knew that would never happen. Ruth Yoder would not stand for an *Englisch* quilt broker coming to a Double Stitch meeting.

"That's a great idea," Lois said.

I shot her a look.

"Oh, I'm sorry," Paula Lee said. "I was so excited to speak with Millie about her quilting group that I didn't see you standing there."

"That doesn't happen to me often because, you know, the hair." She patted the purple spikes on the top of her head.

"It is . . . striking."

Lois beamed. "Thank you!" She thrust out her hand. "Louis Henry. I have been talking to Millie for ages about looking into connecting with a quilt broker and here you are."

Ages?

That wasn't true. Lois had never even heard the term *quilt broker* until this week.

Paula Lee smiled in return. "Well, I'm happy to be the first quilt broker to cross your path, and

Millie's. I would love to talk about working with you. I have to say my commissions are very reasonable and at the industry standard."

"That's great," Lois answered for me. "We want to do our research too."

Paula Lee's smile faded just a little. It was barely noticeable except for the twitch in her cheek. It happened so quickly, I wondered if it was a nervous tick of some sort.

"Millie is so busy with her quilts and Double Stitch—her quilting circle—that she doesn't have time to do much research, but I took it upon myself to make a list of brokers, and I was surprised by how few there are really. I saw your name, and there was also a woman in Millersburg. I can't remember her name, but when I found her, it was through Tara Barron's quilt shop. Terrible shame as to what happened there."

A troubled look passed over Paula Lee's face. "You must mean Sondra Dillard. She was the quilt broker who was working with Tara." She shifted her feet back and forth as if she was suddenly uncomfortable.

"That's right! Sondra." Lois spoke as if she had known the woman's name all along. She smacked herself on her forehead. "How could I forget?"

To me she was overselling her surprise a little bit.

"Should we talk to her?" Lois asked.

Paula Lee pressed her lips together. "You can't."

"Why not?" Lois asked.

"Because she's dead."

My body tensed. The deceased quilt broker had to be the same Sondra that Leah Bontrager had used. The odds of there being two dead quilt brokers named Sondra were slim to none.

Lois placed a hand on her chest and gasped as if she didn't already know this information. "Dead? What happened to her?"

"I don't know exactly. I heard it was a heart attack. It is very sad. She was a great quilt broker and my strongest competition in the county. I actually worked with her before setting up my own business. We also shared information. If she got a chance to broker a quilt but didn't have the time or clients who would be interested in that particular style, she would throw the quilter my way and vice versa. Now that she's gone, it sort of feels like shooting fish in a barrel. Also, I'm just too busy now. With Sondra gone, I am the one who is called to judge all the competitions and give interviews about quilting. To be honest, I am stretched too thin. I'm here today because Sondra's not. Tara Barron would have asked Sondra to be a judge if she was still alive. I know that for a fact. The two of them were very close until they were not."

"What do you mean 'until they were not'?" I asked.

Paula Lee glanced at her wristwatch. "I've said too much already. I have to go. I have a meeting with a quilt shop in Knox County in an hour. If I'm going to make it, I have to leave now." She reached into her small purse and pulled out a white embossed business card. She handed it to me.

"Millie, I would love to talk to you about your quilts and the possibility of coming to one of your Double Stitch meetings. It would be a great honor to see you ladies at work. If you and Iris are any indication, you're a very talented group." She nodded at Lois. "It was nice to meet you too." With that comment, she left.

Lois and I stood in front of the quilts in their massive hanging frames. You really could see every detail in the way they were displayed, and every mistake. I told myself not to scrutinize my own quilt. Ribbon or no ribbon, mine would be the one quilt in the bunch in which I saw all the mistakes.

Lois gave a soft whistle under her voice. "She ran out of here like her tail was on fire."

I nodded. "And she is the third to do so in a very short while."

"The third? Who else left?"

"I thought you would have noticed that both Tyce and Star ran out right after the judging ended."

"Oh, I missed it," she said, sounding disappointed. "After Tyce announced the winners, I ran to the restroom for just a moment. Did they leave together?"

I shook my head. "Tyce went first, and then Star followed him just a few moments later, just as soon as she could leave."

Lois rubbed her chin as though she had an imaginary beard. "Very curious. We will have to find them and discover what happened."

I looked across the room to where Uriah and Zach were chatting on the bleachers. Uriah said something that caused Zach to give a loud belly laugh. It was a wonderful sound. I wondered how long it had been since the boy had laughed like that. A very long time, I was afraid.

"Before we find them, we have to do something about Zach," I said.

She looked over at Zach and Uriah. "Zach? Why?"

I quickly told her about following Zach and our conversation in the hayloft during the quilt judging.

She nodded. "Zach comes first. Then, we catch a killer."

I smiled. "I knew you would feel that way."

Chapter Twenty-five

"I'm going to call Deputy Little," Lois said. "He would be the best one to ask about Zach."

I grimaced. "I don't want him to be taken by child services. He needs to stay with a *gut* Amish family." I had heard too many horror stories about Amish children who had been taken from their community because of accusations of abuse. Some of the accusations were valid. Some were not. But in any case, the Amish children did not do well in the *Englisch* foster system. It was just too different from the lives they knew.

"Then what should we do?" Lois asked.

"I do think you're right that we have to tell Deputy Little. He will be the best one to talk to Hezekiah."

"I can't imagine that conversation going well."

"I can't either, but since Deputy Little has some authority, I believe he'll be able to get more answers than you or I would. But before we do that," I said, "we have to have a plan and a safe place for Zach to sleep tonight."

"Agreed. He could stay with you. You have a spare room."

"That is an idea, but I have an even better one." I paused. "Edith."

"Your niece's greenhouse?"

I nodded. "I think he will be much more comfortable there because he is already friends with Micah, and the other children will be there to play with. They will distract him from his troubles, even if for just a short while."

"Do you think Edith will do it?"

"She might be hesitant at first, but she will agree if we have Deputy Little's approval prior to taking him to the greenhouse. She's a rule follower at heart and wouldn't want to do anything that wasn't following the rules."

"I don't understand that mentality at all." Lois slung her giant purse over her arm.

"How well I know," I said.

Lois left the arena to make the call to Deputy Little so there was no chance Zach would overhear. I didn't want to mention my idea to Zach without the deputy's approval. I didn't want to get his hopes up. I knew he would enjoy being at the greenhouse. He would have plenty to eat and friends too.

Lois came back into the arena. "He didn't pick up, but I know why."

I waited.

"He's over by the axe-throwing booth."

I wrinkled my brow.

"He and a bunch of deputies and crime scene folks are over there."

My eyes went wide. "Did something happen? Was someone hurt?"

"I don't see an ambulance, so I'm not sure. We have to walk over there and find out what is going on."

I nodded and hurried back to Uriah and Zach. "Uriah, would you mind keeping Zach company while Lois and I run an errand? We aren't leaving the fairgrounds."

Uriah tugged on his long beard. "You have some detecting to do. Is that it?"

"Detecting?" Zach asked.

Lois nodded. "You're looking at two crime stoppers."

Zach's eyes were the size of dinner plates.

Uriah put his hand on Zach's shoulder. "Why don't we get some ice cream and look at the games while they are meddling in someone else's business?" He winked at Lois and me to take the sting out of his words.

Zach nodded. "I like chocolate ice cream."

"Then, that is what you shall have," Uriah said and ushered Zach out of the arena. Before he went through the door, Zach glanced at Lois and me one more time, and I could only say there was fear in his eyes.

A small crowd had formed around the axe-throwing cage. Deputies shooed gawkers away the best they could, but as soon as one was encouraged to leave, two more popped up in that person's spot. Lois and I joined the small crowd. As I was so much shorter than almost everyone around me, I couldn't see what happening in the booth.

Lois was a few inches taller than I was and could take a peek if she stood on her tiptoes. I angled back and forth trying to peer through the crowd. "What do you see?" I asked her.

"I don't think there was an axe throwing accident," she reported. "There aren't any EMTs there. It's only deputies and crime scene techs. It looks like they're searching the area."

I saw a gap to my right and went through it.

"Millie," Lois called.

I didn't wait for her. I was too afraid I wouldn't make it through if I waited too long.

When I was within five feet of the axe-throwing booth, a young deputy stepped in front of me. "Ma'am, you aren't allowed here. This is a secure perimeter." He held up his arms.

"I can see that. What happened? Was anyone hurt?"

"Ma'am, I can't answer those questions."

"You can't or won't?"

"Both," Deputy Little said as he approached us. "Chase, you can get back to the scene. I will speak to Ms. Fisher."

Deputy Chase shot me a look as if he doubted the wisdom of his superior's instructions, but at the same time, he wasn't going to argue with him. "Millie, I'm going to ask you to leave the area just as we have everyone else."

"Why are you here? Does it have anything to do with Tara's death?"

He pressed his lips together and said nothing, and in doing so, he gave me my answer.

"Millie," Lois said, hurrying over to us with her purse thumping against her side. "You are as slithery as an eel. I had to tap a man with my purse to make my way through."

I hoped *tap* wasn't a code word for something a little bit stronger like *smack*.

"What's going on, Deputy?" Lois wanted to know. "I was just trying to call you. Millie and I have some information to share."

He arched his brow at this. "About the murder?"

"Not exactly," I said.

"If it isn't about the murder, it will have to wait until after Sheriff Brody arrives. I have to make sure the scene is secure and the search is well underway before he gets here." He looked around as if he was afraid the new sheriff would jump out from behind a tree or game booth.

I knew his nervousness wasn't from fear of the sheriff. He wasn't afraid of Sheriff Brody, but he did want to impress him. Aiden Brody had been Luke Little's mentor since the day Deputy Little joined the force.

"That makes me think that all of this has to do with the murder," Lois said.

"Deputy Little." A female crime scene tech walked over to him. "You're going to want to look at this." In one hand she had a cell phone with a picture on the screen. In the other nylon-gloved hand she held one of the hatchets.

Virgil Rinaldi jogged toward us. "What's going on here?"

Deputy Little turned toward him. "Who are you, sir?"

"I'm Virgil Rinaldi, and this is my business. What are you thinking, crawling all over it?" He glanced around. "Where are Jordan and Amber Lyn? Did they agree to this search?"

Jordan and Amber Lyn ducked behind one of the sheriff's department SUVs. I wondered how much longer they would be Virgil's employees.

Virgil spotted Lois. "Lois, are you all right? What are you doing here?"

"Millie and I are on the case," Lois said proudly.

Deputy Little made a face as if hearing those words pained him somehow.

"Yes, Mr. Rinaldi, your staff did let us into the booth because we have a warrant to search it." He removed a piece of paper from his shirt pocket and held it out to Virgil.

Virgil snatched it out of his hand. "Let me see that. It says you can have all my hatchets. My hatchets? Why would you take those? I need them! How on earth am I supposed to have an axe-throwing booth if there are no axes to throw? Why do you want my hatchets?" Virgil demanded.

"It says on the warrant what we are looking for and why," Deputy Little said.

Virgil held the piece of paper in his hand. "It says it has something to do with murder and you're looking for an item that could be the murder weapon." He waved it in the air. "Are you kidding me? Clearly it wasn't one of my hatchets because the woman was hit on the back of the head. She wasn't cut."

The deputy said nothing.

"Sir?" the crime scene tech said, holding out the phone for Deputy Little. She flipped the hatchet over to examine the blunt side. He held the axe and the photograph next to each other. "Sir, it's a match."

"What's that?" Virgil asked. "What do you mean it's a match?"

"Mr. Rinaldi, I need to see all the hatchets you have here at the fair." Deputy Little's tone was serious. "Every last one of them."

A few feet away Amber Lyn and her future ex-boyfriend Jordan had their heads together, but it didn't look like a romantic conversation. This time it looked much more serious than when Amber Lyn had stormed off to get coffee a few hours ago. They glanced furtively at the deputies, who took pictures of and collected all the hatchets. Once they did that, they handed the hatchets one by one to the crime scene techs, who were dusting and lifting fingerprints off the handles.

"The new sheriff said he supports small businesses in Holmes County. I am a small business, and look how I'm being treated by his deputies!"

"Sir," Deputy Little said. "We have reason to suspect one of your hatchets was used in the murder of Tara Barron, Holmes County Fair board president."

"What? That's impossible. It's completely impossible. My staff and I take safety most seriously. We want our customers to have fun, but we want them to be safe too. All of the hatchets are counted throughout the day and at night before we lock them up. They are kept in a metal tool cabinet with a padlock."

"Who has access to the cabinet?"

He narrowed his eyes. "Only myself and my two

employees, Amber Lyn and Jordan." He pointed at
the young *Englisch* couple standing off to the side.
Amber Lyn was chewing her fingernails down to
the quick, and Jordan continually crossed and un-
crossed his arms. Both their eyes darted in all directions as if they were looking for a means to
escape.

I understood why. They knew very well that one
of the hatchets had been missing . . . Missing on
the day of the murder.

Amber Lyn's eyes locked with mine, and all of
the color drained from her face. She knew that I
knew about the missing hatchet, and I was standing there with a sheriff's deputy.

"There is no mistake. It was one for your hatchets," Deputy Little said. "On the bottom of each
handle, you have the logo of your business carved
into the hatchet—is that true?"

"Yes," Virgil said. "That is true."

"That same mark was indented in the back of
Tara's head."

Lois whistled. "Wow. Someone threw a hatchet
at her, missed striking her with the blade, and she
still died?"

Virgil's face was bright red, and I guessed that
he was seeing red too. I understood why he was
upset. Anyone would be in his position, but I was
uncomfortable that his manner was so combative
with Deputy Little. If he was innocent, why not just
let the deputy take them all? I knew it would be a
loss of business for the day, but wasn't it more important to find the killer? Did he not want Deputy
Little to find the killer?

That thinking sent me back to when I'd first

met Virgil and he said that Tara Barron had given him such a difficult time about having a spot at the fair. Could it be that he was so angry he killed her?

Even if he wasn't a killer, and I prayed he was not, his reaction made me anxious for Lois. She was being courted—or as the *Englisch* say, she was dating this man—and this was how he reacted right in front of her. It wasn't a *gut* sign. Not in the least.

"What is going on here?" a man's voice asked. Rein Pierce, the newly installed fair board president, stomped in our direction. Star was a few steps behind him and looked absolutely terrified.

I glanced at Deputy Little, and he looked as if he was just moments away from fleeing the scene. I couldn't say that I blamed him. If Rein was coming at me like that, I would have wanted to flee too.

"Mr. Pierce," Deputy Little began.

Rein pointed a finger at Deputy Little. "Are you in charge here? Are you the person in charge?"

Deputy Little held up a hand. "Mr. Pierce, I will have to ask you to settle down."

"I should be able to see the warrant. I am the fair board president."

Behind him Star cringed at every word. Maybe it was better for her that he was absent for most of the fair. Having him around certainly wasn't helping her in any way.

"Very well. Mr. Rinaldi, may I have the warrant back."

Virgil handed over the warrant. In turn, Deputy Little gave it to Rein. Rein read the document.

Rein pointed the piece of paper at Virgil. "You? You're the killer? You're the reason for all of this?"

"Hey, where did you get that nonsense? It doesn't say that on the paper," Virgil snapped.

"It says right here that they are searching the axe-throwing booth for a murder weapon. These are your axes, aren't they? I told Tara having your booth here was a terrible idea, but she claimed that it would be a big draw for young people who were bored with the same old games and rides year after year. Now, look what happened! Her stupidity got her killed."

"My booth is not responsible for her death," Virgil said through gritted teeth.

"She's dead because you were here, isn't she?" Rein snapped back. "And I am the one who is left to pick up the pieces and salvage what I can of this mess we call the Holmes County Fair."

I was certain that it was Star who was left to pick up the pieces of the fair, not Rein. In truth, the fair had been running well since Tara's death. That was thanks to Star too. Unfortunately, I doubted she would ever get the credit for it.

"How dare you?" Virgil asked.

Now, the crowd of spectators around the axe-throwing booth was growing even thicker. It seemed that everyone at the fair was wondering what was going on. If I had been just a passerby, I would have been running in the opposite direction to get away from it.

"Gentlemen, please, I don't think you want this broadcast all through the fair."

Rein and Virgil both looked around as if realizing for the first time that people were watching them.

"I need to talk to you about this in private then, Deputy," Rein snapped.

"Very well," the deputy said. "Let's go over to my car and chat." Before leaving, he said, "Now, Millie and Lois, you will have to excuse me. We can talk later about whatever you need. It isn't related to the murder, is it?"

I shook my head. "*Nee.*"

"Then I will catch up with the two of you after I speak with Mr. Pierce." He nodded. "In the meantime, stay out of trouble."

"You got it, Deputy," Lois said and crossed her fingers behind her back.

Deputy Little walked away with Rein.

When Rein realized that Star wasn't following them, he spun around. "Star, let's go."

She ducked her head and dutifully followed him.

"What an awful man," Lois said.

I couldn't agree more.

Virgil turned to Lois. "I have to deal with this. I'm so sorry."

"Good heavens, Virgil," Lois said. "I understand. It's not every day you're a murder suspect. I've been there myself and it really requires all your attention."

He smiled. "I care about you, Lois, and I don't want you or your friend"—he glanced at me—"to get the wrong impression of me because of all of this."

"Of course, we won't," Lois said. "This is an extreme situation."

His shoulders sagged. "Thank you for understanding."

"You can pick me up at the Sunbeam Café at six." She waggled her finger at him. "Don't be late!"

He smiled. "I won't. I have a feeling I will need to have some fun this weekend after this mess." He kissed Lois on the cheek and followed Deputy Little.

Lois touched her cheek. "I feel like a schoolgirl again."

That was what I was afraid of. Lois hadn't been very *gut* at picking her boyfriends when she was in school, or when she was an adult for that matter.

"What are we going to do about Zach?" Lois asked.

"I don't know. We might have to take him to Edith's before we have permission from Deputy Little. It can't be helped."

"Chase, get over here," a crime scene tech called. "I found something."

Deputy Chase hurried over to the makeshift work area for the fingerprinting of the hatchets.

Of course, Lois and I followed, hoping we might overhear their conversation. If Deputy Chase noticed us following him, he gave no indication.

"What did you find?" Deputy Chase asked.

"All the hatchets are covered with fingerprints. Too many people have touched them over the last few days, and it doesn't look like the hatchets are cleaned at all. It's been close to impossible to lift a clear print. They are all smeared and smudged."

"Deputy Little won't be happy to hear any of this," Deputy Chase said.

"This is the odd part. One of the hatchets had clear prints. It had been wiped clean and then picked up afterward."

"This is good news."

"Maybe. The prints were those of a child."

Lois and I shared a look, and my eyes traveled to the ice cream stand near the fairgrounds entrance. Uriah and Zach stood in a long line waiting for ice cream. It appeared that just about everyone else in the fair had the same idea. Nothing hit the spot on a hot August afternoon like an ice cream cone.

"A child? Are you sure?" Deputy Chase asked.

"I'm almost certain because of the size. It could be a small woman, but she would have to be very small, under five feet would be my guess."

Star came to mind when he said that.

Deputy Chase rubbed his chin. "Deputy Little will want to know this just as soon as he's done talking to Virgil. How old do you have to be to throw a hatchet?" Deputy Chase asked.

"Fourteen," the crime scene tech replied. "Fourteen years old. At that age, hands are almost the size of an adult's. This hand was much smaller."

Chapter Twenty-six

Lois and I backed away from Deputy Chase and the crime scene tech. I needed to speak to Zach. I was so distracted by what I had heard, I didn't notice that Amber Lyn had come up to me until she grabbed my arm.

"Excuse you," Lois said to Amber Lyn. "What do you think you are doing to my friend?"

Amber Lyn dropped her hand at her side. "I'm sorry, Millie. It is Millie, right?"

I nodded, keeping my eyes on Uriah and Zach.

"Please don't say anything to the deputies about what I told you this morning. I could get in a lot of trouble."

"What did you say?" Lois wanted to know.

Amber Lyn jerked her head back. "Who are you?"

"I'm her best friend, so whatever it is you say to her, then I know it too. It's the rules."

"You told your friend?" Amber Lyn wanted to know.

I pulled my gaze away from Zach. My stomach was in knots with worry for him. First his mother left, then his *grossdaadi* kicked him out, and now, he might be involved in a murder. Was it any wonder he wanted to hide in the hayloft above the stables? I would too.

"I haven't told anyone, but that doesn't mean I won't. I suggest you go to Deputy Little first. It will be better for you and Jordan if you do."

"What's going on?" Lois wanted to know.

Amber Lyn scowled at her. "I was told to respect my elders, but you're clearly not respecting me, so why should I?" She folded her arms. "I don't have to put up with this. I'm an adult." She said this in a way that only a newly minted adult could.

"Are you calling me your elder?" Lois asked, aghast.

"Amber Lyn, I have to tell the police if you won't. It will help them find Tara Barron's killer."

She grabbed my arm again. "Please. I am begging you. Jordan and I were able to patch things up. I thought that he was just a summer fling, but he's really so much more."

I though their future together was shaky, but I held my tongue. When it came to young people and love, I only shared my opinion if I was asked.

"Also, we could get fired. Jordan would kill me if he lost his job over this." She winced. "That was the wrong choice of words, but you know what I mean."

"Why would it be your fault any more than his?

You said that both of you counted the hatchets and knew one was missing."

"Whoa." Lois held up her hand. "You knew a hatchet was missing?" She directed the question to me. "Why didn't you say anything?"

"We didn't know it was the murder weapon at the time."

"Still . . ."

Across the grounds, Uriah paid for Zach's ice cream and the two of them made their way deeper into the fair. It was getting on to afternoon now, and the fair had picked up. There were more young people and teenagers milling about than there had been in the morning. There were also young families and large groups of children. I let out a sigh and told myself to remain calm about Zach. As long as he was with Uriah, everything would be fine. I could trust Uriah to keep him safe.

"Amber Lyn, I do understand how you feel, but you must tell Deputy Little what you know and when you realized the hatchet was missing. He is going to find out one way or another, even if it's not from me. It would be much better for you if he heard those words from your mouth."

Amber Lyn looked like she might be sick. She then turned around and ran in the direction of the bathrooms.

"Do you think she is okay?" I asked.

"Fair food doesn't really agree with anyone in the long term, and she has been working here all week. Her system is likely in shock." Lois cocked her head. "Tell me what you know about the hatchet."

"All right, but I'll explain while we look for Zach. We have to talk to him."

"You mean we have to talk to him before the police do."

I nodded. "That's exactly what I mean."

"I think I saw Uriah and Zach wander off in the direction of Whac-A-Mole. That's one of my favorites. It's a great game if you have built-up aggression."

"I will try to remember that," I said.

While we made our way to the Whac-A-Mole, I told Lois about overhearing Amber Lyn and Jordan fighting on the opening day of the fair, and what Amber Lyn had told me earlier in the day about the hatchet being returned to the throwing cage with no explanation.

"It has to be the hatchet that had the child's fingerprints on it," Lois said. "Perhaps Zach was the one who put it back. But we have to remember, that doesn't mean he had anything to do with the murder. He's here all the time. He might have just known where it belonged and was kind enough to return it."

"*Ya*, that is very possible, and Zach is a sweet boy. It's something he would think to do."

"I'm sure that's the case. If he saw the murder or knew something about it, why would he be here at all? Out of self-preservation, he would have run away by now."

I knew Lois was trying to make me feel better, but that wasn't the way to do it.

We found Uriah standing in front of the Whac-A-Mole game holding Zach's ice cream. Chocolate melted down the sides of the sugar cone and onto

Uriah's hand. He tried to use a napkin to contain the melting ice cream, but that only seemed to make it worse.

There was no sign of Zach, and I tried not to worry.

"Throw that away, Uriah," Lois said. "When Zach comes back, I will buy him another ice cream."

Uriah tossed the melting cone into a nearby trash bin, and Lois produced a container of wet wipes from her purse. "These aren't just for babies, especially if you love fried chicken as much as I do. You need them within easy reach."

Uriah thanked Lois and cleaned his hands with the wipes.

"How long has Zach been gone?" I asked as he tossed the dirty wipes into the trash.

"Just a few minutes. As soon as we walked into the gaming area, Zach just ran off."

"He ran off without a word?" Lois asked.

"He said that he had to check on his goat and he would be right back. Then he handed me his ice cream and off he went."

"Why didn't you go with him?" I asked. "You just let him go like that?"

"You didn't tell me that I had to keep my eye on him every second. Isn't he here all the time? I thought he knew his way around the fair."

"He does." I closed my eyes. "We have to find him."

"I'm happy to help you look, but what is the urgency?" Uriah asked.

"He might have witnessed the murder," I said.

Uriah's eyes went wide. "In the ice cream line there was a man behind us saying very loudly that the sheriff's deputies were here because they discovered the murder weapon used to kill Tara Barron. Zach wanted to get out of line, but I insisted that we wait because we had already stood it in so long and we were up next to order. He stayed with me, but he didn't seem at all happy about it. His entire demeanor changed. He was a ball of nerves."

This was just what I was afraid Uriah would say. Zach must have been nervous because he knew something.

The three of us split up in order to search the fairgrounds more quickly. I headed to the goat tent. Lois searched the game booths one by one, and Uriah went in the direction of the grandstand, where the motocross races would be held later that night. Even in early afternoon, I could already hear the motorbikes revving up as the riders practiced on the course.

Inside the goat tent, I ran into Micah.

"Hi, Aenti," Micah said with his usual giant smile. "Are you visiting the goats to see how they are? I can assure you that I am taking very *gut* care of them. Phillip is in his glory. He is still so pleased with himself over his win. Peter seems to be cheering up too. Because when everyone comes into the tent to bring Phillip treats for being the winner, they give him some too."

I smiled. "I'm glad. I would not want the goats to be jealous of each other." I looked around the crowded goat tent. "Did you happen to see Zach Troyer recently?"

"*Ya*, he came in here five minutes ago. He didn't really speak to me even though I said hello. He just picked up Scooter and left."

Zach was planning to run, but just as he had said before, he wouldn't leave without his pygmy goat. I was more worried than ever. However, I didn't want to alarm Micah, so I did my very best to control my voice when I asked, "Do you know which way he went?"

Micah shook his head. "Is something wrong, Aenti? Is Zach okay?"

"I'm sure he will be fine. He's just had a difficult day, and I want to check up on him."

Micah nodded but the worry in his eyes said he didn't completely believe me. I didn't blame him for that.

"Do you know where he might have gone with Scooter?" I asked.

Micah wrinkled his nose. "Maybe the stables. I have seen him in there before."

I doubted that was where Zach would have gone this time since I had found him in the hayloft earlier.

"Any other place?"

"He likes the motorbikes. He told me sometimes he hangs out under the bleachers in the grandstand, but I don't know why he would take Scooter there. All that noise would scare the little goat."

I nodded, but of the two options he'd suggested, that was most likely.

"Is Zach really okay?" Micah clasped his hands together. "He's my friend, and I don't want anything to happen to him."

"He's okay. He's just upset about something, and I think he's hiding because of it."

Understanding filled Micah eyes. "It's about his

grossdaadi, isn't it? He hasn't been kind to Zach. If I had a *grossdaadi* like that, I would hide too. He's actually not kind to anyone or any of the goats in the tent. Zach told me his *grossdaadi* is managing the goats because Tara—the woman that died—couldn't find anyone else to do it on short notice, and his *grossdaadi* owed her a favor. What kind of favor could that be? Also, the goats don't need to be supervised by an adult with all the kids here who have a goat in the fair. We know how to take care of them. His being here only made it worse. Thankfully, he's left the fair. I don't think he's coming back. He said he wasn't coming back."

"Where did he go?"

He shrugged. "He just said he wasn't getting paid for this and since Tara was dead, he didn't have to repay his favor now."

"And you don't know what favor?"

Micah shrugged.

I wondered if Zach knew the answer. I would ask him when I found him. And I would find him. Someone had to be looking out for the boy. It wasn't his fault that he was in this mess. At least, I hoped it wasn't his fault.

Could Hezekiah have killed Tara to avoid repaying the favor he owed her? I supposed it depended on how serious a favor it was.

"*Danki* for telling me all this, Micah," I said. "I will go look for Zach in the grandstand."

"Can I go with you?" he asked.

There was so much worry in his eyes for his new friend, how could I say *nee*?

"All right, but Phillip and Peter have to stay here. I can't lose track of them too."

As if the goats knew they were being discussed, they both put their front hooves on the railing of their pen and tried to look as endearing as possible. I shook my finger at them. "*Nee*, you have already gotten in enough trouble this week as it is."

They dropped their hooves back on the ground and pouted. There was nothing quite as gut-wrenching as a pouting goat. The only thing worse was *two* pouting goats. However, I would not be swayed. The fair was not the place to walk the goats on their leads. There were too many sights, sounds, and distractions that might cause them to bolt. If they did that, then I would be missing a boy and three goats. That was far above my quota of missing creatures to find.

Micah and I left the goat tent and walked through the fair to the grandstand. As we went, I looked in every direction for Zach. The deputies and crime scene techs were still with Virgil near the axe-throwing booth. I saw Amber Lyn speaking to Deputy Little. He nodded at what she was saying. Every so often he would interject. I let out a breath. It appeared she was telling the lead deputy about the missing hatchet. At least that was one task I would not be required to do.

Above everything else, finding Zach and making sure he was safe were my primary goals.

Chapter Twenty-seven

Spectators weren't allowed inside the grand-stand during practice time for the riders and drivers who were taking part in the competitions. However, that didn't keep a large group of teen-agers from congregating outside the security fence and trying to watch the practice through the slats.

One of the teens stood off by herself. She was chewing gum and glaring at one of the boys in the group. Even though she appeared to be in a foul mood, she was the most approachable.

"Hello," I said.

She looked me up and down. Perhaps deciding to speak to me was a bad idea on her part. I forged ahead. "Did you happen to see a blond Amish boy go by here? He's about ten."

She frowned. "There are a lot of Amish here. I can't tell one apart from the other. They all dress alike."

I glanced at the group of teens. All the girls

wore very short jean shorts and tight tank tops. I could say the same about her group, that they all dressed alike.

"He was carrying a pygmy goat," Micah said.

The girl looked at him. "With a goat? Yeah, I saw him. I love goats and he let me pet it."

"Which way did he go?" I asked.

"I mean, he went into the grandstand, goat and all. He's in there somewhere." She pointed at the fence.

"*Danki,*" I said. "You've been very helpful."

She shrugged. "If you find him, tell him to bring the goat back out here. I'd love to see it again."

I nodded.

Micah and I walked up to the gate. Through the slats, I could see dirt bikes jumping over mounds of earth and landing yards away. Every landing seemed to be harder than the last one. If I did that, all the fillings would fall out of my teeth.

Micah grabbed on to the bars and stared. "Whoa. Do you think that is something I could do someday, Aenti?"

"Please don't say that to your mother. She would be beside herself."

All the same, Micah stared at the riders. Bringing him to the grandstand had been a very bad idea.

I thought about calling out to someone inside to let them know we were looking for a child, but I didn't think they would be able to hear me over all the revving engines.

"There has to be another entrance."

"Oh, there is," Micah said.

I looked down at him. "How would you know?"

He smiled at me. "I might have been in here before. Zach and I came to look at the bikes. He wants to ride motocross too."

I shook my head. "Show me where it is."

Micah nodded and walked around the grandstand, going in the opposite direction from the group of teens. The structure was huge, and it took several minutes to reach the back of it. Behind the grandstand there was a parking lot, and it was full of motorbikes, trucks with tires taller than any man, and trailers. The back gate stood wide open.

Several riders sat in front of their trailers, drinking and laughing.

"You think Zack went in there?" I asked.

"I know he did." With that, Micah walked through the gate.

I wished I had half the confidence as an adult that Micah had as a boy. I thought Lois might be rubbing off on him. I didn't believe Edith would like hearing that though.

Inside the grandstand, it was even louder if that was possible. I spotted Uriah speaking to a rider who had her pink helmet tucked under her arm. She shook her head.

"Let's go see if Uriah has had any luck," I shouted over the roaring engines.

"If I didn't have my helmet on most of the time, I wouldn't even be in here," the motocross rider said. "The sound is killing my ears."

Micah seemed to be in agreement as he put his hands over his ears. I would like to do the same.

"Millie, did you find him?" Uriah asked.

"*Nee*, but he should be in here somewhere. Someone outside the fence saw him go in with his goat. I would think the goat would make him even easier to find."

The young woman shook her head. "I hate the idea that a kid is missing in here. There are so many places to hide and ways to get hurt. Let me tell the other riders and we'll help you look for him. With all of us searching every inch of the grandstand, we'll find him in no time at all."

"*Danki . . .*"

"I'm Libby," she said. "We'll find him—don't worry about it."

Libby ran off to tell her friends about the search.

Micah rubbed his bare arms as if he was suddenly cold. "I hope we find him."

"We will," Uriah said confidently. "But it doesn't hurt to say a prayer. Let's bow our heads."

Micah and I dutifully bowed our heads, clasped our hands together, and listened to Uriah say a short prayer to find the missing child. As he spoke, I felt my heart swell. He really cared about Zach, even though he had just met him that day. It was just the kind of person Uriah was.

"Amen," Uriah said.

We looked up again, and by the time the prayer was complete, Libby was back with seven other riders ready to search for Zach. "We'll split up," Libby said. "Between all of us we should find him quickly."

Micah decided to join Uriah on the search, so I was alone in looking for Zach. I peeked under bleachers, behind trash cans, and under two of the awnings. I didn't see him. About twenty yards from me, I saw two of the motocross riders walking in my direction, just as a shadow disappeared under the bleachers to the right of the locker rooms. I thought the two riders might have seen the shadow and gone to investigate, but they turned around and went back the other way.

Now I thought I was seeing things.

Even so, I had to satisfy my own curiosity. I went into the locker room, which smelled of sweat, horses, and burnt rubber. It wasn't pleasant at all. Thankfully, I didn't have to be in there long to see no one was there, and with the open wire lockers and benches, there was no place in the room that a ten-year-old boy could hide.

I stepped out, placed a handkerchief to my nose, and nearly ran into Zach, who stood just outside the door.

"Millie, everyone is looking for me." His eyes were huge.

I let out a breath I hadn't even known I'd been holding. It was such a great relief to see him. I hugged him. "Zach, where have you been? I've been so worried."

"I'm sorry, Millie. I had to leave. You have to understand. I wouldn't have run off on Uriah like that if I had any other choice."

"What's wrong, Zach?"

His complexion was deathly pale under his tan skin. "I—I can't say. If I tell you, you might be in trouble too."

"I'm not worried about being in trouble. Lois and I get into trouble all the time."

"But this is worse." His voice was hoarse.

"Let me be the judge of that."

He pressed his lips together and shook his head.

"Zach, I need to ask you a question."

He looked at me with huge eyes.

"Did you take one of the hatchets from the axe-throwing booth?"

He nodded.

"Why?" It was a simple question, but I didn't believe it would have a simple answer. I guessed when it came to Zach's life, there were very few simple answers.

He licked his lips. "For protection."

"Protection? Protection from what?" I asked.

"Everything. Scooter and I needed protection from everything."

He sounded so afraid that I decided to stop my questions there. I was out of my depth trying to help this boy. As difficult as it would be, I knew the sheriff would have to talk to him.

And even though I now knew that Zach had taken the hatchet, and it would be easy to lump him in with the rest of the people on my suspect list, I couldn't do that. I could not believe for one second that this boy had been capable of killing Tara. First and foremost, what reason would he have? Most murders had a motive behind them. What could this boy's motive be?

I decided then and there not to think of Zach as a suspect until I learned otherwise. I decided to try another tactic. "Where's Scooter?"

I knew the way to his heart was through his goat. In many ways, I was the same.

He looked as if he might cry.

"Is Scooter hurt?" I asked.

He shook his head. "*Nee*, but I hid him. It is the best way to keep him safe from my *grossdaadi*."

"You don't have to worry about your *grossdaadi*

any longer. You and Scooter are leaving the fair with me."

"My *grossdaadi* wouldn't like that."

"It's not up to him," I said. "He was the one who abandoned you."

He hung his head. "But he is still my family. He would not like it if I stayed in the county with another Amish family because he would be embarrassed. If I was just gone, he could say I was with my *maam*."

Now, I saw Hezekiah's plan clearly. He had told Zach to leave, and once the boy was gone, Hezekiah would tell everyone that Zach's mother had come back for him just as she'd promised she would. She never had come back though, even though Zach insisted that she would. So did that mean she *couldn't?* Had something terrible happened to her?

"We will talk to your *grossdaadi* about this, but I'm not letting you run off alone with your goat." I put my hands on my hips and gave him my best stern *aenti* voice.

"Oh—okay." He sighed.

"Now, that's settled. Let's go tell the others you've been found, and then we can collect Scooter."

Zach simply nodded. I was relieved he wasn't arguing with me about it anymore, even if it was only for the time being.

It turned out, Scooter had been in the locker room that I'd searched. He had been hidden behind one of the thick bench legs. He was small enough to do that. I was much more used to looking for large goats that were Phillip and Peter's size.

When we returned outside, Libby the motocross rider called off the search party, and everyone clapped for Zach, who was hugging Scooter at my side.

Lois ran the back of her hand over her brow. "Phew. I'm dying of thirst. I'm going to need a lemonade after that. It's way too hot to be running around in a giant tin can looking for a lost boy and a goat."

"I am sorry, Lois," Zach murmured. "I thought I was doing the right thing."

"Running away is never the right thing. You have to learn to stand your ground."

"He's ten, Lois," Uriah said. "I think a little bit of grace is in order for him."

"I have more than a lot of grace for him. If I didn't, I wouldn't be running around in ninety-degree heat with my makeup sliding off to look for him."

"Lois does take her makeup very seriously," I told Zach.

He nodded with wide eyes.

We thanked Libby and her friends again before we left the grandstand. Outside, the group of teenagers was gone.

I wrapped my arms around Micah and Zach. "I have an idea of where Zach and Scooter should go until we figure this all out, and I think you're both going to like it."

Chapter Twenty-eight

Lois had to return to Harvest to help her grand-daughter in the café. Iris hadn't been available to work that afternoon, so Lois had to go.

Before she left, Lois made me promise to tell her everything that happened when I took Zach to Edy's Greenhouse. Since Lois couldn't go along, Uriah offered to drive my buggy to the greenhouse. Zach and Micah loved listening to Uriah's stories as the buggy rolled through the country-side. The boys asked Uriah question after question.

"Why did you move here from Indiana?" Zach wanted to know.

"I grew up here. In fact, I've known your *aenti* since I was a boy half your age."

"Were you and Aenti Millie friends growing up?" Micah asked.

"We were."

"Were you courting?" my great-nephew asked with mischief in his voice.

I turned around in my seat. "Micah, that is not a question you ask an elder. You know better than to be so nosey."

"Oh," Uriah said. "It is all right that he asks. He must know how important you are to me. Micah, my boy, you have a keen eye to observe that I care for your *aenti* Millie."

"You *were* courting?" Micah asked with the same tone in his voice.

I shook my finger at him.

"He might just get his nosiness from you, Millie." Uriah chuckled. "I would say in that case he comes by it naturally."

Zach laughed, and I relaxed a little. I was relieved to see Zach happy, even if it was the result of some *gut*-natured teasing by my great-nephew.

"We were not," Uriah said in mock sadness. "Millie's heart was with Kip Fisher from the moment she saw him. I knew I would never stand a chance with her, so after *rumspringa*, I went to Indiana and met my wife. She was truly the loveliest of women, so compassionate and unassuming; she never would have solved murders even if she had the chance to. She wasn't as brave as your *aenti* Millie, but she had the best heart. She was the perfect mother for my children. They all miss her dearly."

"I wish I could have met her," I said quietly so that only Uriah could hear.

"She would have loved you," he whispered back. "She also would want me to keep living and being happy. That's something I can have with you, Millie."

I stared down at my hands.

"What was Onkel Kip like?" Micah asked. "I never met him."

This was true. Kip died long before Micah was ever born. I opened my mouth to answer his question, but before I could, Uriah spoke.

"He was the best of men. Kind, hardworking, and loved his community. Above that, he loved Millie as a wife should be loved. Her happiness was his ultimate goal. I saw that all the way back to when we were children, and I learned so much about loving someone from the way Kip treated Millie. It is no surprise to me after all this time your *aenti* has not remarried. Who could she meet that would live up to Kip's standard?"

Tears sprang to my eyes because everything that Uriah had just said was true. Well, almost true. Uriah lived up to Kip's standard, and I was beginning to see that. I only had to come to the point where marriage didn't frighten me any longer. I had been a widow for so long, there was comfort in it. I was used to being alone and caring for myself.

I kept my eyes on the road. I didn't want Uriah to see my expression. I needed to sort out my true feelings about Uriah and soon, but it wasn't something I could do until I knew Zach was safe and this murder was solved.

Uriah flicked the reins and turned the buggy into the long driveway that led to Edy's Greenhouse. This time of year, the greenhouse was in its prime. The annuals and perennials flourished in perfectly kept garden beds, awash with every color in the rainbow. The green of the leaves and the grass was bright and vibrant. All the signs were freshly painted, and the Plexiglas siding of the large greenhouse itself shone from a recent polish.

Edith had inherited the greenhouse from her late father, my brother. Her father named it after his only daughter as if he knew that of his two children, she would be the one to carry on his work. My brother had dearly loved plants. In many ways, he loved plants more than anything else. It was in growing things that he took solace after his wife died and left the difficult task of raising his twins, Edith and her brother Enoch, to me, his widowed, childless sister.

In those years, Edith became like a daughter to me. I could not say her brother Enoch was like a son. I pushed memories of that difficult time out of my head. I had done my best with Enoch. I was grateful that my experience hadn't kept me from helping others, helping people like Zach Troyer. I would do better with Zach, I promised myself that.

"You own all of this?" Zach asked Micah. His voice was filled with awe as the gardens seemed to flow one after another all the way up to the greenhouse.

"*Ya*," Micah said. "We have ten acres. Most of the land is for my *maam*'s gardens and hoop houses where she grows her plants. It's so much work. Just to water everything on a hot summer day takes hours and hours. My back hurts just thinking about it."

"You are far too young to complain about back pain, Micah," Uriah said with a laugh.

"It's true! I get a cramp from filling buckets at the well one after another. It's grueling."

This made Uriah chuckle even more.

There were a few cars in the gravel parking lot next to the greenhouse. Edith and her young daughter came out as we pulled to a halt.

"Aenti!" little Ginny cried with her arms in the air. Her long blond braids flew behind her.

For a moment, I was transported back to when Edith was a child and she had greeted me the same way. Ginny was just like Edith. She was all smiles and loved to help. More than that, she adored cats and always seemed to have a kitten or two in one of her apron pockets.

Today was no exception. A small gray tabby kitten poked its head out of her pocket. Ginny scooped the kitten up in her hands and kissed it on the nose. "Isn't he precious, Aenti? Do you want another kitten?"

I petted the kitten. "He is darling, but as tempted as I am, I don't think Peaches would like it all that much. He enjoys being the only cat on my farm."

"But doesn't he need a friend?"

"He has the goats."

"Are the goats nice to him?" Her tone turned serious. There was no greater sin in Ginny's mind than someone or something that was unkind to cats.

"Very kind. In fact, Peaches is the boss and orders them around the farm."

"*Gut.* Cats should always be in charge," she said with feeling.

I thought most cats believed that too.

Micah and Zach jumped out of the buggy, and Zach reached back inside to pull out Scooter.

Ginny pulled her kitten back from me and held him protectively to her chest. "Is that goat nice to cats?"

Zach and Micah joined us. "Oh, *ya*, there are many cats wandering around my *grossdaadi*'s farm, and Scooter is afraid of them. He wouldn't hurt a fly."

The little gray kitten swiped a paw at Scooter. His claws weren't out but Scooter was terrified all the same. He buried his head in Zach's shoulder. Ginny relaxed to see that her kitten could handle the little goat. With her big blue eyes, she looked up at Zach. "Who are you?"

Micah answered for Zach. "This is my friend Zach. He's going to be staying with us until Aenti can find his *maam*."

She looked at me. "Aenti?"

"Let me tell your *maam* before we make any announcements like that," I said to Micah.

Edith came out of the greenhouse then, wiping dirt from her hands with a white cloth. She tucked the cloth in the pocket of her apron. "Aenti, I thought it was you by the way Ginny flew out of the greenhouse. You are always her favorite visitor." She smiled and then spotted Zach standing with us holding his goat. Her brow wrinkled.

"You know what," Uriah said. "I need some more annuals for the square. Some are looking a bit past their prime. You know how Margot wants everything to look perfect all the time. Why don't you kids help me pick some out and then you can tell your friends that you chose the flowers for the square."

Ginny's eyes sparkled at the idea of sharing this news with her friends. "I know just what you need." She ran toward the greenhouse.

Uriah, Micah, and Zach followed her at a much slower pace.

"Zach," I called after them. "Keep a tight hold on the goat around the plants. Don't let him eat anything."

He glanced over his shoulder and nodded. There was worry in his eyes. I thought he must be worried for many reasons, but one of them had to be the possibility that Edith would say he couldn't stay with Micah. I knew my niece; that wouldn't happen.

"Aenti?" Edith asked.

"Let's go sit on the garden bench, and I will tell you all about Zach." I took her arm, and we walked over to the stone bench overlooking a cluster of bright yellow sunflowers. Their broad faces were pointed at the sun, and I thought they seemed to be smiling into the sky. Ruth Yoder would not like to hear such thoughts from me.

Edith waited for me to speak first. She was a *gut* Amish woman and was patient. Patience wasn't an attribute she had gotten from me.

Finally I spoke, telling her about Zach, his *maam*, and his *grossdaadi*. "He has nowhere to go. He could stay with me, of course, but he and Micah have become fast friends. I thought he would be more comfortable here. If you don't want to risk the little goat eating your plants, I can keep him in my barn."

She shook her head. "*Nee*, it is clear to me that the boy loves that little goat just as much as Ginny loves her cats. He likely wouldn't stay here without the goat."

I knew she was right.

"I hate to hear about children who have gone through so much at such a young age. Of course, he can stay here. I have plenty of food. One more child won't make a huge difference, but he has to be willing to work. While he's here, I'll have him tend to the greenhouse just as the other children do."

I let out the breath I had been holding while she spoke. I had never thought for a moment she wouldn't let Zach stay with her, but to hear my belief in my niece confirmed was a great relief.

"*Danki*, Edith. You are storing up treasures in heaven."

She smiled. "I would be happy if some of those treasures could appear here on earth. I won't need them in heaven, where I will be happy and content."

"Gott will bless you for your goodness. It does not mean we live in this world without troubles, but the proverb says, 'Kindness, when given away, keeps coming back,' " I said. "There is one other thing."

She cocked her head and waited.

"No one can know he's here."

Chapter Twenty-nine

With Zach and Scooter comfortably settled at the greenhouse, Uriah and I got back into the buggy. His buggy was still at the fairgrounds, so we had to return there at some point.

"Where to now?" Uriah asked.

"The sheriff's department if you have the time. I know that Margot has a long list of tasks for you to complete before the square dance."

"I always have time for you, Millie."

"What about the flowers?" I asked.

The back of my buggy was loaded with four flats of plants for the square. The children had done a great job helping Uriah pick out the flowers. They were different shades of yellow, red, and orange, the colors of the August sun.

"They're freshly watered and will be fine in the back of the buggy for an hour or two. I can get them into the ground tonight. As long as they are there in time for the square dance tomorrow evening, all will be well."

"Speaking of the square dance, Lois is very much looking forward to it."

"She has a date with a young man?" Uriah asked.

"Younger than we are."

Uriah laughed. "*Gut* for her. Lois doesn't change, does she?"

I smiled. "She is a free spirit. I think that is why we are friends. We are so different from each other."

"You balance one another. I have always thought that. And you are a free spirit in your own way. I can't think of many Amish women who would actively solve a murder or go willingly to the sheriff's office. You're courageous, Millie, and that's something I admire most about you."

As he said this, a proverb came to my mind, "Love always finds a home in the heart of a friend."

I looked at him. "What I admire about you is you don't tell me not to do those things. You help me instead. I don't honestly know if Kip would have done that." It was the first time I had said something even slightly negative about my late husband to anyone.

Kip Fisher hadn't been perfect, not by a long shot. I had begged him for years to stop chewing tobacco. He never did, and it eventually killed him when he was in the prime of life. He also had been a very traditional Amish man. I don't know what he would think of my running all over the county solving crimes, or even having a phone attached to my house. I worried sometimes that he would be disappointed.

As if he understood my anxiety on the topic, Uriah patted my hand, just twice. There was no more contact than that. Then he said, "Those were different times, and you were a different person. I believe Kip would look at things differently now. We all have to as we age. Our views and opinions change over time. I know mine have."

"Mine have too," I whispered.

We didn't speak for the rest of the ride to the sheriff's department. The silence was welcome.

In the parking lot, I climbed out of the buggy as Uriah tethered Bessie to the hitching post.

"Do you want me to go in with you?" he asked.

I shook my head. "If you don't mind, I think it will be better if you stay outside. Zach is a child and I know Sheriff Brody will want to keep this conversation as confidential as possible."

He nodded. "I understand. You will do well. Gott will go with you."

I smiled, put my shoulders back and walked to the hexagonal midcentury building. The glass doors opened into a large empty waiting room. A woman sat at a desk behind a half wall topped by a plastic window. There was a slot in the window just big enough to pass a hand through.

Her eyes went wide when she saw me. I expected that even though it was Holmes County, it wasn't often that an Amish woman came to the department voluntarily.

I cleared my throat. "I would like to speak with Sheriff Brody."

She blinked. "Why?"

I pressed my lips together. I had no intention of speaking about Zach to anyone but Sheriff Brody or Deputy Little. Those two men I trusted implicitly. Although the department was better now that the corrupt former sheriff was gone, I still didn't know who else could be trusted, especially with a child who was potentially in so much danger.

"Please just tell him Millie Fisher is here to speak to him."

"You're Millie Fisher!" she cried. "I have heard so much about you over the years. Oh my, Sheriff Marshall didn't like you at all. He used to rant about you and your friend Louise all the time."

"Her name is Lois, and it is safe to say that the feeling was mutual. However, I can't say I ever ranted about Sheriff Marshall." I paused. "Lois did a time or two."

She picked up the phone on her desk. "If you'll have a seat, I will call Sheriff Brody right now. He just returned from the fairgrounds."

I nodded but instead of taking a seat as she'd told me to, I stood by the window and looked out. Uriah was speaking to Bessie and scratching her nose. Every time he stopped caressing her, the old horse bumped his arm to ask for more scratches. I smiled.

A door behind me opened. I turned to see Sheriff Brody in the doorway. "Millie?" he asked. "I'm surprised to see you here."

"I need to talk to you."

Picking up on the seriousness of my tone, he held the door open for me. I found myself in a room of cubicles that could be in any office building, not exactly what I had imagined the sheriff's department would look like. Perhaps I'd thought it would all be desolate jail cells made of dusty concrete floors, cinderblock, and iron bars.

The men and women working at the desks looked up at me, and a light murmur ran through the room.

"I'll be with Mrs. Fisher in my office," the sheriff announced.

The deputies turned back to their work.

Sheriff Brody showed me to an office with glass walls on every side. He pointed to the chair in front of the desk, closed the door, and then sat behind the desk in the captain's chair that looked as if it might be as old as I was.

I perched on the edge of my chair.

There was an engagement photo of Bailey and the sheriff on his desk. They were both laughing, and Jethro appeared in the corner of the shot. It seemed he always showed up. I nodded at the photograph. "We are all looking forward to the wedding. Have you set a date yet?"

He smiled. "You sound like my mother." He held up his hand before I could protest. "I don't say that as a complaint, just an observation. I know the whole village of Harvest is looking forward to the wedding. We haven't had time to plan anything yet. As you know, we are both terribly busy."

"I wouldn't wait too long to start your life together. Time is precious."

"I know that is good advice coming from you, Millie."

I shifted in my seat. "Advice I should give myself at times."

He removed his cell phone from the pocket of

his uniform and set it on the desk. "Are you here to tell me you have solved Tara Barron's murder?" he asked with a smile. "Knowing your track record with such things, I might just believe you."

I shook my head. "*Nee.* I need to speak to you about Zach Troyer."

"Who is that?"

"A ten-year-old boy in trouble. We have to help him." I went on to tell the sheriff what I knew about Zach's situation, and that he had admitted to taking the hatchet from the axe-throwing booth.

Sheriff Brody tapped his fingers on the table-top. "What else did Zach tell you about that night? Did he see anyone go in or out of the quilt barn?"

I shook my head. "That was all he shared with me. I know there is more, probably a lot more, but I didn't want to press him too hard about it. He has already been put through so much. My main goal is to make sure he is safe and well taken care of."

Sheriff Brody nodded. "You did the right thing, Millie."

I didn't need the praise, but I did feel better getting the approval of the sheriff as he was a man I respected and trusted.

He frowned. "We still don't know why Tara was in the quilt barn at that time of night, but we believe she went there willingly."

"That was to be expected. She was the president of the fair board and appeared to be very stressed over the idea of the quilt judging. Maybe she went inside to check to see if everything was ready for the next day."

"Or she went inside to meet someone there."

"Who?" I asked.

"We don't know." He paused. "You said that Zach is somewhere safe. Where is he now?"

"At Edith's greenhouse," I said.

"How many people know where he is?"

"Edith and her children, Uriah, Lois, me, and now you."

He nodded. "Let's keep it that way. If the killer learns Zach was on the fairgrounds that night, they may believe Zach saw something. He could be in danger."

"Those were my thoughts."

"And we have to be careful when it comes to children as witnesses. I need to consult with the juvenile psychologist we have on call for such situations. I'm going to have to talk to Zach too."

"Can I be there?" I asked.

He folded his hands on his desk.

"I'm the only adult he trusts. His *grossdaadi* will be no help."

"That is an issue too. If his grandfather is his legal guardian, you may have to give him back."

"He told Zach to leave."

"I know, or at least I know that's what Zach told you. We have to confirm with the grandfather and take it from there."

"I would prefer that we hand him over to his mother," I said.

"I would too, but she left him," the sheriff said. "That's worrisome."

"She told Zach she'd come back for him when she was settled."

"But she never did," he finished for me.

"That concerns me. Zach insists that she would

have kept her promise if she could. Can you search for her?"

"We don't have an official missing person's report."

"Can I file one?"

"I don't see why not, but what do you know about her? Have you ever met her? Do you know what she looks like?"

I shook my head. "*Nee.* I have a feeling that her *daed* won't be much help. When you speak to Zach, perhaps he can answer those other questions for you."

He nodded. "A photograph would help immensely in locating her, but I have to assume there isn't one since she is Amish. Add to that the fact there is no social security number, or credit cards, or even a cell phone to trace, it is going to be difficult to find her."

"I have full confidence in you."

"I'll put several deputies on it ASAP, and I'll call that psychologist. I hope to be out to speak to Zack later today. I believe it's wise not to tell anyone else where he is, including the grandfather. Leave speaking to him to me."

"There's one other thing," I said.

He waited.

"There's something interesting I learned about the grandfather. It seems he was volunteering at the fair to pay back a favor to Tara."

"What favor was that?"

I shook my head. "I don't know. Micah was the one who told me."

"Would Zach know the favor?"

"Possibly, I haven't had the chance to ask him."

Chapter Thirty

Later that day, Sheriff Brody left a message on my shed phone to say he would be out to speak to Zach the next afternoon. It was the earliest the juvenile psychologist could be there.

After the long day I'd had, I was relieved. I had to sort out my thoughts about everything that'd transpired over the last day. Uriah had those flowers to plant on the square for the dance the next evening, so I drove him back to the fair to collect his own horse and buggy. After we said our goodbyes, I went into the fair in order to check on Phillip and Peter. I made sure they had enough food and water. The two goats looked as happy as could be as visitors fawned over Phillip's blue ribbon, which was attached to the fence. It seemed Peter had come to view the blue ribbon as his as well.

That was just fine with me. There was nothing worse than a mopey goat.

Before I left, I walked around the fairground in

search of Hezekiah Troyer in case he had come back. I was dying to know what favor he'd needed to repay Tara.

I noted the axe-throwing booth wasn't just shut down—the entire booth and small tent next to it where they sold tickets was completely gone. I wondered if it was now in police custody because of its bearing on the case.

Star walked by me with a clipboard in hand. She appeared to be completely frazzled. All her short hair stood up on her head, and it wasn't because she'd put a long list of products in it the way Lois did.

She didn't even see me when I walked by. She was writing on her clipboard and walking. It was a miracle she didn't run into anyone.

I caught up with her. "Star?"

She turned to face me with weariness in her eyes. I told myself she had grown weary of managing the fair and not of me. In actuality, it was likely both.

"Oh, Millie, you're still here. Someone told me you left the fair for the day."

"Were you looking for me?"

"Not exactly, but I know your nephew was friendly with Zach Troyer. It seems he left the fair and took his little goat Scooter with him without telling anyone. When children check their animals out of the fair, they are supposed to tell the person in charge of the tent before they go. That way we know all the animals are claimed by the correct person and accounted for."

"Isn't his *grossdaadi* overseeing the goat tent? Surely, he would know that Zach and Scooter left."

She pursed her lips. "Yes, well, Hezekiah Troyer

quit early this morning. He said that he wanted nothing to do with the fair now."

"Why is that?"

"He didn't give any reason to me. I saw him storming away from the goat tent and stopped him to see if he was all right. That was a mistake. He practically bit my head off. Honestly, all the tourists who come to Holmes County and think every last one of the Amish are kind and peace-loving farmers don't know a bit about the culture." Her face turned red. "No offense to you, Millie. I'm sorry if that came off as cruel."

"I'm not offended," I said. "The Amish are people just like *Englischers*. We are no better or worse. We sin and make mistakes."

"Yes, well, I suppose you're right. Hezekiah may have decided to remove his grandson and the goat from the fair since he was so upset about it. I don't know why I didn't think of that before." She brushed her dark curls out of her eyes. "I have just been so preoccupied with everything that needs to be done."

"Has Rein been much help?"

She scrunched up her nose. "He has a different view of his role as president than Tara did. He believes his job is to pass out ribbons and raise money for next year. Beyond that, he doesn't have much interest in the fair at all."

"Then why was he so upset when Tara downgraded his responsibilities while he was her vice president?"

"Just between you and me, he wasn't upset about having to do less; he was upset that Tara was running the board. He was just mad that he wasn't the president after so many years on the board."

"How many years was he on the board?" I asked.

"Twenty, maybe more. I just came on a couple of years ago. I moved here from Wisconsin, and always loved my county fair there. I got involved here because I thought it would be a great way to meet people." She sighed. "I wished I had known how dysfunctional this board was before I signed up."

"How is the fair board president chosen?" I asked.

"The person is appointed by the county commissioners."

"And they never chose Rein before, even after so many years of service?"

She shook her head. "I guess not. He doesn't have the warmest personality. You might have noticed that when you met him. Then again neither did Tara." She looked around as if she was about to say something she didn't want anyone to overhear. "From what I heard, one of the commissioners was her former brother-in-law. He convinced the others to appoint her as president to avoid her dragging out her divorce any longer because she told Tyce that was what it would take for her to sign the divorce papers. Apparently they talked about divorce for over ten years."

My eyes went wide. If Tyce and Tara were in such a bad place that they fought with each other for a decade, why would they go into business together? That puzzle piece was the hardest to fit in. Then again, there were puzzle pieces I didn't even have, like the identity of the killer.

Sal rushed up to us out of breath. "Any luck, Star?"

He bent over and held on to his knees to catch his breath.

"Oh my word, Sal. You need to calm down. Your face is as red as a tomato. You are going to pass out from heat stroke," Star said.

Sal stood up, but his face wasn't any less red. "I'm just worried about the kid."

"That is kind of you, Sal," I said. I would have patted his arm if I didn't think the impact would bowl him over.

"One of the other Amish children said he thought Zach was sleeping at the fair at night."

"Oh?" I said.

"He said that he saw him climb down from the hayloft at dawn. The other boy climbed up there and found food and a flashlight."

My chest tightened. How many people knew that Zach slept here, and might have been on the grounds the night of the murder? Could the killer have heard about this by now?

"Did this other child talk to Zach about it?" I asked.

Sal shook his head.

"Well, Zach could have been up in that hayloft for a myriad of reasons. I think every child who grew up on a farm has hidden in the hayloft once or twice to escape."

Sal seemed to relax, and his coloring was finally going back to normal. "I guess you're right. I just felt so bad when I heard that. His grandpa isn't the nicest man in the world, and I heard his mom left him."

"She is going to come get him," I said automatically. I didn't know why I wanted to defend Zach's mother so much after she'd left her only child with Hezekiah. But I did believe she'd thought she was doing the right thing for her son at the time.

"Do you know where he is, Millie?" Sal asked.

I blinked. It was a direct question. "Zach?" I asked to give me time to think.

"Yes," he said.

"I'm sure he's safe," I managed.

Sal looked as if he wanted to press me more on that point, but Star stepped in.

"Most likely," Star said, "Hezekiah took his grandson and the goat from the fair when he quit. We will have to trust that is the case."

Sal blinked. "But he could be in trouble. Millie, don't you think so?"

"I think he's safe." It was impossible for me to come out and speak a direct lie, but it was one of those times when I wished I had the ability.

I left the fairgrounds for home, but just as I was about to turn onto my road, I swerved in the opposite direction and drove to the Yoders' dairy farm. I didn't know how enthusiastic Ruth would be having me pop up on her farm unannounced yet again, but that was a risk I would have to take. I wasn't intimidated by Ruth. I had known her for a long time.

When I arrived, I spotted Bishop Yoder standing in front of his barn, shoeing a horse. The horse placidly stood there as the bishop drove the horseshoe nail home on the gelding's right front hoof.

I pulled Bessie to a stop by the hitching post and climbed out of the buggy. After Bessie was tethered safely to the post, I walked over to the bishop.

Ping, ping, ping came the sound of the hammer's head as it struck the nail. Bishop Yoder glanced at me and nodded. He continued to work on the hoof in front of him. I understood. It could hurt the horse to walk around on a horseshoe that wasn't adequately attached to his hoof.

He added two more nails to the horseshoe and then patted the side of the horse's ankle, telling the animal it was all right to put his foot back on the ground.

The gelding tapped the hoof on the hard ground a few times as if he were testing it, and then stood in place.

Bishop Yoder set his tools back into this tool-box. "Hello, Millie. Ruth isn't here right now. She is at our daughter's home."

Hearing that was actually a relief. I knew all too well that Ruth would want to give her two cents on the conversation.

"That is all right. I'm actually here to speak to you about a sensitive matter, but I can wait until you are done shoeing your horse."

He removed a bandana from his pocket and wiped his hand. "I am done. That was his last hoof. I'm glad of it. Shoeing isn't as easy as it used to be. It's not the horse's fault. My old back can't handle it as well as it used to, but it's a chore I love. It brings you closer to your animal, so I am reluctant to turn the task over to one of my sons or sons-in-law."

"I'd say that is the story for a lot of us now."

He nodded. "Let's go speak at the picnic tables over there."

On the far side of the Yoders' barn were rows and rows of picnic tables. They were set up each summer for meals after the church services at the Yoder home. It felt strange to me to sit at one of the many tables alone with the bishop when I was used to being surrounded by pleasant adult chatter and laughing children.

He sat and folded his hands in front of him. "What is troubling you, Millie?"

I sat across from him and told him Zach's story about his mother.

The bishop shook his head. "It sounds to me as if the girl had man troubles, and I don't doubt it, if Hezekiah is her father."

"You know Hezekiah?" I asked.

"We are close to the same age, and we used to attend the same youth socials. He was always angry about something. It saddens me to hear that he has not changed."

I nodded. "I do have a favor to ask you because I truly believe you are better suited for it than I."

"I'm listening."

"Will you speak to Hezekiah Troyer's former bishop? To find out more about Zach's mother? It might help us to find her. The sheriff is going to speak to Hezekiah himself, but I don't believe he will have much luck learning anything from him."

"I will," the bishop said without hesitation.

"And there is one more thing," I said.

Bishop Yoder pressed his fingertips together in a steeple shape and waited for me to speak.

"I know it is best that Zach be with a member of his own district. It is the Amish way, but for now, please don't tell any of them—including his bishop—where he is. His very life may depend on it."

The bishop's eyes widened. "I will keep that to myself."

"*Danki*," I whispered.

Chapter Thirty-one

The next morning, I was up bright and early. Sheriff Brody said he would be at Edy's Greenhouse that afternoon to speak with Zach, but I wanted to talk to Edith before her greenhouse opened for the day, so I could prepare her for the visit.

I decided to leave Bessie and the buggy home and ride my bicycle the two miles to the greenhouse. Typically, when I went to the greenhouse in this way, the goats trotted after me. They loved visiting the greenhouse, and not just for the chance to eat all my niece's plants. Seeing the children was a highlight for them. I wasn't one to run around a field and good-naturedly chase the goats, but Micah and Ginny were always up for it. Jacob, the more austere sibling, had no interest in such childish games.

Just thinking of the children running around the fields with Phillip and Peter made me miss the two goats more than ever. It was Friday, and the fair would be over on Saturday. I reminded myself that the end would come soon, and Phillip and Peter would be home again to cause trouble and annoy Peaches. I could hardly wait.

The children might not have Phillip and Peter to chase around the grounds, but it seemed to me that they were making use of Scooter. I could hear their shouts and cries as soon as I passed their mailbox, even though the driveway was over one thousand feet long.

The tires of my bicycle bounced on the uneven gravel.

The first person I saw was Ginny, who ran after Scooter with her hands in the air. Her blond braids flew behind her like a banner. Scooter for his part looked like he was having the time of his life as he looked over his shoulder. His ears flapped in the wind to the rhythm of his leaps.

Zach and Micah laughed and ran alongside Scooter, encouraging him to outrun Ginny. I didn't see Jacob, but I wasn't too surprised by that. I bit my lip. I hoped Jacob didn't feel left out with Zach there.

The door to the greenhouse opened, and Edith stepped out. "Aenti, you're here very early this morning."

"I wanted to see how Zach was getting on. How was the night?"

"It was *gut*. He's a very respectful boy, and he's keeping Micah and Jacob from fighting so much. I know it's only been one night, but the children are attached to him. So am I. Have you heard from the sheriff as to what he plans to do?"

I shook my head. "Bishop Yoder is going to speak to Zach's bishop, and the sheriff will speak with Hezekiah. I haven't heard anything yet from either one."

She watched the children playing. "I hope we know something today."

"I do as well," I said. "I also have some news." I went on to tell her about the sheriff's planned visit that afternoon. "I will go into the village this morning to see Lois at the café, but I promise you that I will be back before noon in order to be here while the sheriff and psychologist speak to Zach."

"You don't think they will take him away, do you? Like a foster child?" She bit her lower lip.

"I hope not. I think Sheriff Brody knows that Zach would be more comfortable in an Amish home than he would be in an *Englisch* one." I paused. "I don't know anything about the psychologist."

Her forehead creased with concern.

I patted her hand. "All will be well. Zach's future is in Gott's hands. There is no better place for it to be."

"I know, Aenti." But even as she spoke, she sounded unsure.

The bicycle ride into the village would take me far too long, so I rode my bike back home and collected Bessie and the buggy. I hoped I would have time to stop by the fair to check on Phillip and Peter before returning to the greenhouse that afternoon. I knew they would be well taken care of, but I could not wait to bring the goats home the next day. They had been gone far too long. I thought

Peaches was also looking forward to it. He missed having someone to boss around.

With the fair going on, I hadn't been into the village for a few days, nor had I enjoyed a piece of Darcy's blueberry pie, which was just about my favorite food in the world. I left Bessie and the buggy in the church parking lot. When Reverend Brook's church wasn't having services or events, the lot was open to the public. It might be a small gesture, but it was just another way the church looked out for the community. I tied Bessie up to the hitching post there and made the short walk to the Sunbeam Café, which from the looks of it, was very busy that morning.

It might be because of the square dance that would be happening that evening. I saw Uriah and his assistant Leon rushing around the square setting up tables and chairs. Since he looked so busy, I decided it wasn't a good time to bother Uriah.

The bell over the door rang as I went into the café. Iris Young was at the counter filling a carafe of coffee, and I could see Darcy through the window into the kitchen, flying this way and that in a mad dash to fill all the orders.

"Hi, Millie," Iris said. "Want your usual?"

My usual was black coffee and a piece of blueberry pie. I had it more times for breakfast than I cared to admit, but since I had missed it the last several days, I thought it wouldn't do me any harm to eat it again this one last time. Every time I ate it, I promised myself it was the last time.

"Please," I said. "Where's Lois?"

Iris pointed around the corner. "She's in the back booth with a gentleman."

"A gentleman?" I asked. "Who?"

"I don't know, but she was very excited to see him." She lowered her voice and leaned across the counter. "She giggled, Millie. Giggled! Have you ever heard her do that before?"

Only once or twice, and usually it involved a boy when we were growing up. My curiosity was piqued now. I had to know who Lois was talking to. I assumed it was her app date, Virgil.

"I'll just go say hello. It's what Lois would do," I said.

Iris chuckled. "I will have your coffee and pie on the counter when you come back."

If I were giggling over a man—which would never happen—but if it *were* to happen, I knew for a fact Lois would barge into the conversation to find out the identity of the person I was speaking to. So I had no worries about doing that to her now.

I stepped around the wall into the main portion of the dining room, which was two-thirds full. Most people were there reading and drinking coffee. Only a handful had a full breakfast in front of them.

Lois was facing me, but she was so entranced with the man in front of her that she didn't even notice me, so I went in closer.

I didn't know who the man was, but I knew it wasn't young Virgil. Whoever he was, he had silver hair, not Virgil's long dark locks.

I was just five feet from her when Lois jumped as if she'd been stung by a bee.

"Millie! I didn't see you there."

"I can tell," I said, walking forward. Now, I was in a position to see the face of her companion, and it was none other than the insurance investigator, Rusty Bellwether.

Lois cleared her throat. "Rusty, you remember my friend Millie, don't you?"

"Oh yes." Rusty set his mug on the table. "You were with Lois at the remains of that quilt shop. We were just talking about it."

"What did you learn?" I asked eagerly.

Lois scooted over in her side of the booth, and I sat down beside her.

"It was definitely arson. Kerosene was used to hasten the flames. That's a very common accelerant in Holmes County since so many of the Amish use it in their homes," Rusty said.

"Do you suspect an Amish person set the fire?"

"No, we are almost certain it was the owner of the store."

"Tara?" I asked.

"And her ex-husband, Tyce Barron. The shop wasn't doing well. He increased the insurance policy less than six months ago. Those are both red flags in my line of work."

"He was only open a few weeks," Lois said.

Rusty glanced at her. "You can have insurance on a building the moment you own it even if it's under renovation. He's owned the building over a year."

"Are you sure it's Tyce?" I asked.

"Sure enough to make an arrest. I believe a deputy is on the way to his house right now to pick him up."

"Is there any connection to Tara's murder?"

He shook his head. "That's out of my wheel-house. I just investigate fires and false insurance claims."

"But I wonder," Lois said. "If there is a connection, maybe Tara knew Tyce burned the quilt shop to the ground and was going to go to the police. Or perhaps if she was in on it, she was feeling remorseful and planned to go to the police. To stop her, he killed her."

"Both of those suggestions are possible," I mused. "If one of them pans out, it means this case is solved."

"It feels too easy," Lois said. "It's never that easy."

Rusty chuckled. "You seem to want to do everything the hard way, Lois. I remember that about you."

She shrugged. "What can I say?" She patted my arm, signaling she wanted to get out of the booth. "I should go back to work. I can't leave Iris in the lurch that much longer."

I slid out of the booth, and Lois followed me.

Rusty also got out of the booth.

"I'll see you tonight then?" he asked.

Lois smiled. "You sure will. I'll save you a do-si-do."

"Nice to see you again," he said to me and then left the café.

I followed Lois back to the front counter. "What was that see-you-tonight comment about?"

"Rusty asked me to save him a dance tonight."

"I thought you were going to the square dance with Virgil," I said and held back what I really wanted to tell her—that Virgil wasn't a *gut* fit for her—but I held my tongue yet again.

"I am, but we aren't exclusive. I just met the guy. And it doesn't mean I can't flirt and take a spin around the square with another man."

I shook my head; I would never understand Lois's rules to dating. They were so different from the way the Amish did things. "Just try not to get too invested," I said. "Until you are sure."

"You worry too much, Millie."

I guessed she could say that because she wasn't the one who had to comfort Lois when a relationship ended. A task I had taken on with epic amounts of cookie dough to help. Lois loved hard, but she broke up hard too.

As promised, my generous piece of blueberry pie and black coffee were on the counter.

"Iris, I'm sorry I was gone so long," Lois said.

Iris smiled. "It is all right, Lois. Did you have a nice chat with your friend?"

"Very nice, and we learned a thing or two about the investigation too. I would call that a win," Lois said. She then grabbed a carafe of coffee and headed into the seating area.

Usually when I came to the café, I liked to sit at one of the tables along the window and watch the square. However, when the café was busy as it was today, I stayed at the counter in order to free up the tables for paying customers. Since the café had opened, neither Lois nor Darby had allowed me to pay for a single bite. I told them they couldn't keep it up forever or they were sure to go into blueberry debt, which I thought was quite serious.

I perched on a stool at the end of the counter

and ate my pie. It tasted even better than I remembered. That could be because it was a week since I'd had my last slice. Absence makes the heart grow fonder, as they say. It wasn't an Amish proverb. Perhaps the statement had come from a greeting card long ago.

And the sweet tangy taste of pie was just what I needed to catch a killer.

Chapter Thirty-two

The bell over the door chimed, and an *Englisch* woman walked in. I was surprised to see it was the quilting judge, Paula Lee. Before she said a word, I knew she was there to speak to Iris. It certainly wasn't to speak with me.

Paula Lee's eyes brightened as soon as she saw Iris. "Mrs. Young?" she said. "I'm so glad I found you here. I would love to talk to you a little more about your quilts and how I can help you grow your business."

Iris, who was rolling silverware into paper napkins on the counter, looked like a deer in a buggy's headlights.

I jumped off my stool. "Paula Lee, I'm Millie Fisher. I met you at the quilt judging yesterday."

"Oh, yes, third place." She said *third place* as if it was equivalent to last.

I wasn't too offended. I knew my quilting was very *gut*, but it couldn't hold a candle to Iris's work. She was just that talented with her needle.

"I promise to speak to you too, but I'm really here to talk to Mrs. Young. I have been trying to find her again for the last day, and finally learned that she worked at this café. I came straight here after that."

"I can see that," I said.

"I—I'd like Millie here while we talk. She is a very *gut* friend of mine and a member of my quilting circle. She knows my work just as well as anyone." She kept rolling the silverware as she spoke as if she needed something to do with her hands.

Irritation flashed across Paula Lee's face but soon melted away. "Of course. I would love to chat with both of you. As I told Millie before, I am very interested in your quilting circle. You have so many talented quilters in one group. I would love to meet with all of you and share what I can offer as a broker."

"We would have to see if the members of Double Stitch would be open to that," I said. "I know that some might be." Leah came to my mind. "But it would make others uncomfortable." I was speaking of Ruth, of course.

Iris stacked her napkin-wrapped silverware into a wicker basket on the counter. "I would like to speak to you, Paula Lee, but I don't know that now is the right time. I am at work, and there are tables that need to be tended to."

"Nonsense," Lois said as she came around the corner from the dining area. "Take a break and chat with Paula Lee. I'm sure you and Millie"— Lois gave me a meaningful look—"can learn something helpful."

About the murder, I hoped. I knew Lois hoped the same.

The café was noisy, so I suggested we go outside and sit in the park, which consisted of a small playground and little else. The park was peppered with picnic tables where the parents and babysitters could sit while watching their children. At the moment, there were only two young *Englisch* sisters playing on the jungle gym. The girls challenged each other to more and more dangerous flips on the monkey bars. The teenager who was with them watched with growing concern.

"This is a nice spot," Paula Lee said as we sat at one of the picnic tables.

"I've always liked this park," I said. "It has a lovely view of the square. The village is having a square dance tonight if you're interested in coming. I believe it starts at six."

Paula Lee wrinkled her nose. "I'm not much for dancing and wouldn't think the Amish would be either."

"The Amish aren't." I brushed a stray leaf from the top of the table. "I don't think you'll see many there, and they certainly won't be dancing."

"Are you planning to go?" Paula Lee asked.

"I'll be at the café helping Darcy. Iris is off in the evening, and Lois has a date for the square dance."

"Hmm," Paul Lee said. "Do you know how she met her date? I have been striking out terribly. It's not easy to date in your forties."

"She met him on an app," I said. "But I don't know which one, nor do I have any idea how it works."

"Maybe I will ask her," Paula Lee mused. "And maybe I will come to the square dance too. It would be a great way to meet some people."

Iris sat next to me with her hands clasped so tightly in her lap that her knuckles turned white.

"Before I begin, do you have any questions for me, Iris?" Paula Lee asked.

When Iris didn't say anything, I spoke up. "How does a quilt broker work exactly?" I asked.

She pressed her lips together. I knew she had hoped to have this conversation with Iris alone, but from what I could tell, Iris wasn't going to be able to work up the nerve to ask any of the important questions that had to be answered before she went into business with Paula Lee. Someone had to do that for her, and that someone had to be me.

Paula Lee cleared her throat. "It's very simple really."

As soon as she said that, my guard went up. Lois had said to me once that any time an *Englischer* said something was *very simple*, it was the opposite, and they typically spoke in a way that was meant to be ambiguous.

"Iris makes the quilts like she already does, and I take them to the highest bidders. That includes stores, collectors, and other individuals. I have customers not only in this county but all over the world. I just sold an Amish quilt to a buyer in Italy if you can believe that, and the buyer was willing to pay top dollar too. Both the quilter and the buyer were very happy with my service. They never would have connected without me."

"That is very impressive," I said.

Paula Lee appeared to relax somewhat when I said this. "Thank you. I have spent years and years trying to grow my business, and I take great pride in the success I have had."

"How are these buyers introduced to Iris's work in particular?"

"I take quilts to them," she said. "When at all possible."

"You have to take the quilts?" I asked. "You can't just show them pictures?"

"Buyers who are paying top dollar want to see what they are buying up close." She sniffed. "Of course, for the clients who are farther away, I send pictures and the best description I can. I still have the quilt in my possession while I'm in the process of selling it because I video chat with the buyer too. I need to have the quilt in my possession for the best chance of a sale. I have to study it and know it as if I made it myself in order to convince someone to buy it. The prices of the quilts I sell are high and it takes work to reach that price point. Eventually, Iris will become so well-known as one of my clients that she will get commissions to make quilts for high-paying customers. In those cases, I would not have the quilt beforehand. As a quilter of her caliber, she will receive commissions in no time at all. Of that, I'm sure."

"Is that how Tara Barron's quilt broker, Sondra, operated?"

She blinked at me. "Yes. Sondra taught me everything I know about selling quilts. She was a great mentor to me. I learned everything I could from her." She sighed. "I know that there was even more to learn."

"Oh?" I asked.

Next to me, Iris relaxed as the conversation shifted away from her. She hated to be the center of attention for any reason at all.

"She had the quilt-brokering business dialed in. I have seen her sell a quilt for top dollar to a person who was determined not to buy it. It was something to watch. I worked for her for a few years before branching out on my own. She had an amazing eye for quilts and other handicrafts. She taught me to recognize hand-stitched from machine-made. She was gifted in finding talent, and she had an extensive list of clients. She had some of the best quilters in Ohio on her list. Most of them were Amish in Wayne, Knox, and Holmes counties, but there were English quilters too. To be represented by her, a quilter had to apply with a reference, and there was a long waiting list."

I nodded. This matched what Leah had told us at the Double Stitch meeting about having to apply to be one of Sondra's quilters.

"So you were competitors when you started your own business? Was that difficult for Sondra when you went out on your own?"

She frowned. "In a way, yes, but I don't think either of us looked at it as a bad thing. Sondra was a friend and a sweet older woman. She had to be nearing eighty when she died. I think she was proud when I was able to go out on my own. Our customers didn't overlap too much. I went farther away, whereas she sold more things locally. I always thought her child would go into the business with her, but that never happened. I believe it comforted her to know someone would be able to take over the work when she was gone." She stood up. "I've told you all I can tell you about what I do." She pulled a business card from her purse. "Mrs. Young, give me a call when you're ready. I really believe we can work together in a way that would benefit both of us. It was so nice to talk again. I understand that you are a busy wife and mother and I'm sure you spend a lot of time quilting, so I am happy to meet with you again at your convenience. Call me night or day."

Iris took the card in her hand and looked down at it as if it just might spontaneously combust. It seemed to me that I would have to find out a lot more about this quilt-broker business before Iris committed to it. Perhaps having Paula Lee at the next quilting circle meeting was the best idea. Ruth Yoder and the ladies wouldn't let her run off without answering their questions. We all wanted what was best for Iris and her family and for each other too.

"I don't know how Carter is going to feel about all of this," Iris said after the other woman had left. "Paul Lee made it sound like it would be very *gut* for my family, but maybe it's too *gut* to be true. If having a quilt broker is such a wonderful help, why don't more Amish women use them, and why haven't we heard of them before Leah Bontrager brought up her old quilt broker, Sondra?"

Those were all very *gut* questions that I didn't have the answers for.

Iris stood up. "I should get back to work. I don't want to leave it all to Lois."

"Lois will be fine," I argued. "You managed everything while she was talking to Rusty."

"Even so." She started toward the café. I followed her.

When I caught up with her just outside the café, I said, "Iris, you don't have to make any decisions now or even tomorrow. Paula Lee needs you for her business. *Ya*, she can help you sell more quilts for higher prices, but she can't quilt herself. She needs you and people like you for her livelihood. You are the talent, and ultimately, what you do is your choice."

"*Danki*, Millie. From the way Paula Lee talked, I can tell there is much money to be made by doing this. That is not my ultimate goal. I need money to pay my bills and take care of my family. I don't need anything more than that." She paused and then added quietly, "And I don't want to come to hate quilting. Sometimes when a person turns their passion into an occupation, they begin to resent it. I don't want that to happen to me."

I could understand that. I thought of my own passion for matchmaking. It was something I did to help the young and sometimes not-so-young people in my community. It was a joy to be able to help make a good match. I don't know how I would feel if paying my bills depended on it.

An Amish proverb came to mind: *You are only poor when you want more than you have.*. That was what Iris was saying she didn't want to happen to her.

I was about to share all these thoughts with her. Iris opened her mouth to say something, and I guessed it would be something about her husband not agreeing to her using a quilt broker, when Lois burst out of the café. "Millie!"

"Lois, what's wrong?" I asked.

"I just got a call from Rusty." She was out of breath. "Tyce Barron has been arrested."

"For arson?" I gasped.

"No, for the murder of his ex-wife."

Chapter Thirty-three

That afternoon, Bessie was safely tucked into her barn at home with a fresh bag of feed and plenty of water when Lois picked me up at my farm. We had agreed that it was best to go together to Edy's Greenhouse for Zach's interview with the sheriff. Well, actually Lois said I wasn't going to go without her. Not that I minded. No one would keep Edith's children more distracted during the interview than Lois. She was more like another playmate than a parental figure.

The two-mile car ride from my farm to the greenhouse was brief, but I still managed to ask Lois if she was able to gather any more details about Tyce Barron's arrest from her insurance investigator friend, Rusty.

Lois turned her car onto the greenhouse drive. "Rusty didn't know any more than he told me in the initial call. I'm hoping the sheriff will tell us."

I was grateful to see that Lois and I had beat

Sheriff Brody to the greenhouse. Jacob, Micah, and Zach were all sitting outside repotting mum seedlings. It wouldn't be too long before the sunflowers would fade and the chrysanthemums would bloom. Every year seemed to go by a bit quicker than the one before. I blinked and another season had all but passed.

Scooter napped under a garden bench not too far from the boys. It seemed to me that he was fitting in quite well.

"Aenti!" Micah cried, jumping up from his task.

"Micah, get back here. Maam said that we had to stay until the job was done," Jacob said.

His younger brother ignored Jacob and galloped in our direction.

Zach looked as if he wanted to run to us too but stopped himself because he was afraid of what Jacob might say.

"Any news about the goats? How are they? Maam said that I had to stay home today to help with the greenhouse. I wish I was at the fair." Micah's words came out in a rush.

I patted his shoulder. "The goats are fine," I reassured him. "I'm looking forward to having them come home tomorrow."

"I'll miss going to the fair though," Micah said. "We will have to wait an entire year for it to come around again."

"That's how fairs work," Lois said. "And their happening only once a year is what makes them special."

Micah gave a dramatic sigh. "I guess. Maam said you were coming back today because the sheriff wants to talk to Zach."

"Oh," I said. "Did she tell Zach this?"

He squinted. "*Ya.* I might have been listening when she told him. Why does he need to speak to the sheriff?"

As if this question beckoned him, a sheriff's department SUV came down the long driveway. Through the windshield, I saw Sheriff Brody was driving, and in the passenger seat was a woman I didn't know. I had to assume she was the juvenile psychologist.

Edith came out of the greenhouse. Ginny was on her heels but stayed back when she saw the psychologist and sheriff climb out of the car. The little girl didn't care much for strangers. She plucked a kitten out of her apron—a solid white one this time—and carried it back into the greenhouse. I thought that was for the best. Ginny was too little to understand what was going on, nor did she need to know.

However, Zach seemed to think retreating like Ginny was an excellent plan. He stood up and ran into the greenhouse after her.

Sheriff Brody walked toward us. "Have you told Zach that we need to speak to him?"

"I did," Edith said. "Why don't the two of you wait on the back porch and I will bring Zach to you."

The sheriff nodded.

Micah went to sit with Scooter the goat, and Jacob, after a resentful glare at his brother, went on with his task of repotting the long line of plants in front of him.

Edith and I went into the greenhouse. We found Ginny and Zach sitting on the concrete floor teasing the kitten with a piece of twine. The kitten's tiny claws peeked out of his paws as he tried to dig into the twine time and time again. Every time, he missed.

"Are you sure you don't want another kitten, Aenti?" Ginny asked me as she looked up at me with her bright blue eyes.

"I'm sure, but you keep tempting me with all these adorable little kittens all the same."

She giggled.

"Zach," Edith said. "The sheriff is here to speak to you."

He was looking down at the kitten. "I know."

"We shouldn't keep him waiting."

"I know," Zach said but made no effort to move.

"He said I could be there when you speak with him," I said. "Will that help?"

He stood and brushed off the back of his trousers. "*Ya*, that will help."

Zach and I went out of the greenhouse, and by the time we reached the back porch, Lois was already there sitting with Sheriff Brody and the psychologist. Zach stopped along the way to pick up Scooter for comfort. Maybe the Amish could have comfort animals after all, but they certainly wouldn't call them that.

"Hi, Zach," Sheriff Brody said in a friendly voice. "My name is Aiden, and this is Miss Carrie, and we just want to talk to you about the first night of the fair, so we can understand what happened."

Zach perched on the edge of a chair with his goat. "Can Lois and Millie stay with me?"

Sheriff Brody frowned. "I already said that Millie could, but . . ."

Carrie looked at us and then at the sheriff. "That would be fine. We are happy to do whatever it takes to make you comfortable. I see you brought a friend with you. What is its name?"

"This is Scooter." He laid the goat across his lap.

I let out a sigh of relief and sat next to Lois on a resin bench.

"Can you tell us about that night?" Sheriff Brody took over the conversation again. "You took a hatchet from the axe-throwing game?" Carrie asked.

He nodded. "My *grossdaadi* said I couldn't go home with him that night. He wanted me to stay at the fair. There were a lot of people there, and I was afraid. I borrowed one of the hatchets for protection."

"When was this?" Carrie asked.

He wrinkled his brow. "A few hours before the fair closed. The two people working at the axe-throwing booth were fighting. It was a boy and a girl. I just slipped my hand into the cage and took one. I always planned to put it back. I was just borrowing it."

That must have been Amber Lyn and her summer boyfriend. That romance really didn't have any chance of lasting. I hoped Amber Lyn would break it off sooner rather than later. To draw a bad match out only made dissolving it that much worse.

"And you left the hatchet in the hayloft?" Carrie asked.

"Not at first. When the fair ended, I slipped into the quilt barn. I thought I would be more comfortable there with all the quilts. It felt safer. More like a home than the hayloft did." He swallowed. "I hid in the quilt barn while Sal checked it and locked up."

"Sal is the security guard," the sheriff said for Carrie's benefit.

I smiled at Zach. He was doing a great job, and so was Lois. She hadn't interjected once during the entire conversation.

"After he was gone, I wanted to sleep on one of the quilts but they were all hanging up. Then I saw one quilt not hanging, so I laid that on the floor and tried to sleep."

"Did you sleep?"

He shook his head.

"Then what happened?" the sheriff asked.

"I was just lying there on the quilt trying to sleep, but I couldn't rest. Every little noise I heard made me jump. I couldn't settle down. It was *gut* that I didn't sleep because some time after the fair closed, I heard someone unlock the door. I jumped up and rolled up the hatchet in the quilt and then slid behind one of the largest quilt displays to hide."

"Someone came into the quilt barn," Sheriff Brody said.

He nodded. "It was Tara. She came inside and started fiddling with each quilt. She was examining each one like she was looking for the tiniest of tiny flaws."

"How did she seem?" the sheriff asked.

"She was nervous. That's what I thought, and then a man came into the barn too."

I tensed up.

"Who was it?" Sheriff Brody asked.

He shook his head. "I don't know. I've never seen him before. She called him Tyce."

Lois and I shared a look. Was this more evidence to prove Tyce Barron was the killer?

"I remember because I had never heard that name before. He was an *Englischer* like her."

"Then what happened?" the sheriff asked.

"They started arguing. He called her a bunch of bad names and told her that she ruined everything, and she told him it was his idea to burn down the quilt shop and he was the one who ruined that. She also said that they would never see the money because he messed it up."

My eyes went wide. This was proof that Rusty had been right. The former couple had set the quilt shop on fire, most likely for the insurance money.

"Then he told her that she had to clean up the mess or she would be sorry," Zach went on.

"And then?" the sheriff asked.

I could feel Lois tense up beside me. I knew we were both thinking this was the moment when Tyce threw the hatchet at the back of her head. Had he found it in the quilt?

"He left." He scratched his goat between the ears.

Sheriff Brody blinked. "He left?"

Zach nodded. "He called her one more really awful name and stormed out. I can't say what he called her. It would be wrong."

"What did Tara do?" the sheriff asked.

"She stomped around and went back to fixing the quilts." He shrugged. "While she did that, I saw my chance and slipped out the door." He hung his head. "But I left the hatchet wrapped in the quilt. I just wanted to get out of there. I thought I would go back for it later when she was gone."

"Where did you go?" Carrie asked.

"I wanted to go see Scooter in the goat tent, but Sal was in there moving around. He was in the tent for a while, so finally I hid in the hayloft. After an hour or so, I was worried about the hatchet. I knew I had to put it back, so I gathered up the courage to go back to the quilt barn. I heard Sal running around trying to catch Phillip and Peter, who had escaped again."

The sheriff shot me a look. I shrugged.

Zach started to speak faster as if he just wanted to get the story out. "I went into the quilt barn. She was lying on the floor on the quilt, and it was all torn up. The hatchet was on the floor next to her. I—I took it. I was afraid that I would be blamed for what happened if the hatchet was found there." He started to cry. "It's my fault she's dead, isn't it?"

Sheriff Brody knelt in front of Zach. "It's not your fault."

"But it is. If I hadn't hidden the hatchet in the quilt barn, she'd wouldn't have been hit with it. She would still be alive."

Sheriff Brody scratched Scooter's cheek, and Zach relaxed some. I supposed he felt he could trust someone who was kind to his goat. I thought he was right that kindness was a *gut* measure of who could be trusted and who couldn't be trusted. "When someone makes the decision to hurt another person, they find a way. If it hadn't been the hatchet, it would have been something else," Sheriff Brody said.

"So what are we thinking?" Lois asked. "Tyce came back and killed her?"

"That's one possibility," the sheriff said. "He did admit to being there that night, but he said Tara was still alive."

Carrie stood. "Zach, why don't we walk over there and chat for a moment?"

Zach looked at me.

"Go ahead," I told him.

He held Scooter tight and followed Carrie. They sat crossed legged under a large tree. Scooter fell asleep in Zach's lap.

Sheriff Brody watched them for a long while. "We found his mother."

"Where is she? Is she planning to come back for him?"

"She's dead." The sheriff shook his head. "She was killed in a pedestrian car accident in Akron not long after she left. She was listed as a Jane Doe since she didn't have an ID or dental records. She was wearing English clothes, so the Akron police had no way of knowing she was Amish."

"How awful," Lois said.

I felt sick. "What does this mean for Zach? His *grossdaadi* doesn't want anything to do with him."

Sheriff Brody nodded. "That is true. I spoke to Hezekiah and told him about his daughter. He was angry and said he didn't want anything to do with the boy."

"Can he stay with us?" I asked. "I would have to talk to Edith, but we wouldn't want him to go into the foster system. I spoke with Bishop Yoder yesterday, and he's going to talk to Hezekiah's bishop to see if a family there would welcome Zach into their home."

Sheriff Brody stood up. "He can stay here for now. I have to talk to some people and see what I can do. This is a delicate situation. We need to tell Zach about his mother, but Carrie will be the one to know the right time. She's evaluating him now. Until she says we can tell him, we need to keep it to ourselves."

Lois and I nodded, but I didn't wholeheartedly agree that it was the right thing to do.

Chapter Thirty-four

Margot Rawlings rushed about the square just as the dance was about to begin. Her short curls bounced on the top of her head the way they always did when she was especially agitated, and Margot was very agitated at the moment. The weather was not cooperating.

After leaving Edy's Greenhouse, where Zach was happily settled in with Edith's children, Lois and I went to the fair to check on Phillip and Peter, both of whom were fine and still basking in their fame, or Phillip's fame. Don't tell Peter I said that. However, when we left, there was a definite shift in the weather. The sky grew dark, and it rained off on and on. Lois checked her phone and found there was a good chance of thunderstorms that evening just when the square dance was about to begin.

The square dance was scheduled for six, so the sun should have still been high in the sky. It was, but it was shrouded in black clouds. The promised storm was coming, but you couldn't tell Margot Rawlings that. She bounced around the fair like a ping-pong ball that had gotten loose from a game board, barking orders at Uriah and Leon through her bullhorn.

The two Amish men were frantically trying to raise a large awning in the middle of the square to protect the dance floor, which was just wooden tiles that had been laid over the grass. However, the increasing wind was making the task difficult.

Lois put her hands on her hips. She was in full square dance garb—a purple bejeweled plaid shirt, jeans, and purple cowboy boots that were the same color as her spikey hair. Her dangly earrings were the shape of cowboy boots too. "Someone has to talk some sense into Margot. This is ridiculous. The dance has to be postponed."

I couldn't agree more as rain hit me in the face. Lois and I had walked over to the square from the Sunbeam Café when we noticed how much Uriah and Leon were struggling with the tent. We wanted to offer our help.

"You know Margot," I said. "I think she would go ahead unless there was lightning, and she would be annoyed to call it off even then."

I looked up at the sky. "I'm glad I will be safely inside the café during this, but I want you to be careful. Don't stay out in the bad weather."

"Don't worry about me, Millie. I never take such risks."

I snorted.

"Millie, Lois?" Uriah asked as he hammered one awning post into the ground. "What are you doing out here? The weather is getting bad."

"We can see that," Lois said. "We wanted to lend you a hand."

"We will be all right," Uriah said.

As he spoke, there was a gust of wind that ripped the awning cover from Leon's hands. The young Amish man ran after it.

"On second thought," Uriah said. "A second set of hands would be a big help."

Among the four of us we got the awning up over the dance floor and secured to the ground.

Margot came over when we were finished. "Thanks for helping, Millie and Lois," she said. "Can you believe this weather? Why do things like this happen to me?"

Lois arched her brow. "We live in the Midwest and it's the summer. This is the time for storms."

"Not on my watch," Margot snapped and stomped away with her bullhorn at her side. "Leon, come with me," she called over her shoulder. "You need to get the microphone in place for the dance caller."

Leon stumbled over his own two feet to run after her.

"Sheesh," Lois said. "She grows more and more like Ruth Yoder every day."

Lois had a point even though the two women would hate the comparison.

"I think that's the best we can do," Uriah said as he wiped sweat from his brow with his bandana. "I can't imagine that many people are going to show up, but you know Margot. She never says surrender."

"Why don't you come to the café and take a rest until the dance begins," Lois suggested to Uriah.

"*Danki*, but I had better stay here in case anything else needs to be adjusted. You know Margot and her adjustments."

We did.

Across the square, a car parked in front of Swissmen Sweets, and Virgil Rinaldi climbed out. He wore jeans, cowboy boots, and a denim shirt. Just like Lois, it seemed that he was taking this square dance seriously.

"Oh, my word," Lois said. "There is my date. How do I look?" She patted her hair, which did absolutely nothing since it was cemented into place.

"You look lovely," I said. "But I thought you weren't sure of Virgil any longer," I said, wondering if I should tell Lois at this point that I thought they were a poor match. I had been avoiding it all week.

"That's true, but I want to look good. There is no shame in that."

Uriah chuckled.

I pressed my lips together.

Virgil walked over to us, and he was holding a bouquet of sunflowers. "Lois, you look gorgeous."

Lois looked down at her bejeweled outfit. "Oh this?"

Uriah was looking at the dark sky at that point. I was convinced it was because he was trying so very hard not to laugh outright.

"You look like a cowgirl princess."

Lois placed a hand to her chest. "I have never been called that before, so I thank you! And you look quite dashing yourself." She smiled.

"The weather doesn't look so good," Virgil said. "Are you sure you want to stay for the dance? We could do something else."

"Let's stay until we are forced to leave. I feel it's the right thing to do for Margot's sake. If no one shows up at all, she might lose her mind. We can't have that," she said. "If the weather turns too sour, we can dash into the café." She looked at me. "That's where you will be, right, Millie?"

"Darcy and I will both be there," I said. "I'm headed there now." I took the flowers from Lois. "Let me put these in some water in the café. They will look so nice on the counter."

"Oh, they will," Lois said. "They are gorgeous, Virgil. It is so old-fashioned of you to bring me flowers."

He smiled. "I would do anything to bring a smile to your face."

I found myself standing there wondering if what he was saying was sincere. I didn't have any reason to doubt him, but there was just something about Virgil that made me feel a little ill at ease.

I waved to Uriah, Lois, and Virgil, doing my best not to worry over what a poor match Virgil was for my dearest friend.

As soon as I was inside the café, we were hit with a rush of customers. I quickly put the flowers in a vase with water and picked up a notepad to start taking orders. It wasn't often that I donned an apron in the café and acted as waitress. Most of the time, I was sitting, nibbling on blueberry pie, or chatting with Lois, Darcy, Iris, or all three of them at once.

I waited on tables in the café enough to know the ropes and how Darcy liked to receive orders through her pass-through window into the kitchen. When I helped out like this, I never let Darcy or

Lois pay me. They never charged me for eating there, so it was a two-way street.

It seemed that Margot's square dance had brought many *Englischers* to the square, but instead of braving the elements on the dance floor, they were all piling into the café for coffee and pastries. I couldn't say that I blamed them.

I rushed about for the next hour as dancers came and went. When I had a moment to catch my breath, I peeked out the window and saw people twirling around on the dance floor under the awning. Through the glass pane, I heard the up-beat rumble of country music and the dance caller shouting terms like "promenade!" I had no idea what that meant, of course, but it seemed the dancers knew because they didn't miss a beat.

The sky was still black as ever, but at least it had stopped raining. Maybe the worst of the storm would hold off until after the square dance. The wind, however, was relentless, and I saw a *gut* number of cowboy hats fly through the sky. One was trapped high in a pine tree.

Darcy joined me at the window. "Grandma is determined to have a good time even if a major thunderstorm is coming. Sometimes I wish I was that adventurous."

"Your *grossmaami* is one of a kind. There is no doubt about that."

She laughed. "Would you like a piece of blueberry pie?"

"I thought you would never ask. I think it's quiet enough in here to take a bite or two."

"Or four," Darcy teased.

I didn't deny it.

Over the next thirty minutes the weather got worse and worse. Through the window, I watched Uriah trying to keep decorations from blowing away. Margot's curls stood on end, and then the rain that had held off for so long poured down in one great bucketful. The brave souls who had come out for the square dance despite the predicted bad weather dashed off in all directions.

Margot stood at the top of the gazebo steps. Although I could hardly see her through the rain, I could certainly hear her, thanks to the bullhorn. "Stay close. Stay close," she cried. "The weather should pass soon and we can get back to the dance."

The weather did not look like it was going to pass anytime soon. The Sunbeam Café was inundated with a group of wet dancers. Lois was among them, but Virgil wasn't. Instead Rusty was at her side. I pulled Lois aside. "I thought you went to the dance with Virgil." I glanced in Rusty's direction. He was using napkins to wipe rainwater from his face.

"I was, but Rusty cut into the dance. Virgil stormed off when I agreed to dance with Rusty. I don't need that kind of attitude. We weren't exclusive. Just because a man is handsome doesn't mean he is the right fit. At my age, I am looking more for character and kindness."

"I'm glad to hear that, Lois. I've wanted to tell you that Virgil was a bad match."

She put her hands on her hips. "Well, why didn't you? I could have used that information a few days ago."

"You know I don't make comments on matches unless I'm asked."

"That might apply to strangers but not to me. I want to know what you really think, Millie. That is what true friendship is."

"You're right," I agreed. "Next time, I will tell you just what I think even if you never ask."

"But I'm asking," she paused. "What do you think about Rusty?"

"I like him. He has potential."

Her eyes sparkled. "Excellent! Now, let me get back to my date."

I shook my head and decided I would head home just as soon as the rain passed. I wanted to stop at the greenhouse and see how Zach was doing. He had gotten a lot of information that day and I knew he must be overwhelmed. However, he had yet to be told about his mother's death. I didn't agree with the psychologist, Carrie, that it was best to wait to tell him, but I had promised Sheriff Brody I wouldn't say a thing.

To my surprise, the quilt broker Paula Lee was among the people who took refuge from the rain in the Sunbeam Café. She'd said that we'd see her at the square dance, and it seemed she had kept her word.

She looked up from the mug of hot cocoa in front of her. "Millie, it's nice to see you."

"Would you like to order any food?"

She shook head. "No, this is fine. I'm just waiting for the worst of the weather to stop, so that I can go home. The square dance was a bust for me, as expected." She sighed.

"Did you meet anyone at the dance?" I asked.

She pursed her lips. "No. I struck out again. I'm going to end up alone."

"I could help you with that," I said.

She stared at me. "With finding a date?"

"I'm a matchmaker. I usually match Amish couples, but the same rules apply to the *Englisch*, I would think. It just comes down to compatibility."

She wrapped her hands around her mug. "Well, I just might be in a place where I'm desperate enough to use an Amish matchmaker. I'll try anything at this point."

"I've been thinking about what you said earlier today."

"Oh, something else about my sad dating life?"

I shook my head. "You mentioned that you thought Sondra's child would work with her selling quilts, but they never did. Where is that child now?"

"You know him. It's Sal Dungle, the security guard at the fair."

I stared at her. "Sal Dungle?"

"Oh yes. He and his mother were very close. They did everything together, which was why I was surprised they never worked together. I know that quilt brokering isn't usually considered man's work, but Sal never struck me as someone to be concerned with that."

The front door of the café slammed open. "Aenti!" Micah cried. "Zach is gone!"

Chapter Thirty-five

I hurried over to Micah's side. He was dripping wet. Before I could even ask for help, Darcy was there with several clean kitchen towels. Micah's body was narrow enough that I could wrap his shoulders in one. "Micah, I can't believe you came out in this storm. How did you get here?"

"I rode my bike."

"In this weather?"

"The weather wasn't this bad when I left," Micah said. "It wasn't raining then, just a little windy."

A little windy was an understatement, I thought, as I noticed the awning on the square had toppled over. Uriah and Leon were trying desperately to get everything out of the rain. Meanwhile Margot sat on the gazebo steps with her bullhorn looking completely deflated.

"Does your *maam* know you are here?" I asked.

He shook his head. "She had a plant society meeting tonight, so she left Jacob in charge." He wrinkled his nose at this. "I told Jacob that I couldn't find Zach, and he said we had to wait until Maam got home to look for him. That would be hours. I did the only thing I could think of—I came here. I knew you were at the café tonight."

"I'm glad you did. Darcy, can you take care of Micah? I'm going to go look for Zach."

Lois stepped forward. "Not without me, you're not. I can drive."

"Can I help?" Rusty asked.

"Yes," Lois said. "Call the sheriff."

With Micah safely in Darcy's care, Lois and I ran out into the pouring rain to her car. "Where are we going?" Lois asked.

"To the fair."

"That's what I thought you'd say." She revved the engine.

As we drove there, I told her what Paula Lee had revealed about Sal. "Wow. I never would have guessed Sal was into quilts," she said.

"He acted like he didn't know Tara well, but if his mother was her quilt broker, he must have known her, right?"

Lois leaned forward, peering through the rain. "I would think so."

When we reached the fair, there was a mass exodus of visitors. The weather gave no sign of improving, and everyone was hightailing it home. Sal wasn't at his post at the gate, and his absence—especially with so many people going through the gate at one time—made me nervous.

Lois and I went into the fair. We were the only people going in rather than coming out. Luckily, we both were fairly dry because Lois had a set of emergency ponchos in her purse. It really was amazing everything she was able to fit in there. Darcy once told me that she thought her *grossmaami*'s purse had a secret compartment to hold all the stuff inside it. I thought she was joking. Now, I wondered if it was true.

"Let's start with the goat tent," I suggested.

We went to the goat tent and found the goats agitated but dry inside. Phillip and Peter perked up as soon as they saw me. "You're going home tomorrow, boys. I promise. Did you see Zach?"

Where Ruth Yoder would have thought I had lost my mind to ask a goat such a question, Lois didn't even bat an eye.

Phillip made a kicking motion in front of him. I looked in that direction and saw the quilt barn through the rain. I swallowed.

"Let's look in the quilt barn," I said.

"Whatever the goat says," Lois agreed.

The quilt barn had not been reopened since the murder, and the door was locked.

"I got this," Lois announced and pulled out her favorite investigating tool, her lock picks.

When we were inside the barn, we heard a voice.

"I never saw you," a child said. I knew it was Zach, and my stomach immediately dropped into my black sneakers.

"You're lying. The deputies told me that you were talking to the police."

"*Ya,* but I never saw you." Zach's voice shook. "Please let me go. I won't tell anyone that you were here."

"Don't lie to me, boy!" Sal shouted.

"You're the one who is the liar. You said when you picked me up at the greenhouse that my *maam* was here waiting for me. Where is she?" Zach asked through tears.

My heart constricted. If we had told Zach about his mother's death earlier, he would not have gotten into the car with Sal because he would have known Sal was lying.

Lois and I needed to formulate a plan, but Lois wasn't going to wait for that. She jumped forward, holding her purse as if she was ready for the hammer toss. "What's going on in here?"

Both Sal and Zach turned to us. Zach had climbed on top of one of the ten-foot quilt frames, clearly in an attempt to escape Sal, but now he was trapped high in the air with nowhere to go.

"Stop where you are or I will shake the boy right off this thing." He gave the quilt frame a shake as if to prove his point.

Lois froze, and I did too.

My mouth felt dry. If Zach fell from the quilt frame, he might not die but he could be seriously hurt. At the very least, Sal would have a chance to grab him while he was dazed from the fall. There had to be a way to get him down or get Sal far enough away from him so Zach could climb down on his own. Neither Lois nor I was agile enough climb up there after him, and that was assuming the rack could hold our combined weight in the first place.

"Sal, what are you doing? Let Zach go," I said.

"So he can tell the police I killed Tara?" he spat back.

"I didn't expect him to come right out and say it like that," Lois muttered to me.

I inched forward. "Why did you kill Tara, Sal?"

He glared at me. "I didn't mean to kill her. I was just so angry. She didn't care what she'd done to my mother. When I spoke to her, I was trying to make her see that. That she'd put undue pressure on my eighty-year-old mother. She didn't need that."

"How did she put pressure on her?" Lois asked.

He narrowed his eyes at Lois. "She didn't like any of the quilts my mother brought her to stock her shop. She wanted more and better quilts. She just wanted more and more and drove my mother into an early grave. My mother should have been retired at her age, but she kept brokering quilts because it was what she loved to do. Tara took all the joy out of it. To her it was just about making money. It wasn't about the relationships with the quilters or the buyers like it was for my mother. My mother had a heart attack from the stress and died. It was all Tara's fault. My mother told me on her deathbed that she wished she had never met her. That night in the quilt barn, I wanted to talk to Tara and tell her what I knew about her. I went into the quilt barn. She was alone. I told her about my mother, and do you know what she did? She laughed in my face over my dead mother. I have never been so angry."

"So you hit her on the head?" Lois asked.

"As I was leaving, she picked up a quilt that was all bunched up in a corner. When she did, the hatchet fell out and slid across the concrete. I—I picked it up to return it to the axe-throwing booth."

"Then what happened?" I asked in the most soothing voice I could muster.

"She was folding the quilt and said that even if my mother hadn't died, she had planned to find a new quilt broker. She said my mother wasn't living up to the promises she'd made about what she could deliver." He took a shuddering breath. "I had the axe in my hand and I just flung it at her. I wasn't trying to hit her. I was just so mad!"

"But it hit her on the head," I said. "You could have called for help. She might have lived."

"Even if she were alive, I would be blamed. I am always blamed for everything."

I wanted to ask him what he meant by that but wasn't sure it was a route I should take. All I cared about at the moment was getting Zach, Lois, and myself out of that quilt barn in one piece.

While I was speaking to him, Lois was inching away from me and closer to Zach.

"In my position, anyone would do what I did," he claimed.

That wasn't true.

Lois was moving along the wall now. This just might work.

"What about the quilt? Why was it shredded?" I asked.

"I did that after I hit her because I thought the police would look for an angry quilter or someone like that. I had to cover my tracks. I thought the shredded quilt would buy me some time until I figured out what to do." His voice shook.

And it had. The first suspect had been Ruth Yoder.

"Is that why you let my goats loose too, to cover

your tracks and make it seem as if you were just the distracted security guard that night?"

"I didn't know they would find their way into the quilt barn. They are the most disobedient animals I have ever seen."

Those were fighting words.

"Why did you stay, Sal?" I asked.

"What do you mean?" He squinted at me as if he was trying to determine why I was speaking in riddles.

"You could have gotten away from the fairgrounds. You could have been away from here on the run."

"And leave my life? Leave everything I've ever known because of one mistake?"

But that one mistake had taken another person's life.

"Hey!" Sal cried when he noticed Lois moving along the wall. He ran at her and pushed her against one of the heavy wooden quilt frames. Her head connected with the frame, and she slid to the floor.

"Lois!" I cried, running to her.

"Now I have no choice but to get rid of all three of you," Sal said. "I'm not happy about it, Millie. I really liked you."

From the floor, Lois winked at me. I stifled a gasp. She was faking being hurt. My heart raced and heat crept into my cheeks.

"What you need to do is run out the door," Lois whispered. "You can make it out and call for help."

"I'm not leaving without both of you."

"Fine. Step back and watch me work," she said.

I took a few steps back.

Lois jumped to her feet. "Leave her alone." Sal clutched his chest in surprise. It gave Lois just enough time to swing her massive purse and knock him to the ground. His head hit the concrete and he was out like a light.

She held up her purse. "And that is why you carry a brick everywhere you go."

I reached up and helped Zach down off the quilt rack. He clung to me.

She looked down at Sal. "You know, for a killer he goes down like a ton of bricks. Pun intended."

By the time the sheriff's deputies arrived, Lois and I had Sal tied up with the ribbon and yarn she happened to have in her purse. Zach was tucked under my arm as if I would never let him go.

"How were you able to tie him up?" Sheriff Brody asked.

"I hit him with my purse," Lois said matter-of-factly.

Sheriff Brody glanced at her purse. "That will do it. Maybe I should get some of those for the department."

"Not a bad idea," Lois agreed.

Sal came to and looked at me. "Millie," he said in a hoarse voice. "I am sorry, Millie."

I held more tightly to Zach's shoulders.

I looked into the eyes of the man who just an hour ago had thought that he could kill my closest friend, Zach, and me. Even so, compassion filled my heart. I thought of the times after Kip had died when I had wanted to lash out and blame others for what had happened to him. It had happened to me. I knew if it had not been for my faith, I would have given in to my anger and grief. Gott's steady hand in my life had kept me from straying outside of His will. It seemed to me that Sal hadn't had faith in his life. But that was a question only Sal could answer. I didn't know, and it wasn't my place to know.

However, what I did know was forgiveness was not just a gift for Sal, it was a gift for myself as well. "I forgive you, Sal."

He nodded, and Deputy Little escorted him out of the quilt barn one last time.

Epilogue

Sheriff Brody narrowed his eyes at Hezekiah Troyer. "You will agree to it, or you will be charged with child neglect and abandonment. After the way you treated Zach, the courts would take him away from here and put him into the foster system. Do you want that for him?"

Hezekiah's face was turning even redder with fury.

Phillip, Peter, and Scooter, who were now the best goat friends, jumped around and chased each other in the background. Edith had built a pen for Scooter and let my goats inside it when they came to visit the greenhouse. The juxtaposition of the happy goats and furious Hezekiah was jarring.

"This is your one chance to make things right by your grandson. I suggest you take it."

The two men were squaring off in the front yard of Edy's Greenhouse. Zach and Edith's children were inside the house, but I knew they were watching through the windows, waiting to see what Hezekiah would do.

Hezekiah glared at me. "Meddling childless women like you are the ones who destroy families. You can have the boy. I do not care. Do what you want with him. I have no use for the child. I never have. He will come to no *gut* because of his *Englisch* blood." He stomped away to his buggy.

As he drove off, Lois balled her fists at her sides, but I was proud that she didn't punch Hezekiah in the mouth. If it had been fifty years ago, she would have clocked him.

Edith, who had been holding my hand like a vise, whispered, "He can stay."

"He can stay," I whispered back. I looked behind me and was greatly relieved to see Zach and the other children standing in the doorway to the farmhouse. He had a home.

Edith let go of my hand and ran to the house. All four children burst out and hugged her. For the first time in weeks, my heart was light.

Lois went to talk to her new boyfriend Rusty, who was waiting by his car. I was grateful that he was here to support us. I thought he was a *gut* match for her. Speaking of *gut* matches, I had one of my own.

Uriah came to my side. "Don't you want to go be with your family?"

I shook my head. "I want to give them a moment together first."

"You did a *gut* thing by placing Zach with Edith," Uriah said. "You should be mighty pleased with yourself."

I gave him a weak smile. "I am, but I am sorry he

had to go through so much pain. No child should be treated the way he was."

"You're right," he agreed. "What we can do is help the ones we can reach, as you have. You have a big heart, Millie, and it is one of the things I love about you the most."

"I love the same about you," I said.

He stared at me. "Did you say *love?*"

I nodded.

He grinned from ear to ear. "That's a word I thought I would never hear from you as much as I prayed for it."

"I love you very much, Uriah. I just had to let myself accept it. It took time."

He nodded. "I understand that. We have both experienced loss." He swallowed hard. "Will you marry me, Millie? I'm ready for your answer, whatever it might be. I will respect and honor whatever it is you decide. If your answer is *nee*, please know that I understand, and I will leave Harvest. I do not want you to feel uncomfortable in your hometown. I will always be welcome back in Indiana. My children still don't understand why I left after you rejected me once. A second time is all I would need to know that you are serious." He bowed his head as if he was ready for ridicule or for a blessing. He stared at the ground.

"*Ya.*"

"*Ya?*" he asked.

"*Ya*, I will marry you." I looked into his deep blue eyes. "I want to be your *fraa.*"

He wrapped his arms around me and lifted me in the air. When we were young, he might have spun me around a few times, but we weren't young any longer. He set me back on the ground and held me in a tight hug.

Lois noticed and called out to us. "What's going on?"

Neither of us answered, because in that moment we were in our own little world.

"When should we get married? When should we talk to the bishop?" The excited questions spilled out of him.

"Why don't we get married tomorrow?" I asked. "At our age, why wait?"

"You're right, why wait?" He had the widest smile on his face. "I have been waiting to marry you, my beloved Millie, for fifty years. I can last one more day."

Suddenly, Phillip and Peter butted into us. It seemed the two rascal goats had leaped over the side of Scooter's pen. They hopped joyfully around us, and I couldn't help but start laughing. For the first time in a very long time, I felt as joyful as my goats.

I looked up at Uriah, who was laughing too.

"What's going on?" Lois wanted to know. "What's so funny? Will someone tell me what's happening?"

But Uriah and I couldn't stop laughing.

Finally, I managed to say, "Are you ready to be a goat *daed?*"

He grinned. "So very ready, my *fraa.*"

Please read on for an excerpt from Amanda
Flower's new Katharine Wright Mystery series,
coming soon!

TO SLIP THE BONDS OF EARTH

Chapter One

How dare Bufford Lyons make such a fool of me at the teachers' meeting this afternoon? As we were coming to the end of the fall semester, I had made a formal request to teach Greek III in the spring. The language was one of my first loves and the reason I took my teaching position, but ever since I had begun teaching at Steele High School, I had been relegated to the introductory classes in languages. First year Latin was a painful course to teach. Most of the students didn't want to be there and had no interest in learning any language, especially not a dead one.

I had thought after so many years teaching and the upcoming retirement of Mr. Wellings, the current Greek III teacher, I would be allowed to take on a more demanding course.

"We can't have a woman teaching upperclassmen," Bufford had said when I'd made the formal request in front of the faculty assembly. "The young men in these courses are far too close to Miss Wright's age. They won't take a young woman seriously, and they need to concentrate on their lessons, as our students of Greek are the most likely to go on to college. Steele High School has a reputation to uphold."

I stood up. "I studied Greek at Oberlin College and graduated with top honors in the course. I am more than cap—"

"You are still a *woman*." He said the word as if it was some sort of slur.

I put my hands on my hips. "Should I be pointing out the obvious, that you are an old man?"

The principal, Mr. Mellon, took his mallet and banged the table in front of him. "Miss Wright, please calm yourself."

I balled my hands at my sides. Why was I asked to calm myself but Bufford wasn't? I knew why— because, as Bufford had pointed out, I was a woman. That was reason enough for them to reprimand me, and that truth set my teeth on edge.

"I do understand your educational background," Mr. Mellon went on. "But the school board has already decided it would be best if the upperclassmen were taught by Mr. Lyons."

Bufford sat back down in his chair with a smug look on his face.

"What?" I asked. "He doesn't know half the Greek I do."

Mr. Mellon held his gavel in his hand as if he was contemplating rapping it on the table again. "A veteran teacher is best for the course. You are still early in your career."

"You mean a veteran *male* teacher," I corrected.

"Miss Wright," the elderly principal said. "The matter is settled. Now we must move on to other topics of concern."

"Yes, Miss Wright," Bufford said. "You should stick to selling Christmas trees. That's more appropriate for a female teacher." He smiled at me, and his gray mustache twitched as if he was holding in a laugh.

"Excuse me for caring about the students and wanting them to have access to an arts program while in high school. I am willing to make that extra effort for my students rather than sitting on my laurels and accepting positions I'm unqualified for simply because I am the oldest man in the room."

"Miss Wright," Mr. Mellon exclaimed in shock.

The smile had faded from Bufford's face. I had successfully hit my mark. He'd made me look like a fool, but he was the fool. He couldn't even conjugate in Pig Latin.

At the end of the meeting, I stormed from the room. Typically, after school I went home like the dutiful and obedient daughter and sister I was, but on that day, I was just too spitting mad to face the demands of my family.

It was a crisp December day, and a walk into town was just what I needed. Fresh snow dusted the lampposts and street signs, but was not yet thick enough to stick to the ground. The shop windows were all done up for Christmas with evergreens, red ribbons, and toy trains.

I let out a sigh. I should be concentrating on my holiday shopping instead of what Bufford Lyons had said. His comment about the school fundraiser steamed me the most. I'd been working for weeks to make sure the Christmas Tree Sale and Carol Singing went off without a hitch, and it was set for a few days before Christmas. All the proceeds would be going to the music department.

Even though music wasn't my specialty, I loved listening to it and knew it was an important part of a public education. I was working with the Parent Teacher Association and association president Lenora Shaw to organize the fundraiser. The PTA was in its infancy, but I recognized what a vital partner it could be in achieving our fundraising goals. When I'd told Principal Mellon of my enthusiasm, he'd appointed me as the teacher liaison. It wasn't until later that I learned he'd chosen me because I was a woman, not because of my support of the group.

Bufford, Principal Mellon, and all the men in that building were the same. They believed I should be grateful I even got to be in the same room with them and completely ignored the fact I had more common sense in my left pinkie than all of them combined.

I had to put the incident at school behind me, if only for a little while. Winter recess would be here soon, and I needed the break as much as my students did. This afternoon, I hoped to visit the book shop and find something new to read to take my mind off the ridiculous school rules I had to abide by as a female teacher. I might find a gift for my father and brothers as well.

A gentleman I recognized from town but could not name tipped his hat to me.

"Good afternoon, Miss Wright. We heard your

brothers are at it again. What are they thinking? That they can fly like a bird? It goes against nature. If God wanted us to fly, he would have given us wings."

"Are you suggesting humans should not swim because we do not have fins?"

He blinked at me as if my retort was some sort of riddle he couldn't make heads or tails of. "I beg your pardon?"

I adjusted my spectacles on my nose. "If anyone can achieve flight in our lifetime, it will be my brothers, Wilbur and Orrville Wright."

"Two boys from Dayton?" he snorted. "That is as likely as Old Saint Nick walking down the street."

I lifted my chin. "Well, I suggest you make up for being on his naughty list because I heard he is out on a stroll checking off names." With that, I marched away.

I left him there and headed into the bookstore, browsing for a long while. There was nothing like books to put my mind at ease.

"Kate, I didn't see you there," a kind voice said. "You were so hunched over that book. What is it?"

I held up the tome in my hands to show my old school friend, Agnes Osborn. "A history of Rome."

Agnes snorted. "I should have known you would be engrossed in something of that sort."

I smiled. "My interests have not changed, Ag."

"You're nothing if not consistent." She tugged on a lock of hair that had fallen from its hairpin. "Have you heard from your brothers? I would be interested to know how they are getting on in North Carolina."

"They write, of course, though not as often as I would like," I replied. "They write more often to Father than they do to me, but they seem to be getting on fine. They said they are very close to heavier-than-air, powered flight."

She cocked her head. "Haven't they said that before?"

"A time or two," I admitted.

"Why aren't they happy with the bicycle shop? Why isn't that enough for them? Would they not be happier to settle down and marry? Don't they want children?"

I shook my head and said nothing. These were questions I received often in regard to my brothers, and I had tired of answering them after so many years. I was grateful when Agnes changed the subject.

"Will you be at the Shaws' party this Saturday?" she asked with sparkling green eyes.

"I plan to go as long as Father doesn't need me. Lenora Shaw is hosting and inviting everyone on the Steele PTA."

"I heard of lot of young men will be coming home to see their families for Christmas and they'll be at the party. You know the Shaws' party is the real start of the holiday season in Dayton. This will be the first time I have had an opportunity to go."

"The presence of young men is of no concern to me. I'm far too busy with my teaching, caring for Father, and minding my brothers' bicycle shop to have time for such things."

She clicked her tongue. "You need to have a life

of your own. You are too wrapped up in others' lives. Haven't you ever cared for a man who wasn't a family member? Have you thought about being in love?"

My friend gave a little swoon at the very idea, but Agnes Osborn had been dreaming of love since we were in pigtails. I knew this because I had heard about it ad nauseum for the last twenty years.

I pressed my lips together. When I was in college, I had briefly been engaged. My family never knew about it, and I didn't love the man. It just seemed getting engaged was what senior men did, and as a sophomore, I'd gone along with the proposal. Thankfully, both of us had realized our foolishness before it was too late or before I made the mistake of telling Father or my brothers. They would never have forgiven me, had I married. However, there had been another man whom I'd cared for deeply. Unfortunately, he was now married to someone else.

I said none of this to Ag and was thankful she'd never visited me at Oberlin College, where I had attended school, so she knew nothing of either man. No one in Dayton knew of them. I looked at the small watch pin attached to the lapel of my coat. "I should be heading home. Father will wondering where I have been so long."

"I hope I didn't upset you, Kate," Agnes said with a frown. "That wasn't my intention."

"I know." I smiled at her. "But I would appreciate it if you would not bring the idea of romance up again."

She didn't give me an answer one way or another as we said our goodbyes.

Taking the Roman history I had purchased at the shop, I made my way home to number 7 Hawthorn Street. The white house with green shutters came into view. I noted that some of the greenery and red bows I had wrapped around the posts on the wide front porch had come loose. I would need to fix those before I entered the house. Ever since my mother had died when I was fifteen, I had been determined to keep a nice home for my father and brothers. That went for both the inside and the outside. Everything had to be just so.

I stepped onto the porch and set my satchel on the white rocker, but before I could even pick up the first bow, the front door flew open.

"Miss Wright, you're home!" exclaimed Carrie Kayler, our seventeen-year-old maid. She wore her bright blond hair in a bun at the back of her head and a simple gray dress with a white apron. Her green eyes were the size of dinner plates.

"Carrie, what is wrong? Is Father all right?" Fear clawed at my chest. Had my father fallen ill?

"I'm fine," my father said in his booming bishop's voice. He stood in the foyer holding a telegram. He kept looking down at it.

A new fear overtook me. Had something happened to my brothers? "Are the boys all right?"

He handed the Western Union telegram to me. What I read took my breath away.

SUCCESS FOUR FLIGHTS THURSDAY MORNING ALL AGAINST TWENTY-ONE MILE PER

HOUR WIND STARTED FROM LEVEL WITH
ENGINE POWER ALONE AVERAGE SPEED
THROUGH AIR THIRTY-ONE MILES LONGEST
57 SECONDS INFORM PRESS HOME CHRIST-
MAS. ORVILLE WRIGHT.

The paper fell from my hands. It seemed that
everything in the world was about to change.